1001
ULTIMATE
Brain
Booster
Activities

www.pegasusforkids.com

Published by Kuldeep Jain for B. Jain Publishers (P) Ltd., D-157, Sector 63, Noida - 201307, U.P.
Registered office: 1921/10, Chuna Mandi, Paharganj, New Delhi-110055

Printed in India

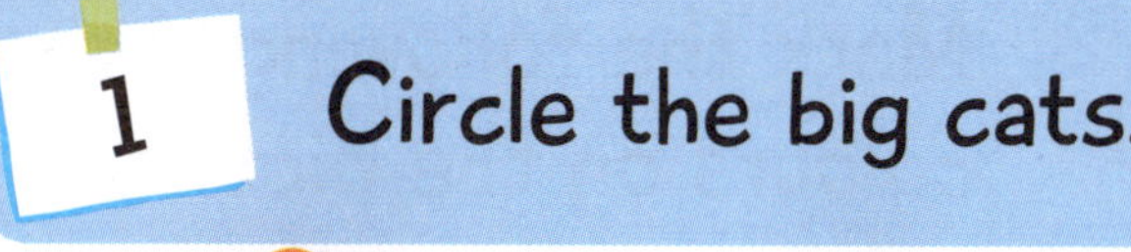

1 Circle the big cats.

2 Colour by numbers.

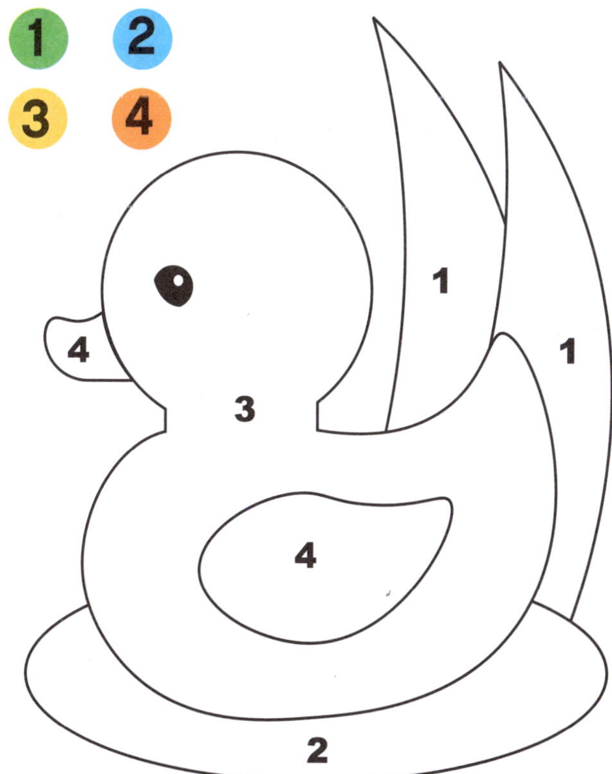

3 Match the animals to their skin patterns.

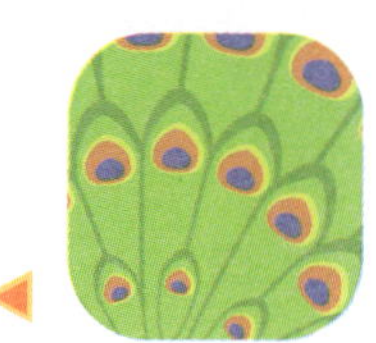

4 Count and write the number of freshwater animals.

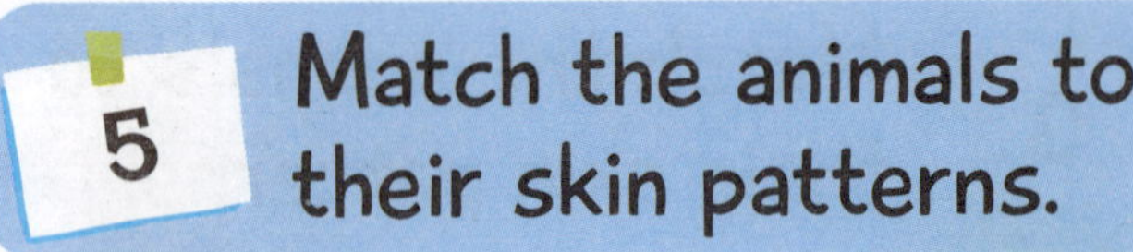

5 Match the animals to their skin patterns.

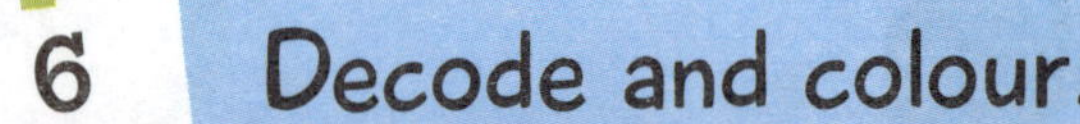

6 Decode and colour.

8

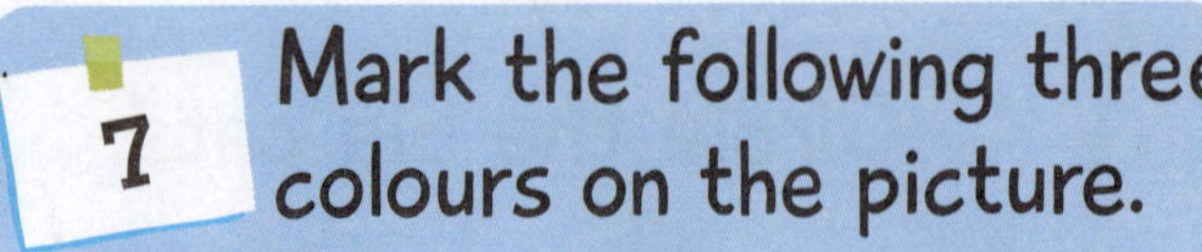

7 Mark the following three colours on the picture.

8 Complete the crossword.

						3			
						4		5	
1			2						
				6					
						9			
		7		8					
	10								

9 Count and write the number of farm animals.

10 Circle the things not needed in a photo shoot. One has been done for you.

11 Count and write the number of animals.

12 Find 10 differences.

13 Take the animals to their homes.

14 Circle the grasshopper.

15 Draw lines to join the parts of the same animal.

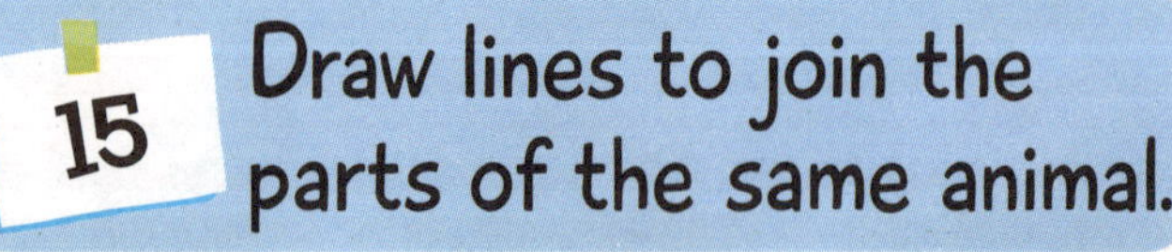

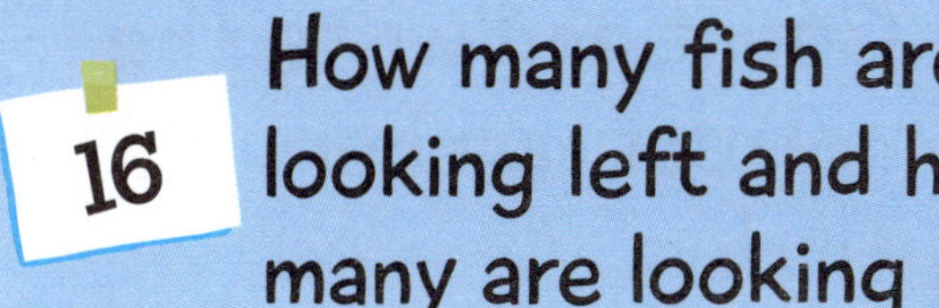

16 How many fish are looking left and how many are looking right?

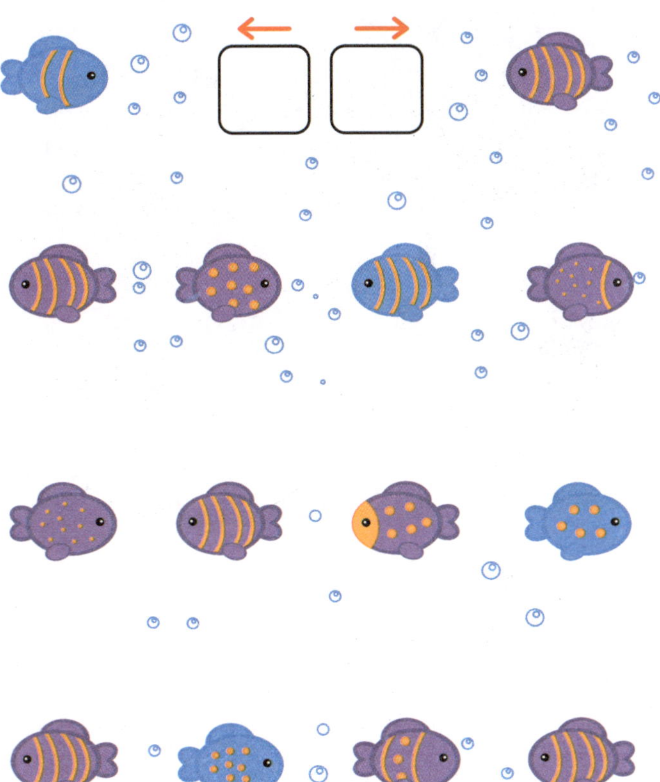

18 Look at the picture and do the following:

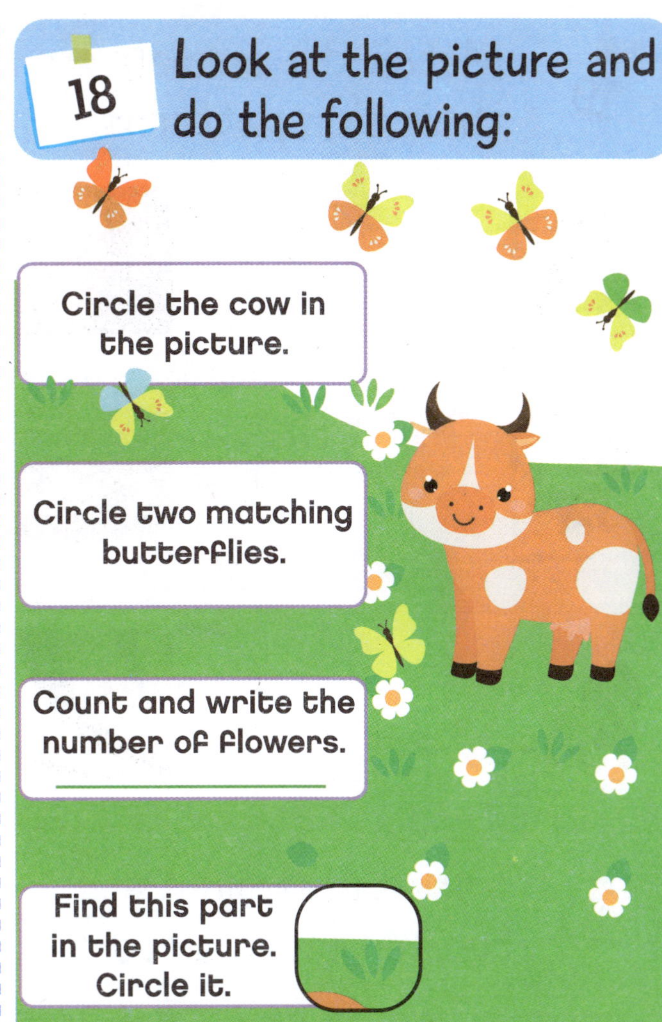

- Circle the cow in the picture.
- Circle two matching butterflies.
- Count and write the number of flowers. ____________
- Find this part in the picture. Circle it.

17 Find these farm animals in the grid.

HORSE

GOAT

CHICK

SHEEP

COW

PIG

CAT

G	O	A	T	P	B	N	C
J	K	I	S	Z	R	M	A
E	S	C	O	D	W	H	T
D	H	L	H	P	D	H	O
I	E	V	P	I	C	O	W
H	E	Z	I	O	H	R	G
K	P	I	G	T	I	S	R
W	U	X	Q	C	H	E	A
D	U	C	K	F	Y	M	O
G	P	S	C	H	I	C	K

19 Match the animals to their skin patterns.

20 Trace the straight and curved lines, then colour.

21 Count and write the correct numbers in the circles.

22 Join the dots in order and colour the picture.

23 Count and write the correct numbers in the boxes.

24 Mark this part on the picture.

25 Count and tick (✓) the right answer.

1 2 4 3

6 7 9 8

3 4 5 2

5 7 6 9

26 Circle the things not needed in a classroom. One has been done for you.

27 Match the animals to their foods.

28 Which animal comes next?

29 Trace the lines and help the animals grab food.

30 What does my name begin with?

_ulture — W U V

_at — B V W

_abbit — R Q P

_orm — W U V

_wan — S K X

_-ray Fish — K X Z

31 Write the missing numbers.

51, ___, ___, 54

___, ___, 57, ___

32 Add and subtract to make a path from 1 to 10.

33 Match the animals to their names.

Flamingo

Sloth

Lion

Zebra

Monkey

Tiger

34 Match the animals to their skin patterns.

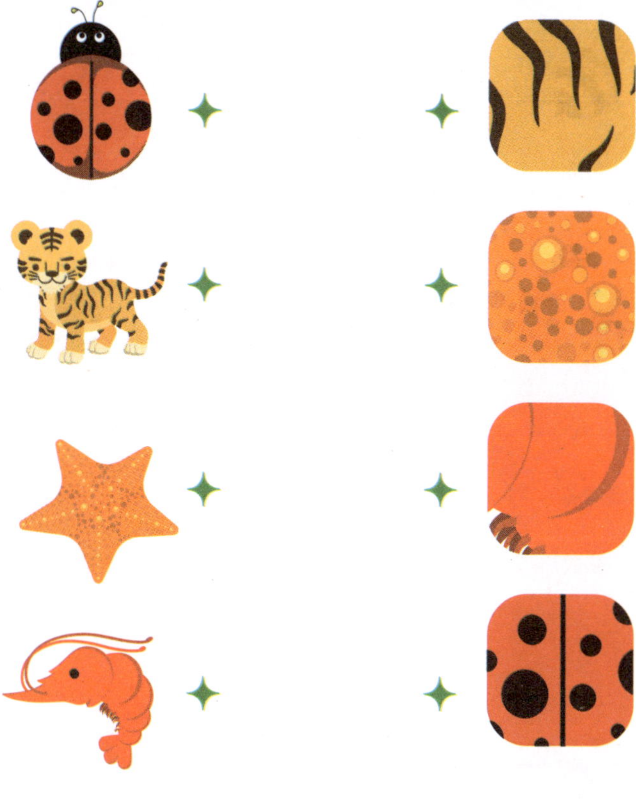

35 Which number shows the honeybee's home?

36 Find the matching shadows.

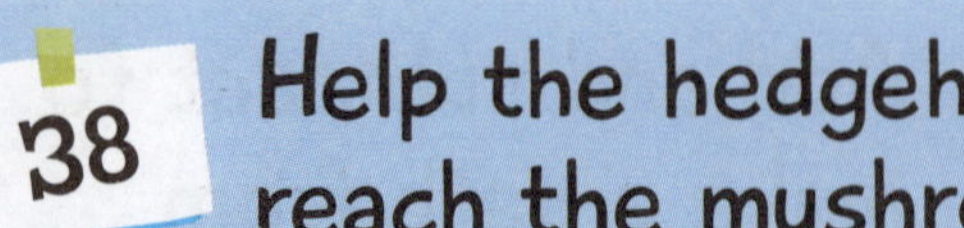

38 Help the hedgehog reach the mushrooms.

37 Colour by numbers.

39 Count and write the number of animals.

40 Complete the ocean crossword.

41 Complete the sudoku puzzle.

42 Circle the things that begin with the given letter.

M...

N...

O...

P...

43 What tools will a baker use? Tick the objects.

44 Circle the farm animals.

45 Match the animals to their tails.

46 Which animal comes next?

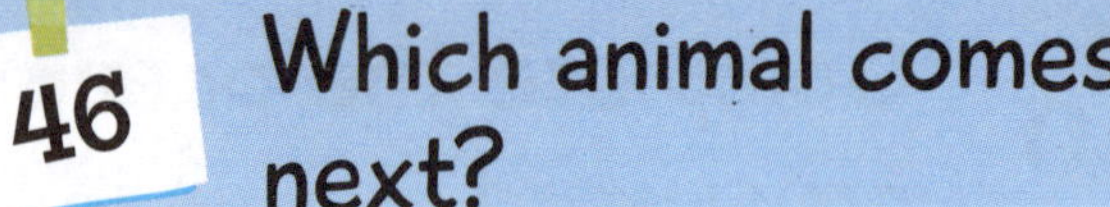

47 Connect the numbers and colour the picture.

48 How many fruits each? Count and write in the boxes.

49 Match the animals to their foods.

50 Trace the lines.

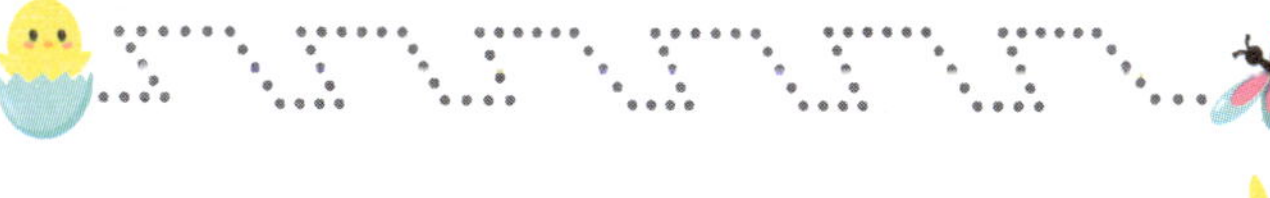

51 Match the bodies to their faces.

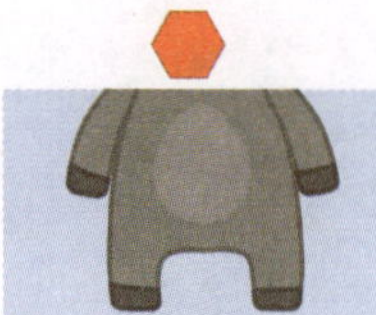

52 Colour by numbers.

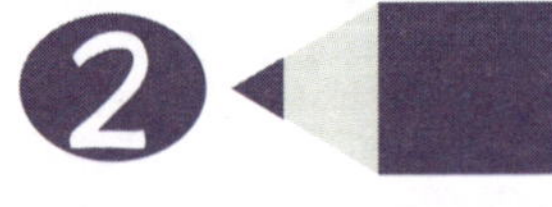

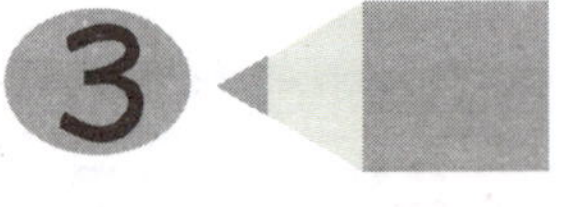

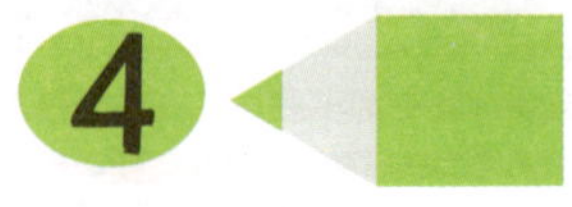

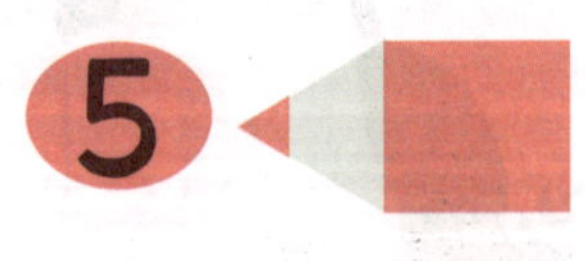

53 Which insects don't have wings? Circle them.

54 Trace the lines and practise drawing.

55 What will a postman use? Tick the objects.

56 Colour the picture.

57 Count the penguins and circle the correct answer.

58 Colour the sparrow.

59 Match the animals to their foods.

60 Find any one pair of identical ladybirds.

61 Help mama reach her baby. Add and subtract to make a path from 1 to 10.

62 What time is it?

3:30 6:40 5:00 11:40 1:45

63 Choose the right spellings.

64 Circle the one not in a pair.

65 Trace the lines.

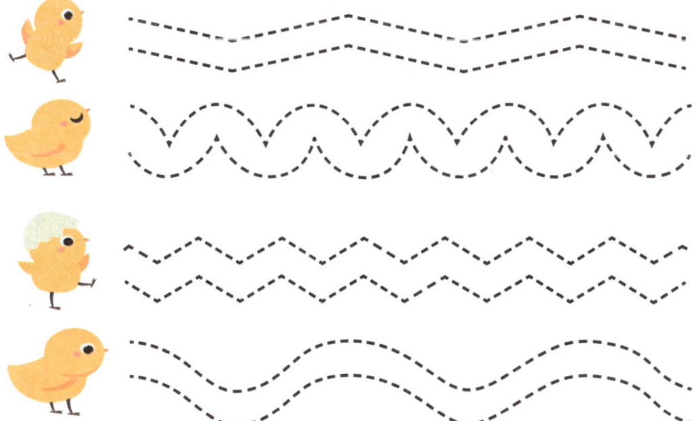

66 Make a word with the hidden letters.

A	B			E	F
G	H	I	J		L
M	N	O	P	Q	R
S	T		V	W	X
		Y	Z		

D			

67 Circle the living things.

68 Find a path for the bear to reach the tree.

69 Find 10 differences.

70 Colour by numbers.

1 2 3 4 5 6 7 8 9

71 How many cars do you see? Write in the box.

72 Find the matching shadows.

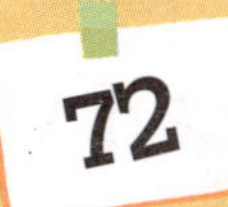

73 Identify the pictures and complete their names.

74 How many birds can you see? Write in the box.

75 Take them to their homes.

76 Trace and colour.

77 Who is behind the bush?

78 How can mama dino reach her hatchling?

79 Trace the lines and colour the pictures.

80 How many shapes each?

81 Match the fronts to the backs.

82 Colour by numbers.

83 Find the sum.

Match each animal to its name.

KOALA PENGUIN RACCOON LEOPARD

Sort the land and the sea animals.

86 Colour the picture.

87 Copy the pattern.

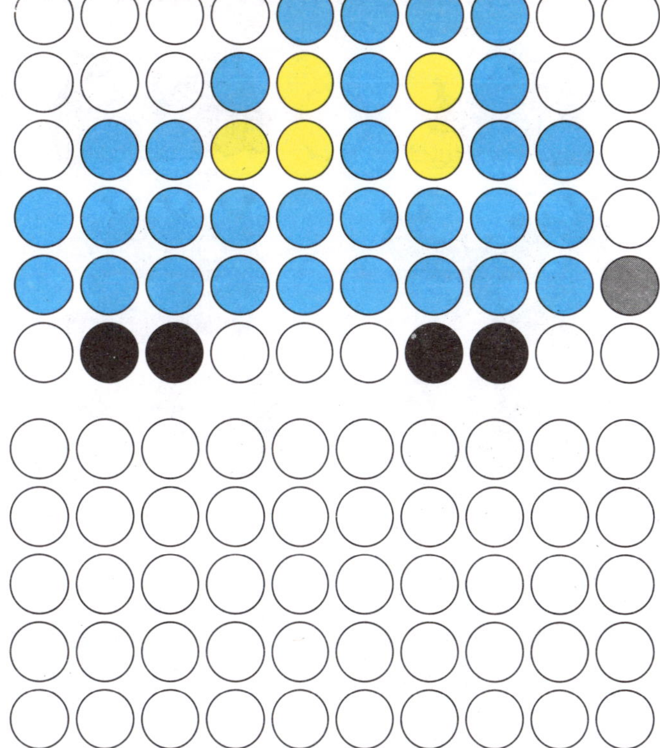

88 Join the dots and colour.

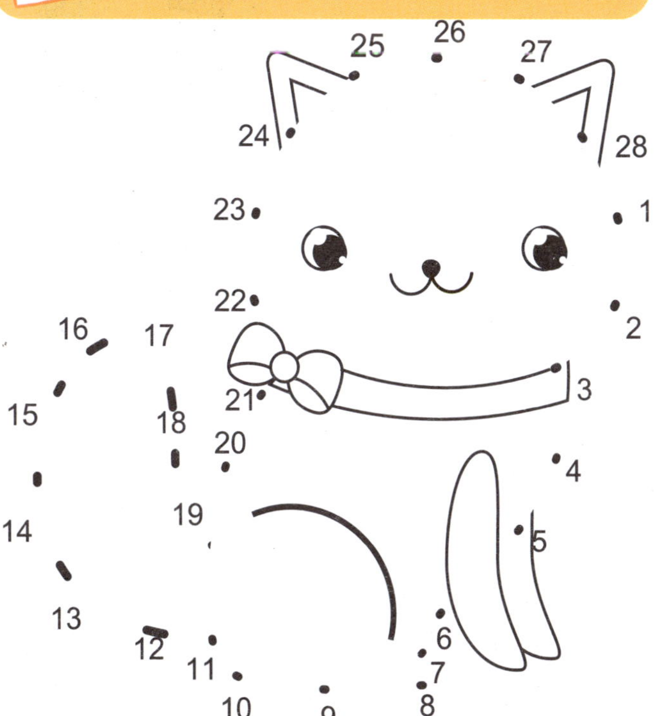

89 More, less or equal to? Put the correct symbols in the circles.

90 Colour the duck in the pond.

91 Which leg belongs to whom?

92 Count and write the number of insects.

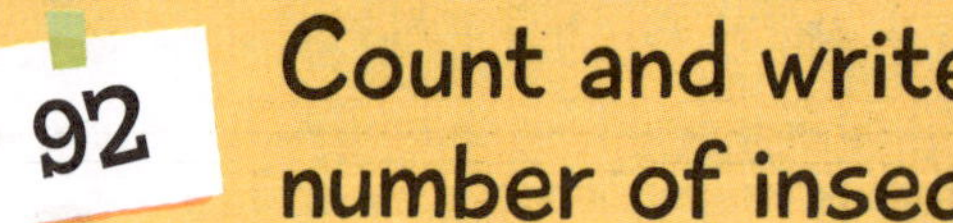

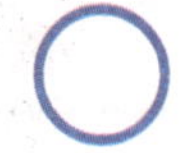

93 Trace the ducklings' paths to their feed.

94 >, < or =? Tick the correct symbol.

96 Rearrange the letters to find my name.

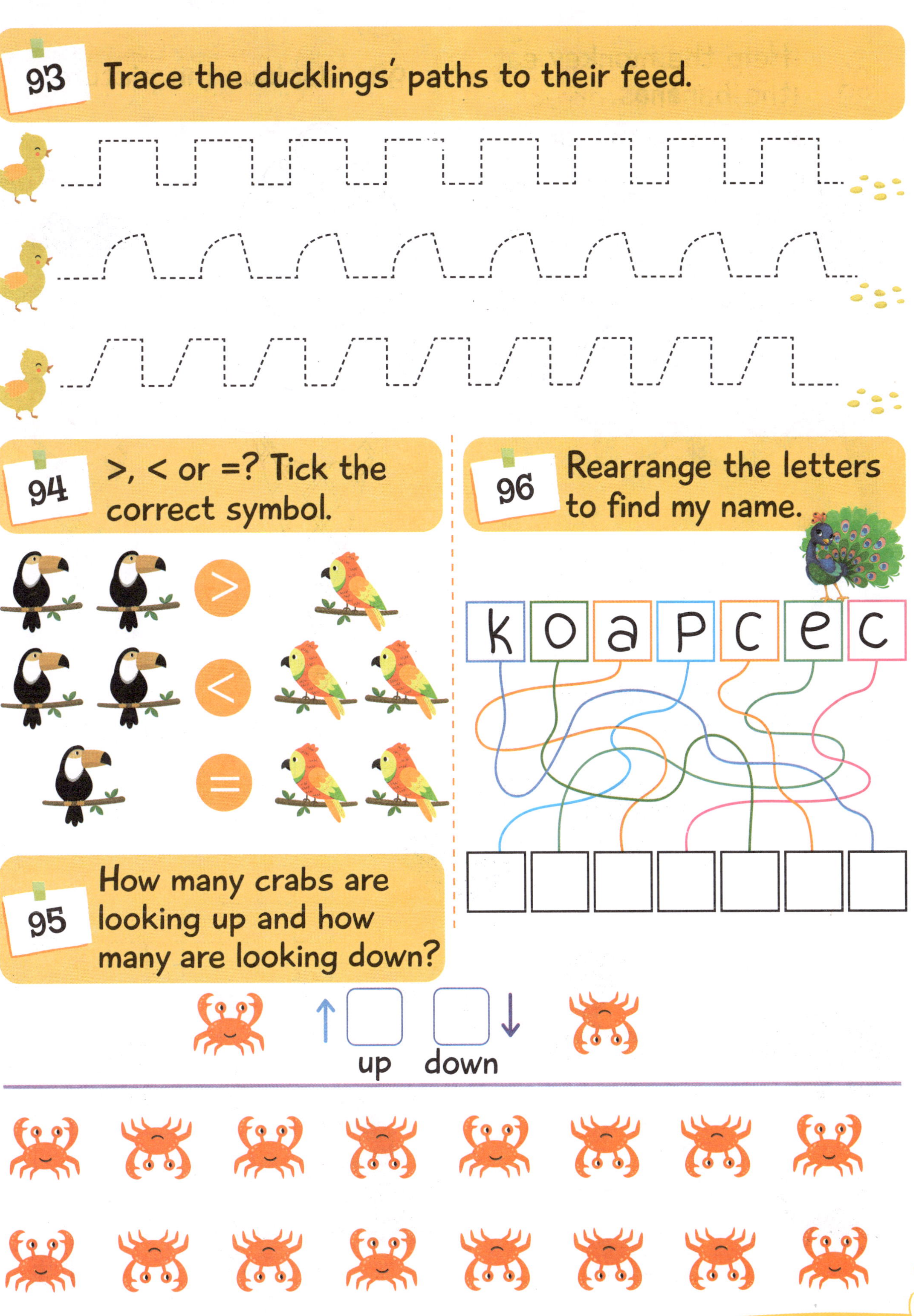

95 How many crabs are looking up and how many are looking down?

97 Help the monkey eat the bananas.

99 Colour the picture.

98 Fill the grid.

100 Find 8 differences.

101 Circle the odd one out.

102 Match the animals to their feet.

103 Trace the lines and colour the picture.

104 Find 6 differences and colour the picture.

105 Match the sea animals with their names.

 ★  ★ CRAB

 ★ ★ 

 ★ ★ 

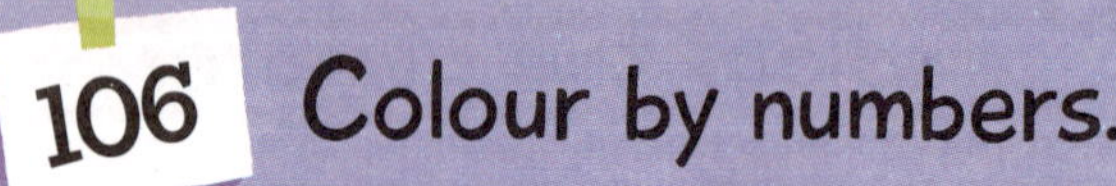

106 Colour by numbers.

107 Add and write the answers in the boxes.

1 + 0 = ☐  8 + 2 = ☐

4 + 6 = ☐ 7 + 0 = ☐

3 + 2 = ☐  9 + 1 = ☐

108 Rearrange the letters to find my name.

109 Trace the loopy lines from the birds to the birdhouse.

110 Add and subtract to make a path from 1 to 10.

111 How many birds are flying?

112 Match the creatures to their tails.

Pair the birds and colour them.

Copy the colour pattern.

115 Connect the dots in order and colour the picture.

117 Fill in the missing letters to find my name.

T		R		E	

116 Help each bird get back to the bird village.

118 Find the identical two.

119 Colour by numbers.

120 Colour the avocet.

121 Match the pieces by drawing lines to the bird.

122 Match the birds to the correct shadows.

123 Number each block as per the dots around it.

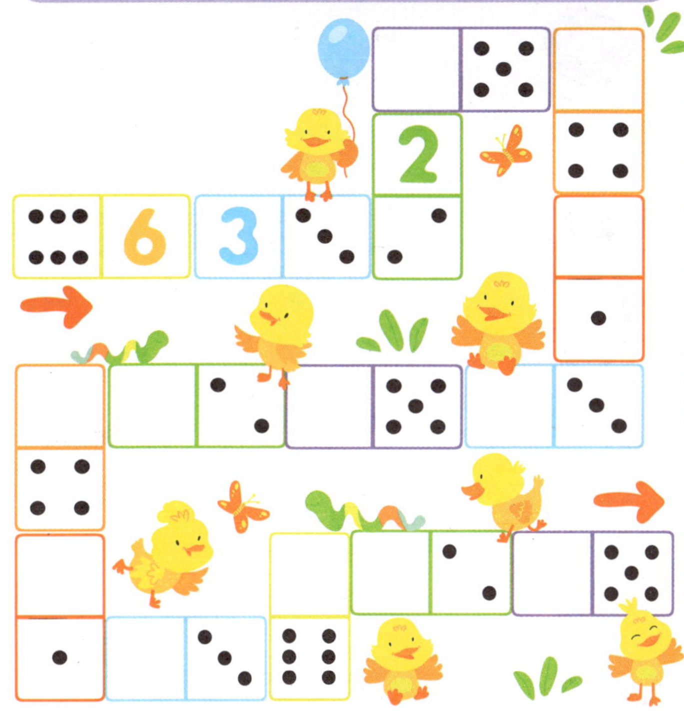

124 Join the dots in order and colour the clown fish.

125 Draw a trail from 1 to 16.

		1	0	3	5	4
			1	2	8	7
3	2	1	5	3	4	0
4	7	3	10	11	9	8
5	6	7	18	10	13	19
8	10	8	9	15	12	17
9	15	11	10	18	11	16
18	13	12	11	16		
17	14	15	16	→		

126 Make a word with the hidden letters.

A	B	C	D	E	F
	H		J	K	L
M		O		Q	
	T	U	V	W	X
		Y	Z		

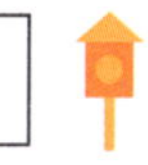

127 Which bird comes next?

A  B  C 

128 Colour the chameleon brightly!

129 Match the animals to their young ones.

130 Trace the lines.

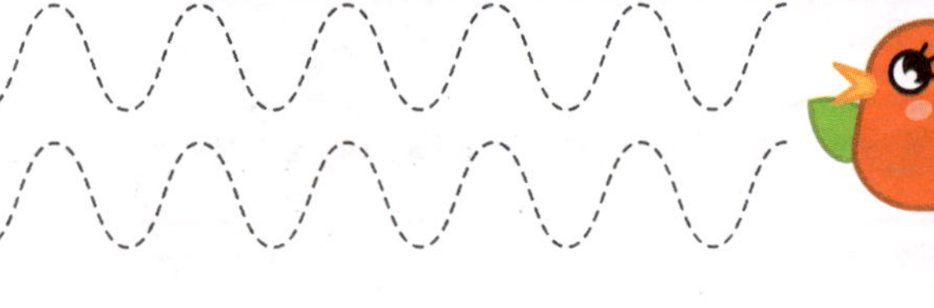

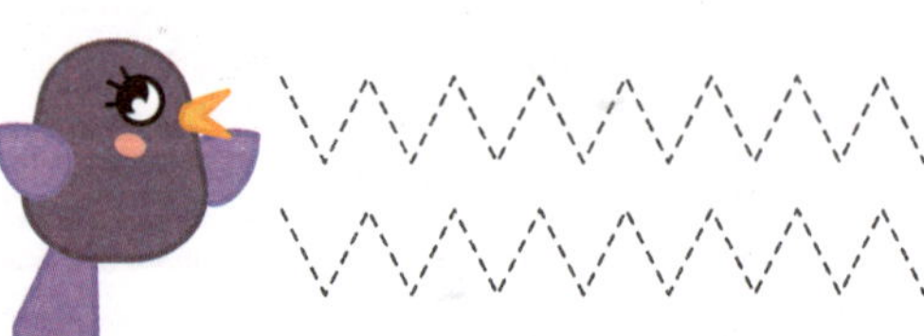

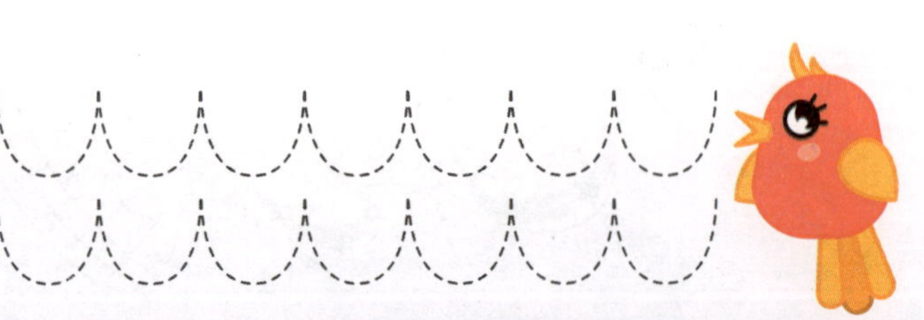

131 Connect the dots from 1 to 10 and colour.

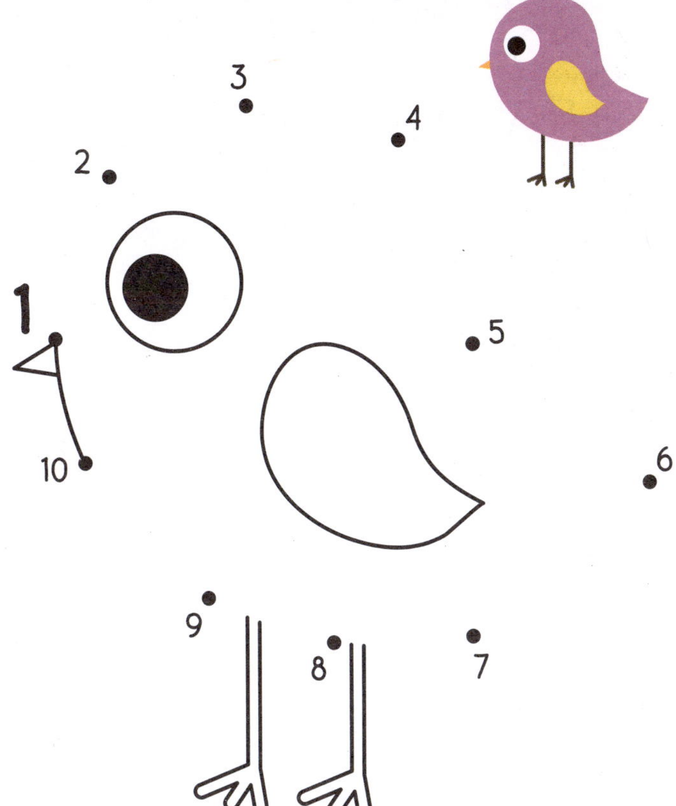

132 Help the little penguin join his friends.

133 Make a word with the hidden letters.

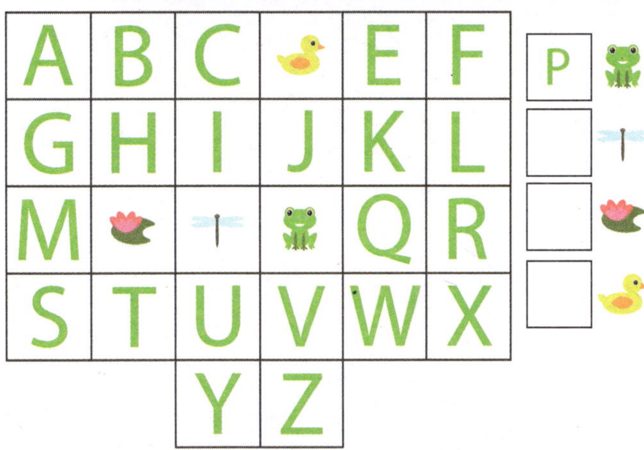

134 Trace the paths.

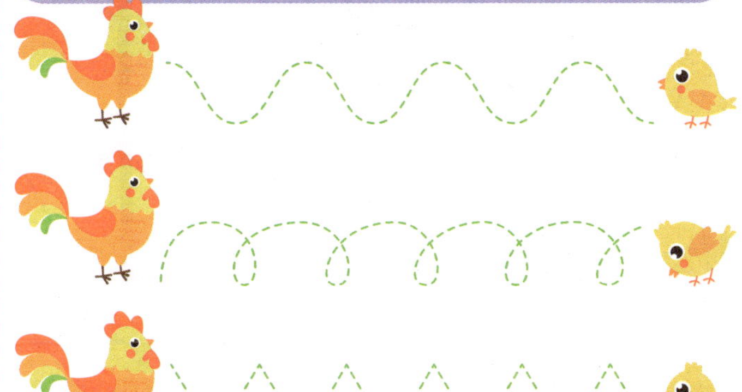

135 Match the animals to the food they eat.

136 Colour by numbers.

1-Pink

2-Green

3-Red

4-Yellow

5-Blue

137 How many snails are there? Write in the box.

138 Trace the lines and circles. Then, colour the bird.

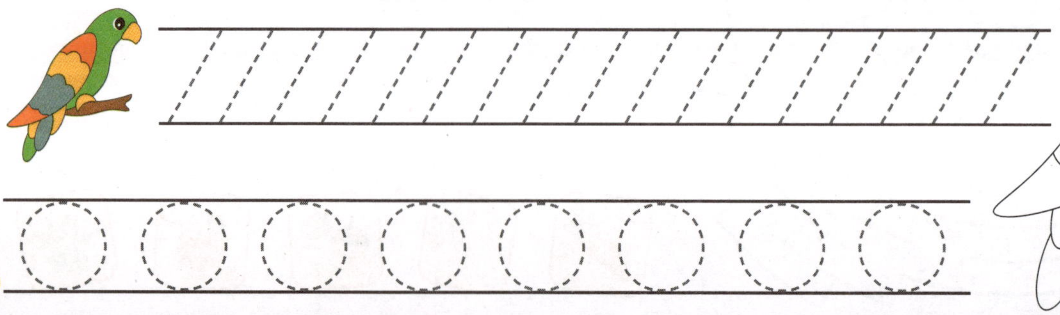

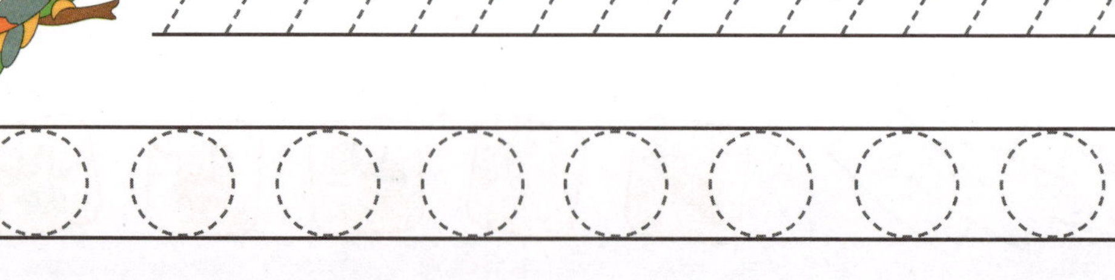

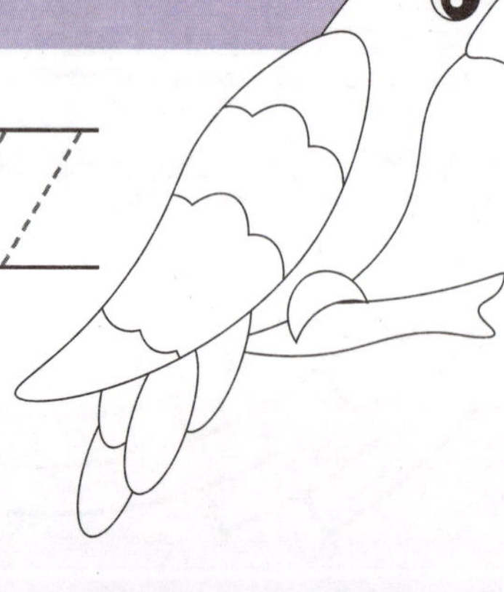

139 Look at the picture and colour.

141 Find the matching shadows.

140 Draw the other half.

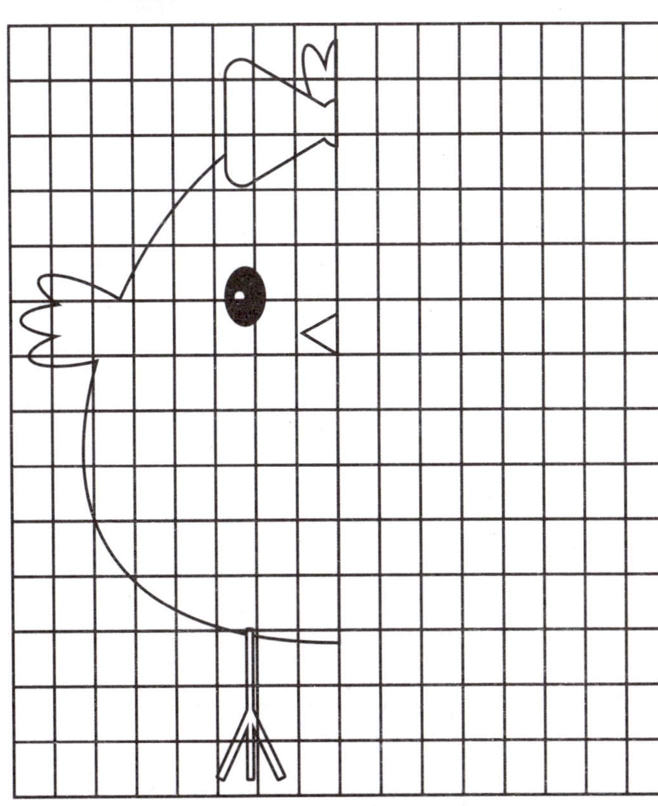

142 Spot the flamingo.

143 How many fruits are there? Write in the boxes.

144 Help the duckling waddle over to its mama.

145 Practise number writing.

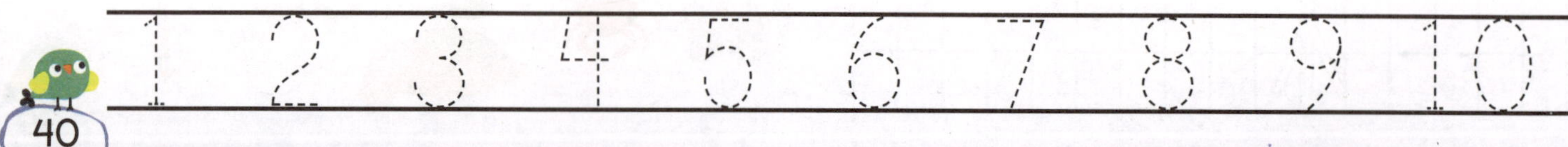

146 Make a word with the hidden letters.

B

147 Join the dots and colour the goose.

148 Match the fronts to the backs.

149 >, < or =? Write the correct symbol in the circle.

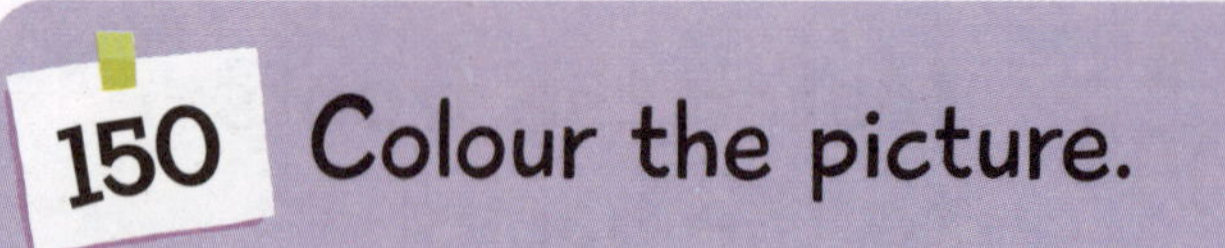

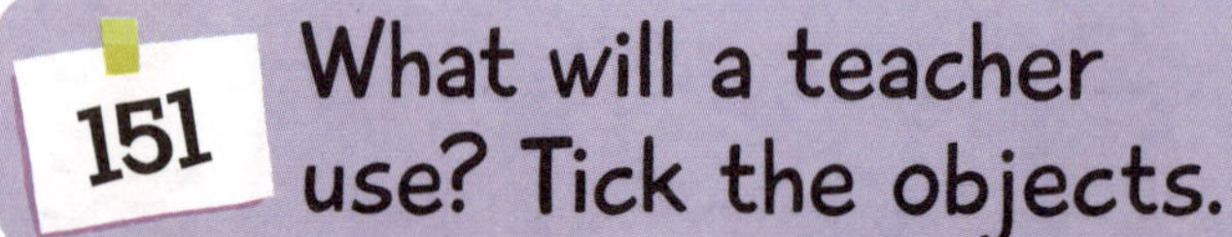

152 Trace only number 4s.

9 4 7 1 8 3 6 1 5 10 1 7 3 2 3 5 8 10 5 8

2 1 9 4 1 9 7 1 2 1 6 6 1 2 6 4 8 7 6 3 4 9 5

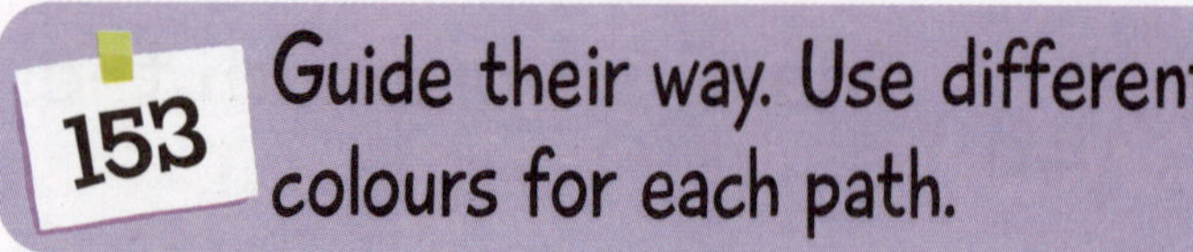

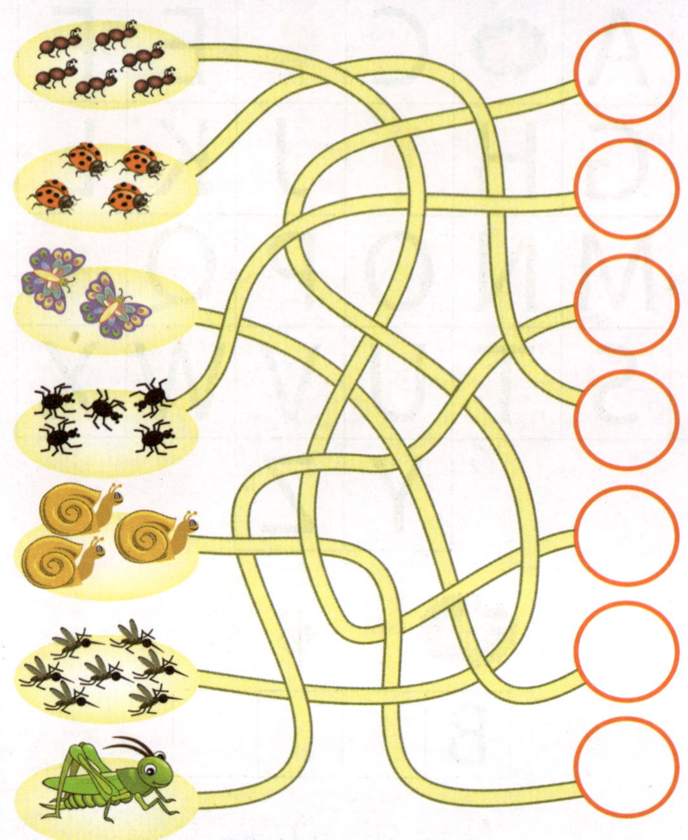

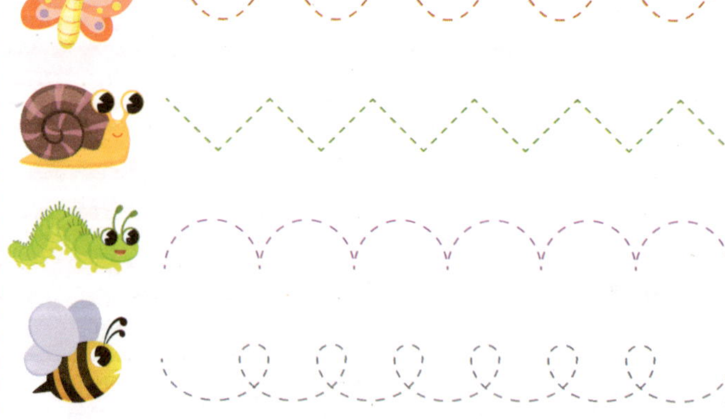

155 Connect the dots from 1 to 20 and colour the flamingo.

156 Fill in the missing letter.

157 Help the goose waddle over to the pumpkin.

158 Colour all the small o's yellow.

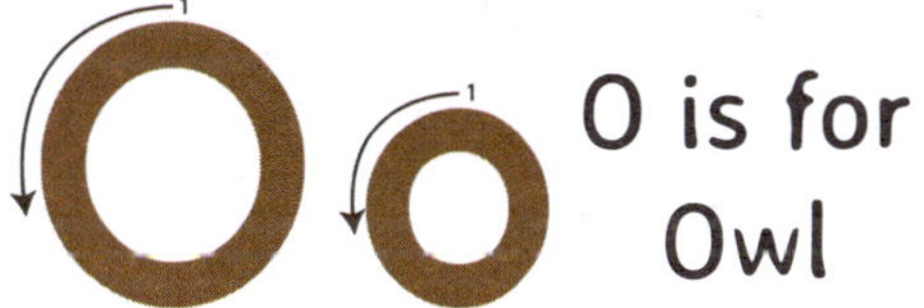

k O w a P a E
o m Y o o o E
v Q w x y A m
t b s h O
p w
d f k y
a b
c o c O
h h o y o f w

159 Join the dots from 1 to 16 and colour the picture.

160 Help the pair get back together. Trace a path from 1 to 22.

				2	5	6	8	3	10
			→	1	2	3	9	7	9
			10	8	7	4	6	9	10
17	8	16	14	11	9	5	8	9	11
14	15	20	9	13	14	6	7	12	10
10	9	13	12	11	10	9	8	18	20
22	23	14	17	19	21	23	26	29	32
28	25	15	16	20	23	27	30		
19	17	14	17	13	21	22	→		
12	10	28	18	19	20	10	12		

161 Match the sea creatures to their body parts.

162 Which Easter eggs have birds drawn on them? Colour them.

163 Match the swan to the correct shadow.

165 Trace and colour the parrot.

164 Trace all the lines and colour the picture.

166 Add, subtract and solve the sum.

			8	+	3	+
						2
						-
						9
						+
1	+	6	-	7	+	6
-						
3						
+						
7						
+	4	-	5	=		

167 Connect the dots from 1 to 30 and colour.

169 Draw and colour the other half.

168 Follow the instructions to make an origami dog.

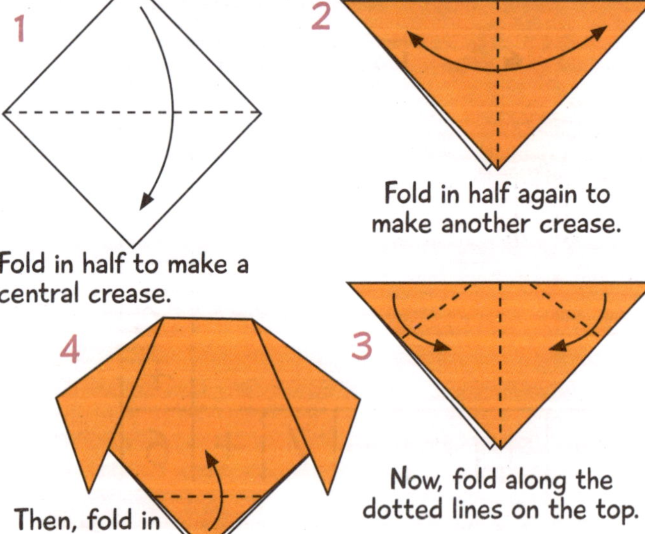

1 Fold in half to make a central crease.

2 Fold in half again to make another crease.

3 Now, fold along the dotted lines on the top.

4 Then, fold in the bottom tip dotted line.

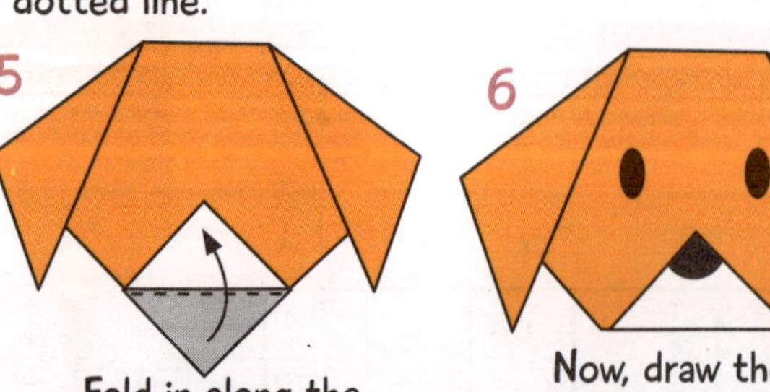

5 Fold in along the dotted line.

6 Now, draw the eyes and nose as shown.

170 Help the dinosaur reach the eggs.

171 Colour by numbers.

1 2 3 4 5

172 Write the missing letters.

p_a_ p_ac_ l_m_n or_n_e a_p_e

173 Circle only the non-living objects.

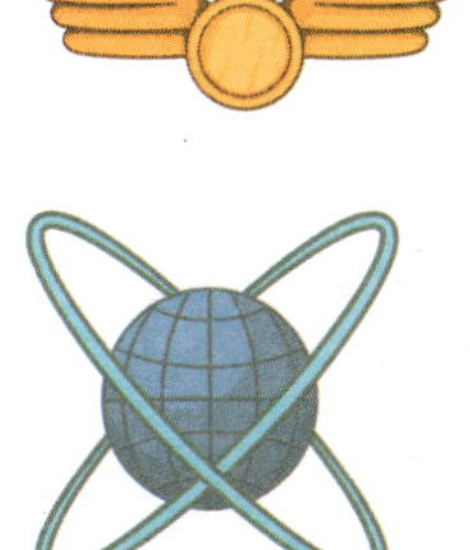

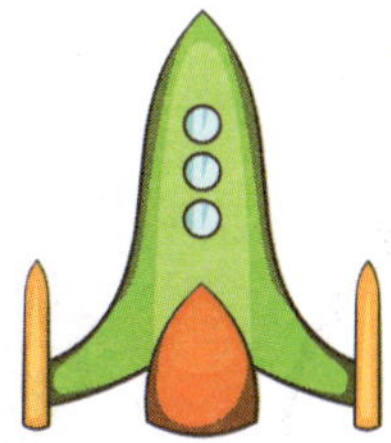

174 Which image comes next?

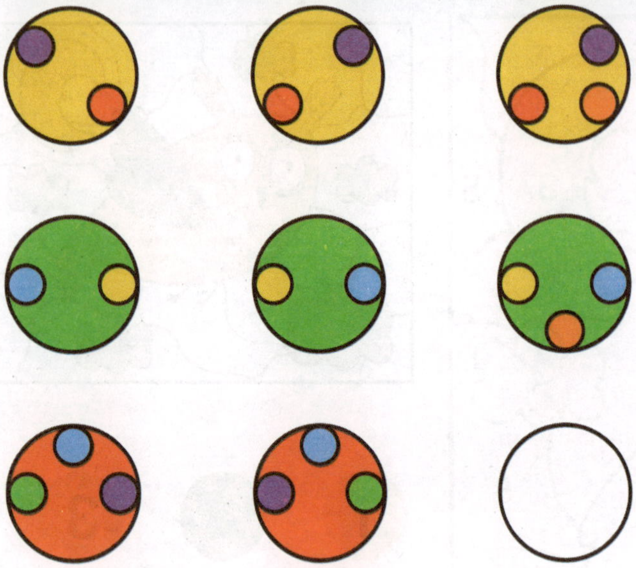

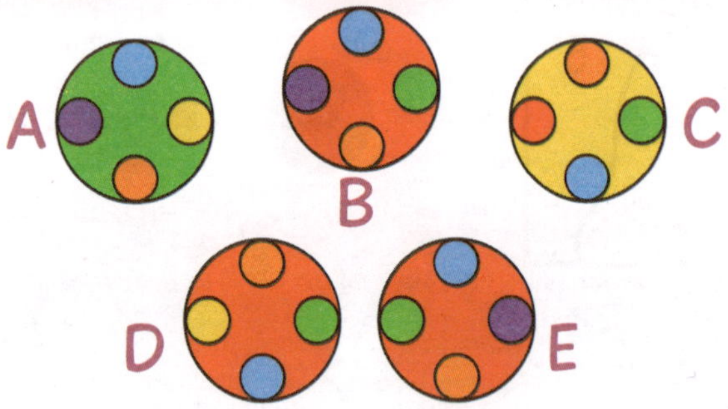

A B C D E

176 Match the names to the pictures.

- Bird
- Butterfly
- Balloon
- Banana

175 Can you trace these numbers?

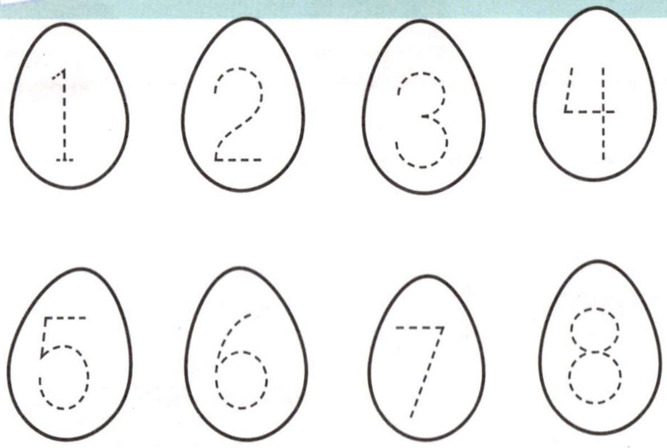

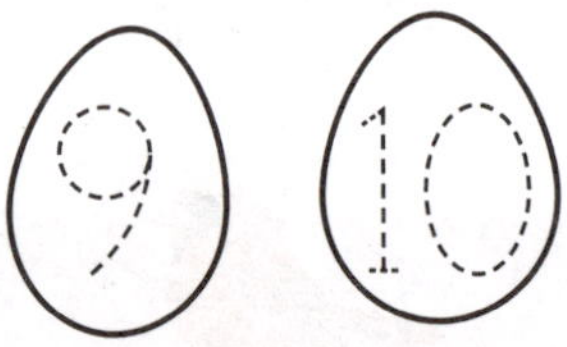

1 2 3 4 5 6 7 8 9 10

177 Look at the image and colour.

178 Count and write the number of slices.

180 Circle the correct shadow.

179 Calculate and write the answers.

181 Connect the matching pairs of butterflies.

182 Find the names of these birds in the grid.

D	T	H	A	F	L	A	M	I	N	G	O
O	W	L	T	R	E	I	N	D	I	E	R
V	O	T	W	E	A	T	S	K	G	A	K
E	A	T	O	U	C	A	N	F	H	L	D
T	C	A	O	G	E	S	Z	L	T	N	P
Y	R	Z	D	X	R	B	E	A	I	P	A
R	A	I	P	E	L	I	C	A	N	A	R
U	N	K	E	O	M	O	U	S	G	R	R
P	E	A	C	O	C	K	A	F	A	Q	O
F	U	W	K	R	U	B	E	A	L	W	T
K	I	L	E	E	R	W	H	A	E	P	H
X	N	Y	R	G	S	W	A	N	W	K	I

183 Circle the things not found in a laboratory. One has been done for you.

184 How many bugs are there?

185 What will a basketball player use? Tick the objects.

BASKETBALL PLAYER

186 Connect the dots from 1 to 15 and colour the picture.

187 Match the coloured shapes to their colour names.

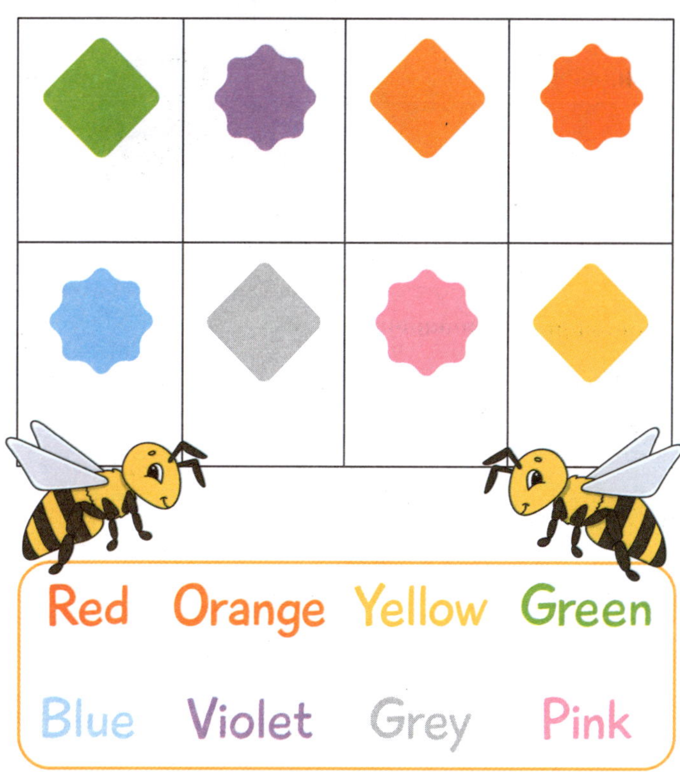

188 Circle the twin parrots.

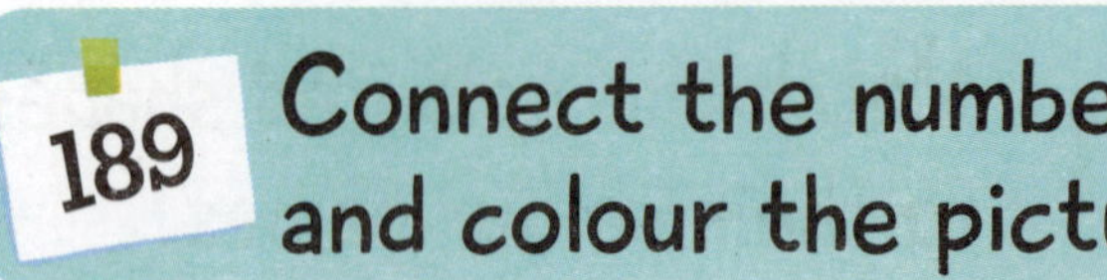

189 Connect the numbers and colour the picture.

190 Colour by numbers.

191 Trace the wavy, raguly and cloudy lines.

192 Help the caterpillar eat through the apple.

193 Complete the sudoku puzzle.

194 Count and write the number of fruits.

195 Find the matching shadows.

196 Circle the things not needed by a priest. One has been done for you.

197 Connect the dots from 1 to 5 and colour the picture.

198 Spell out my name.

199 Write the names of the shapes.

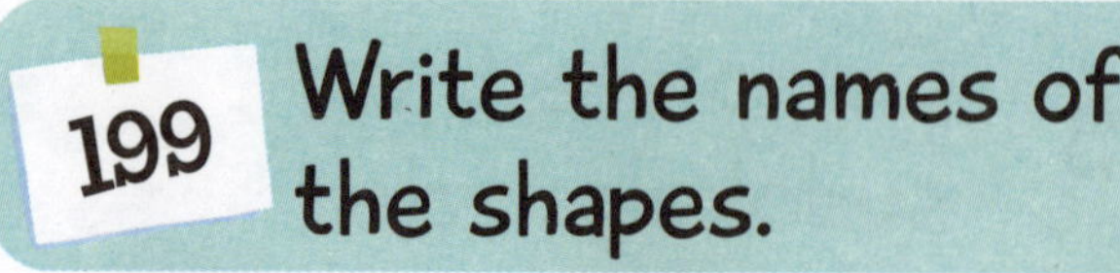

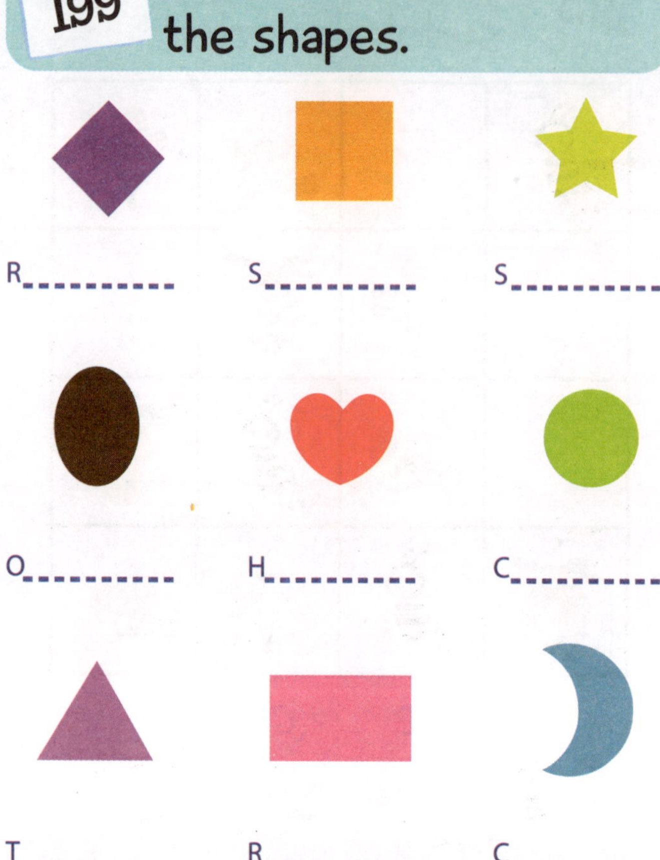

200 Colour the picture.

Count the baked goodies.

Find the matching shadows.

How many honeybees are there?

Match and write the missing letter.

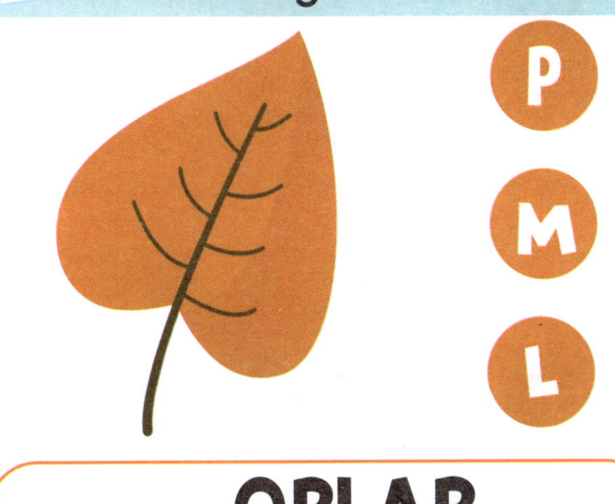

205 Colour by numbers.

207 Add and write the answers in the boxes.

206 Match the creatures to their shadows.

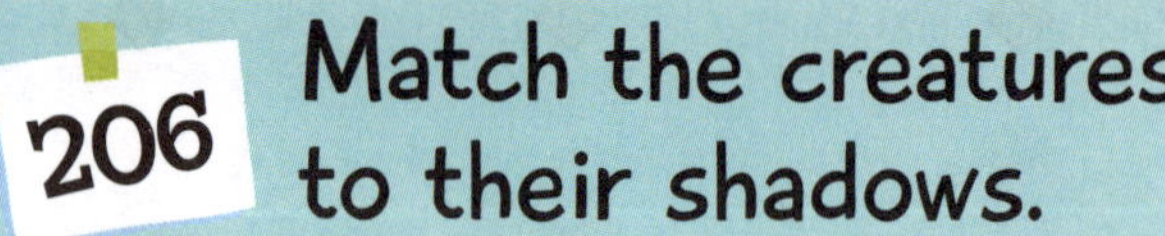

208 Solve the sudoku puzzle.

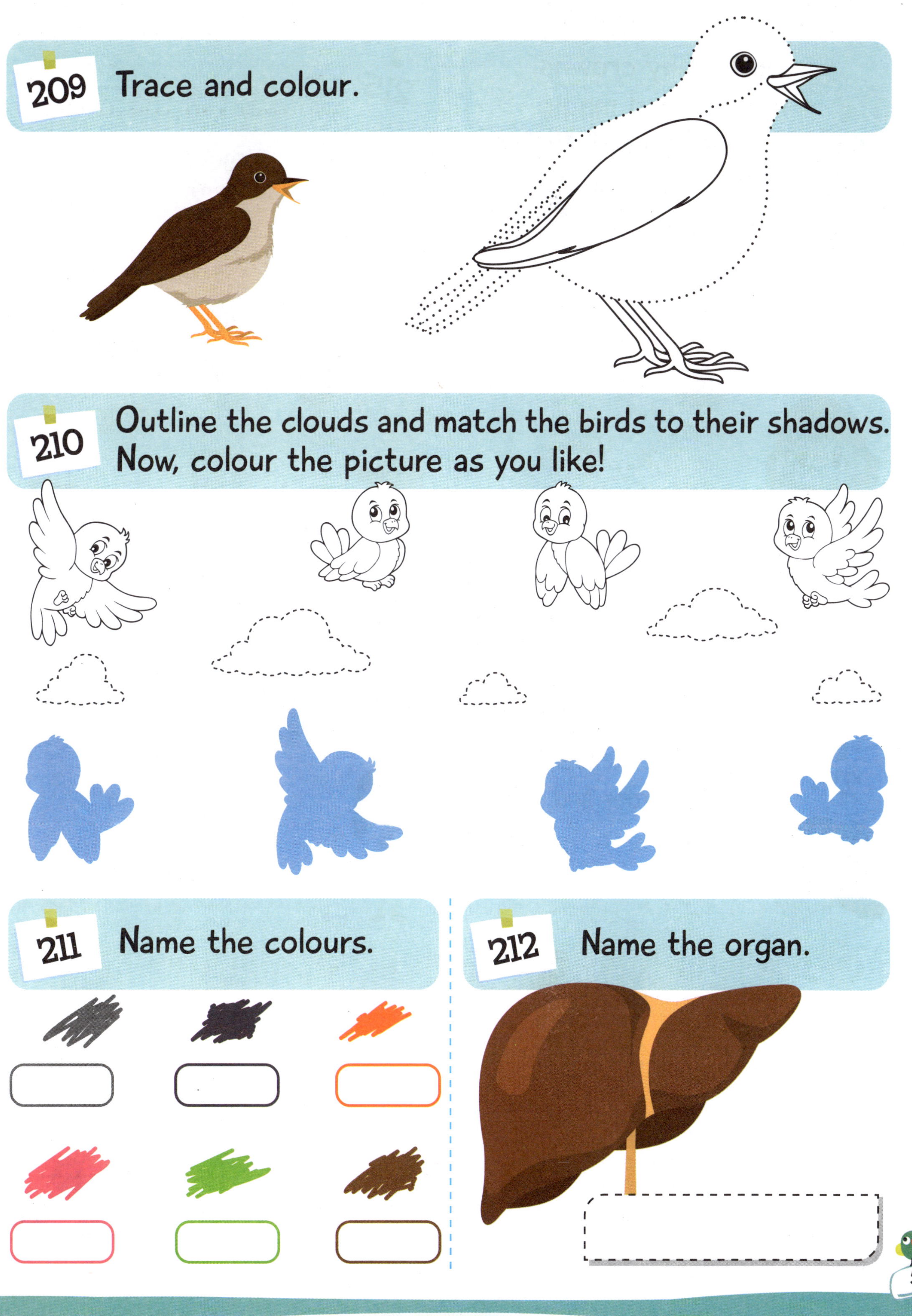
209 Trace and colour.
210 Outline the clouds and match the birds to their shadows.
Now, colour the picture as you like!
211 Name the colours.
212 Name the organ.

213 How many crowns, mirrors and magic wands lie next to the little mermaid? Count and write.

214 Connect the numbers in ascending order and colour.

215 Circle the rib cage.

216 Help the doctor treat the virus.

Circle yes or no in the following:

The car is moving without a driver.

The plane is floating in the sea.

218 Write the missing letter.

H

G

__UPITER

Count and write the number of clothes.

220 Colour only the fish.

221 Can you find at least 10 birds in the grid? One has been done for you.

S	P	I	G	E	O	N	H	K	Y	R	W	A	X	F
B	H	U	N	A	I	M	A	W	S	S	E	O	W	L
K	S	E	A	G	U	L	L	G	W	R	E	W	S	A
T	G	U	T	L	S	E	S	K	A	A	N	D	H	M
G	S	B	P	E	L	I	C	A	N	U	H	B	N	I
T	A	R	E	V	C	D	O	Q	Z	E	N	P	I	N
U	P	Y	N	P	S	N	N	E	R	R	G	E	V	G
R	R	S	G	E	T	U	D	P	I	Y	R	A	X	O
K	A	U	U	G	S	T	O	R	K	Q	E	C	U	O
E	H	R	I	I	P	S	R	H	K	C	R	O	W	N
Y	Q	R	N	P	D	H	L	C	P	W	T	C	A	F
V	T	E	R	L	W	O	O	D	P	E	C	K	E	R

222 Colour all the capital Qs purple.

Q is for Quail

a q p x Z f

F q Q h s B a x

r n Q r y g y

b s f x e j h

p M h e R Q

q a A p a q r

p p B d i b

B w f M

c D E r f

r x Q q s x

223 Colour by numbers.

1 2 3

224 Write the missing numbers.

225 Trace the lines.

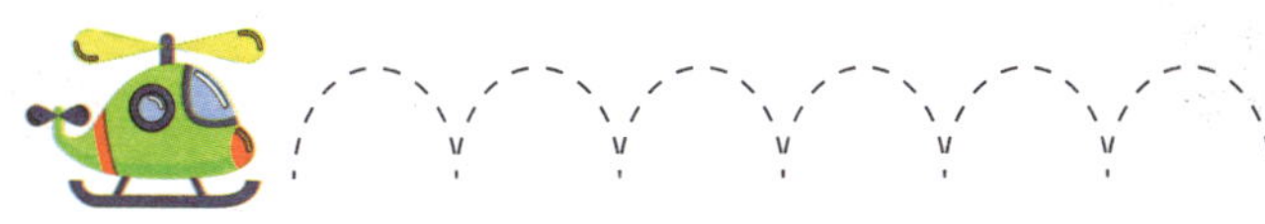

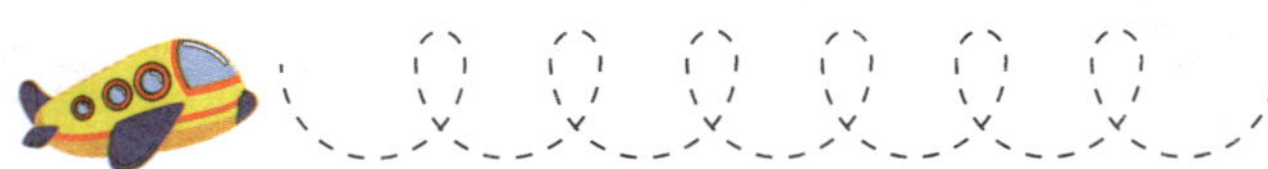

226 Write the first letter of each word to make a new one.

227 How many road vehicles are there? Write in the boxes.

228 Find 10 differences between the two images and colour them.

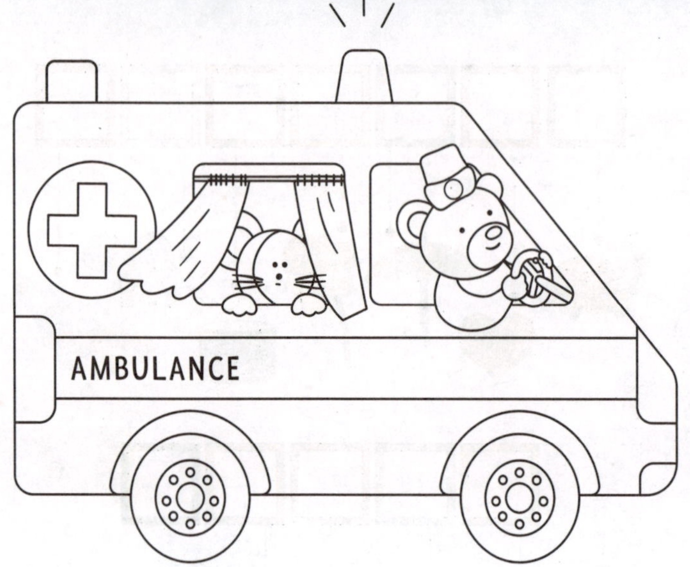

229 Copy the colours.

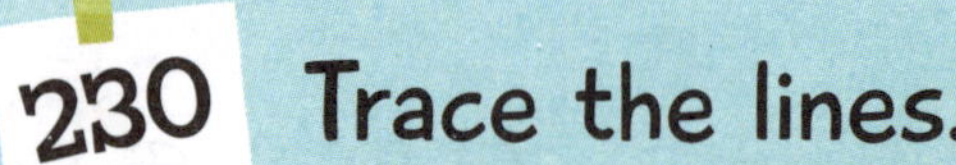
230 Trace the lines.

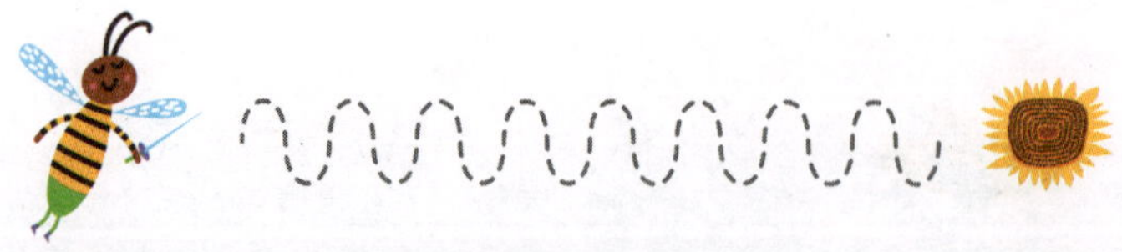

231 Help the water drop and the caterpillar reach the plant.

232 Connect the dots from 1 to 20 and colour the picture.

233 How many butterflies of each type are there?

234 What is each part known as?

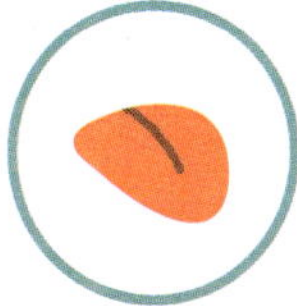
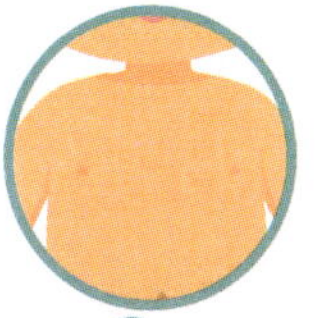
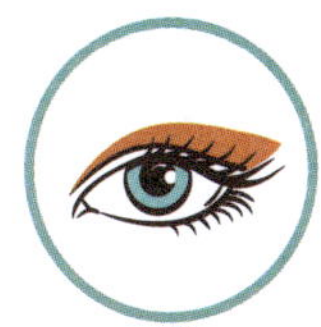

chest ear eye tongue

235 Identify the body part.

Connect the numbers and colour.

Help the bees get to the flowers.

Can you find these insects in the grid?

D	O	N	K	O	Y	P	D	I	P	S	A
R	B	R	T	E	R	M	I	T	E	I	N
A	O	L	C	S	A	T	G	K	M	A	T
G	R	A	S	S	H	O	P	P	E	R	D
O	B	D	A	G	E	S	N	L	R	N	C
N	P	Y	L	A	R	B	E	A	T	P	E
F	O	B	U	T	T	E	R	F	L	Y	I
L	N	I	U	O	M	E	O	L	E	R	M
Y	G	R	S	G	W	H	A	Y	A	K	O
F	U	D	L	R	U	B	E	A	G	E	T
K	I	L	C	O	C	K	R	O	A	C	H
C	A	R	P	E	N	T	E	R	A	N	T

239 Match as per colour combinations.

241 Sort the insects into the jars by their type.

240 Colour by numbers.

1 - Red

2 - Yellow

3 - Brown

4 - Purple

5 - Green

6 - Blue

242 Make a word with the hidden letters.

244 Look at the picture and colour.

243 Trace and colour.

245 Colour all the small and capital Cs green.

C a c p C Z C c T
N C Z p K J s m
W c b H c C Q E C C
t D C N h
c T f E Q s C s
Z A H s p J m
C p K c K c p C

246 What will a diver use? Tick the objects.

247 Number the steps in sequence.

248 Trace the path and colour the butterfly.

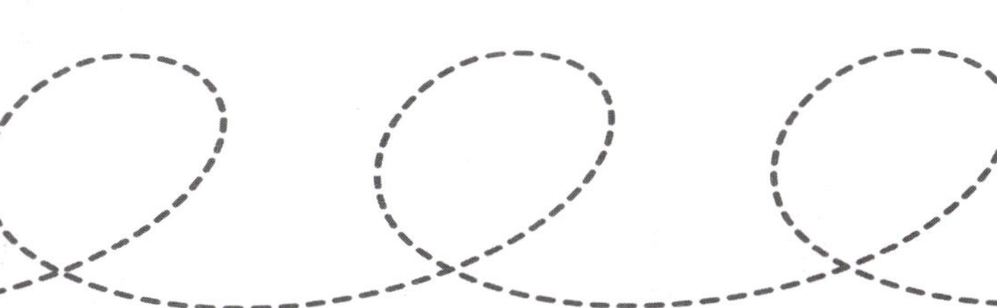

249 How many stationery items are there?

250 Write the missing letter.

E__RTH

251 What will a policeman use? Tick the objects.

252 Trace the lines.

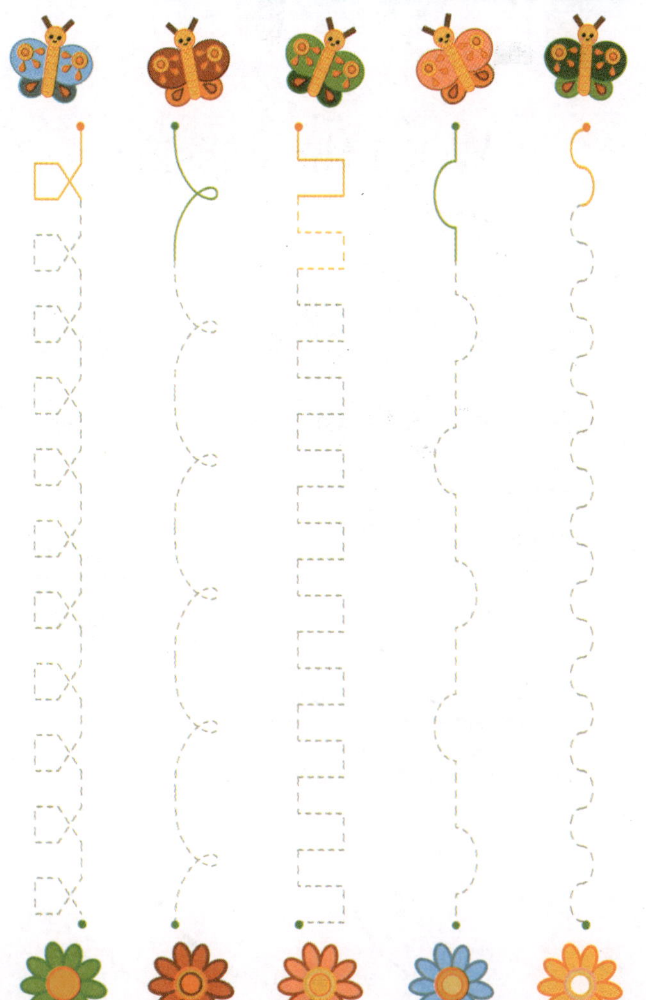

253 Trace and colour the picture.

254 Add and write the answers on the leaves.

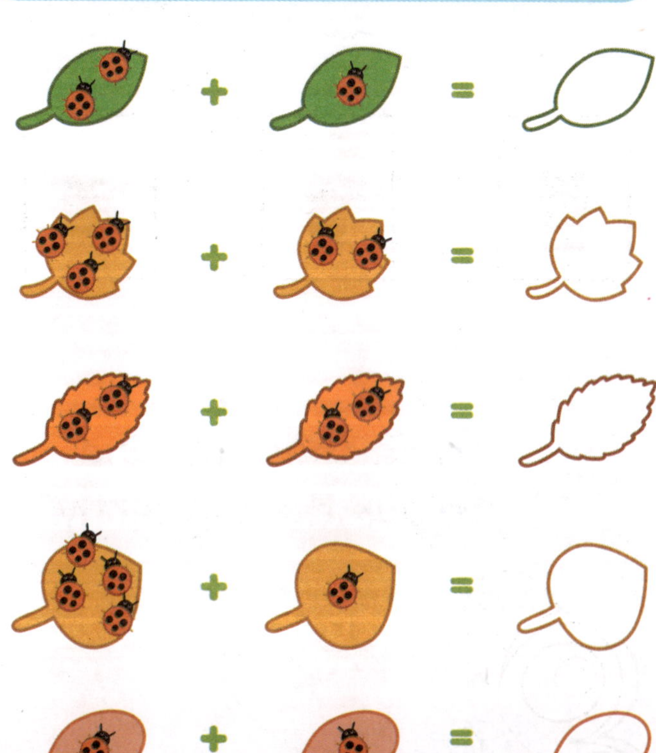

255 Write the missing numbers.

256 Help the friends meet by tracing the dotted lines.

257 How many crawlies are there?

258 Connect the dots from 1 to 10 and colour the dragonfly.

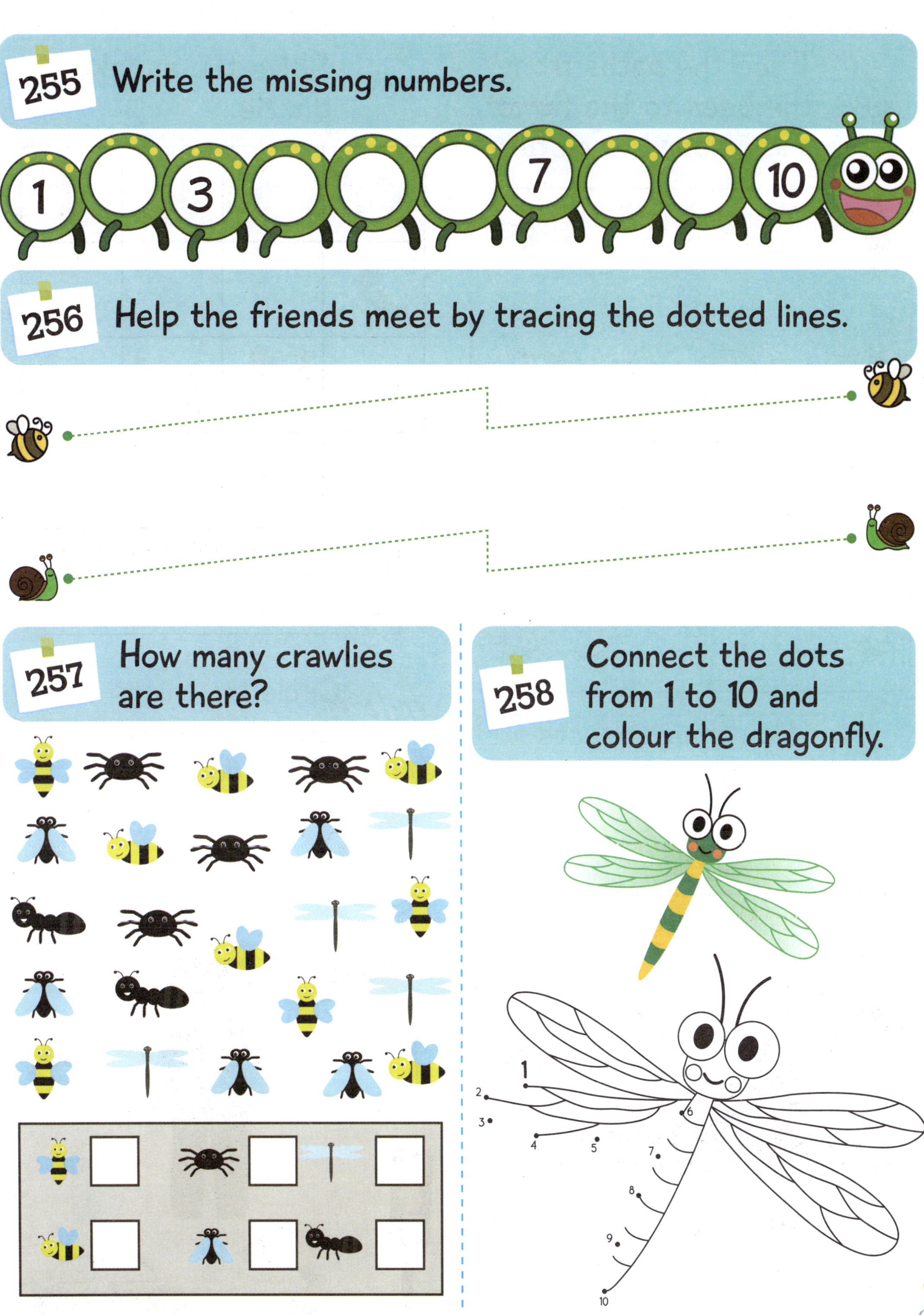

259 Trace the paths from the bees to the flower and colour the picture.

260 How many insects are there?

261 Solve the sudoku puzzle.

262 Circle the things not needed by a taxi driver. One has been done for you.

263 Which mode of transport comes next?

264 Find the matching shadows.

265 Trace numbers from 1 to 16 to create a trail.

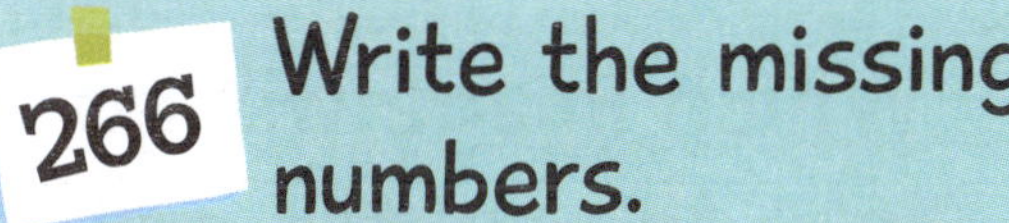

266 Write the missing numbers.

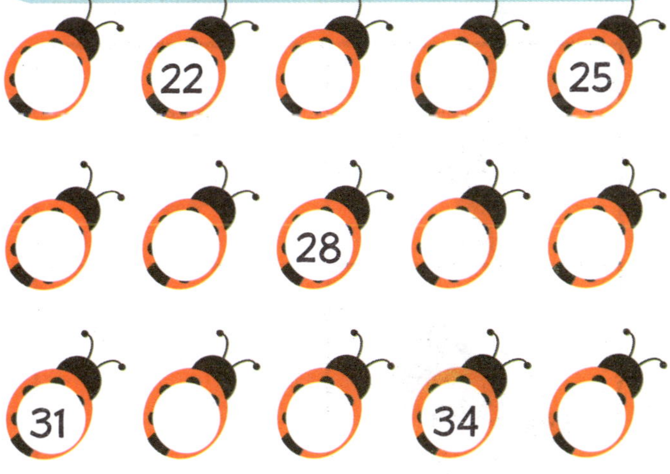

267 Trace the lines and colour the picture.

268 Which image will go into the fourth cell?

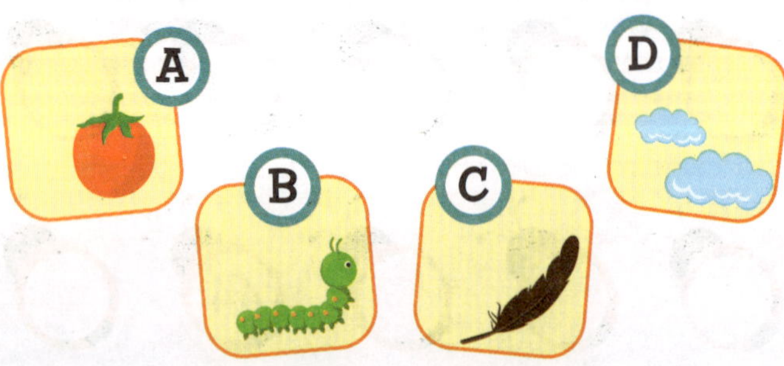

269 Colour by numbers.

1 2 3

270 Subtract and write the answer in the box. One has been done for you.

4 - 1 = 3

3 - 1 = ☐

4 - 2 = ☐

2 - 1 = ☐

4 - 3 = ☐

3 - 2 = ☐

271 Connect number wise and colour.

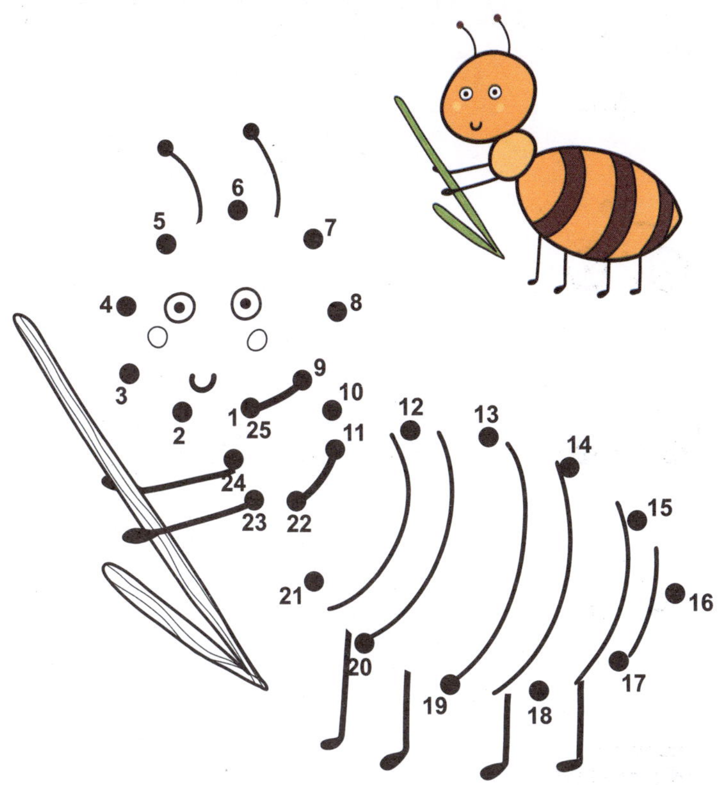

272 Complete the equations.

273 Calculate using logic.

+ = 6

+ + = 13

+ + = 10

– + – =

274 Count and write.

275 What will a baseball player use? Tick the objects.

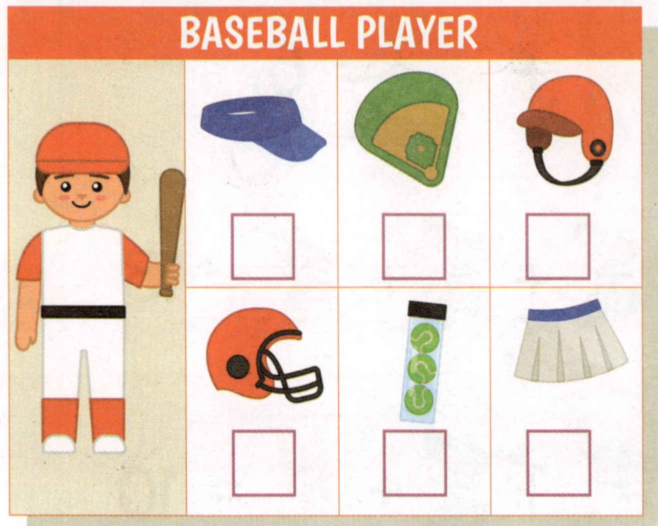

276 Colour by numbers.

1 -  2 - 3 - 

4 - 5 -

277 Trace the words.

helicopter

bicycle

ambulance

scooter

school bus

278 Guess what comes next.

1	2	3	4

Match according to the size.

Trace over the lines.

Solve the sudoku puzzle.

1 2 3 4

Trace the lines and colour the picture.

283 Help the butterfly reach the flower. Trace the numbers.

		2	3	4	7	5
		↓	1	2	9	6
3	2	1	4	6	7	9
4	9	8	6	10	9	18
5	6	3	7	11	17	19
8	7	5	14	16	13	17
15	8	9	14	15	14	16
17	12	10	13	16		
14	13	11	12	↓		

284 Find the matching shadows.

285 Tick the things that a doctor will use.

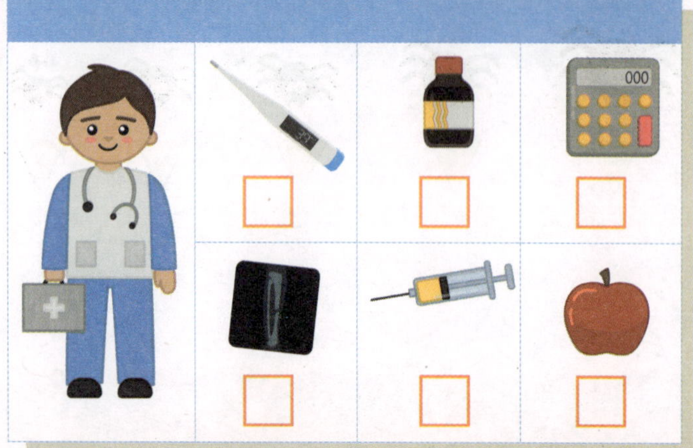

286 Circle the insect that is neither big nor small.

287 Cross (X) the odd one out in each row.

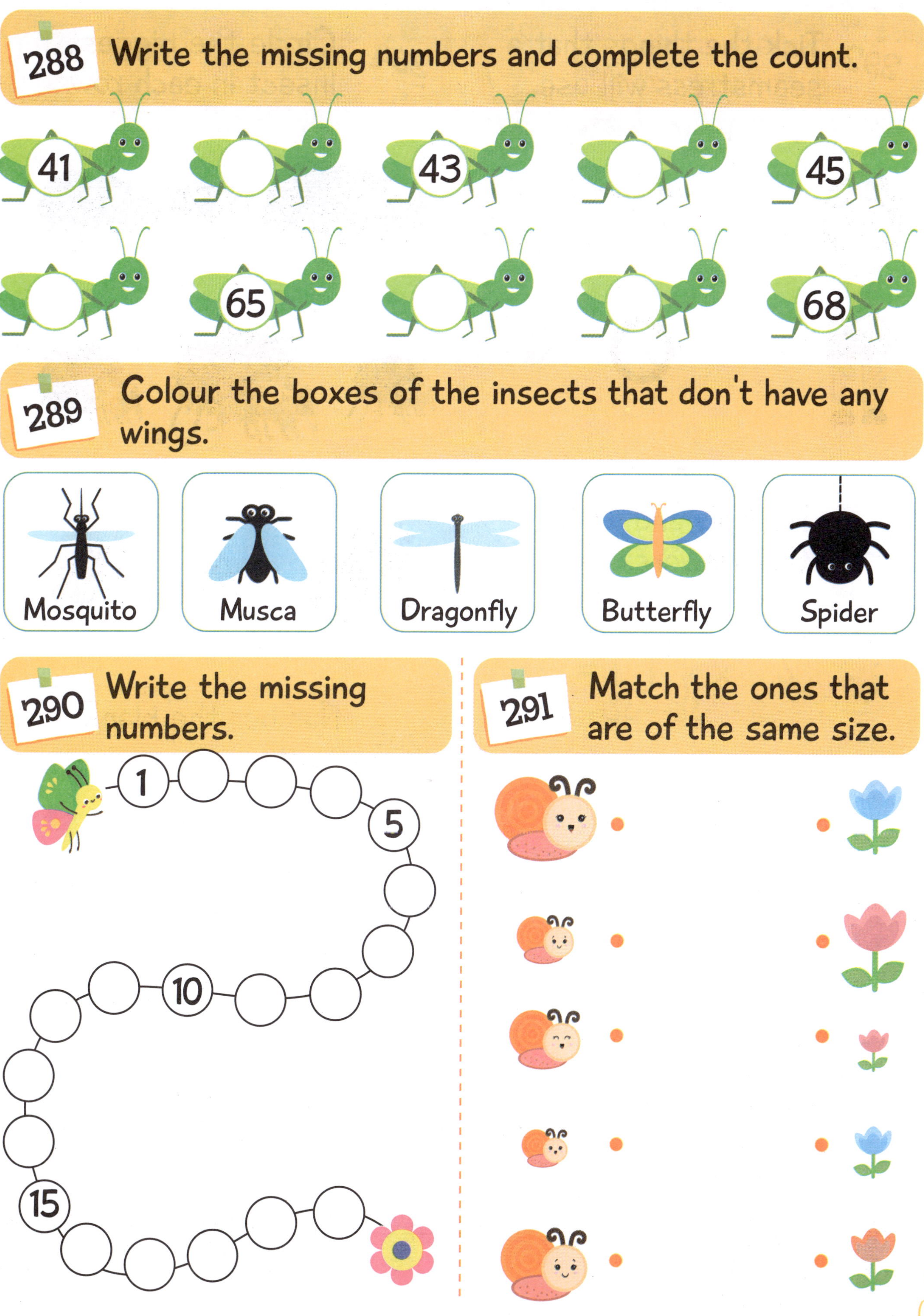
288 Write the missing numbers and complete the count.
41
43
45
65
68
289 Colour the boxes of the insects that don't have any wings.
Mosquito
Musca
Dragonfly
Butterfly
Spider
290 Write the missing numbers.
1
5
10
15
291 Match the ones that are of the same size.

292 Tick the things that a seamstress will use.

293 Multiply and write the answers.

294 Circle the biggest insect in each row.

295 Number the blank spots.

296 Match the ones that are of the same size.

297 Colour the baby firefly.

298 Trace the path to make different shapes.

299 Decode the puzzle to find a way to exit the maze.

300 Spot and circle the insect.

301 Number the blank spots.

302 Colour the caterpillar.

303 Solve the sudoku puzzle.

1 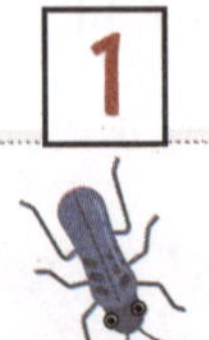 2  3  4 

304 Tick the things that an artist will use.

305 Match the paintings to their sketches.

1

2

3

4

5

6

306 Match by colour.

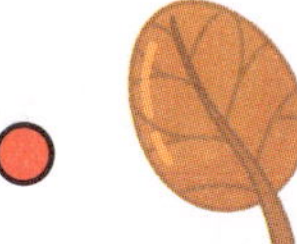

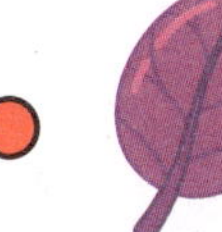

307 Colour the picture.

308 Tick the things that a boxer will use.

309 Match the paintings to their sketches.

310 Colour the ladybird.

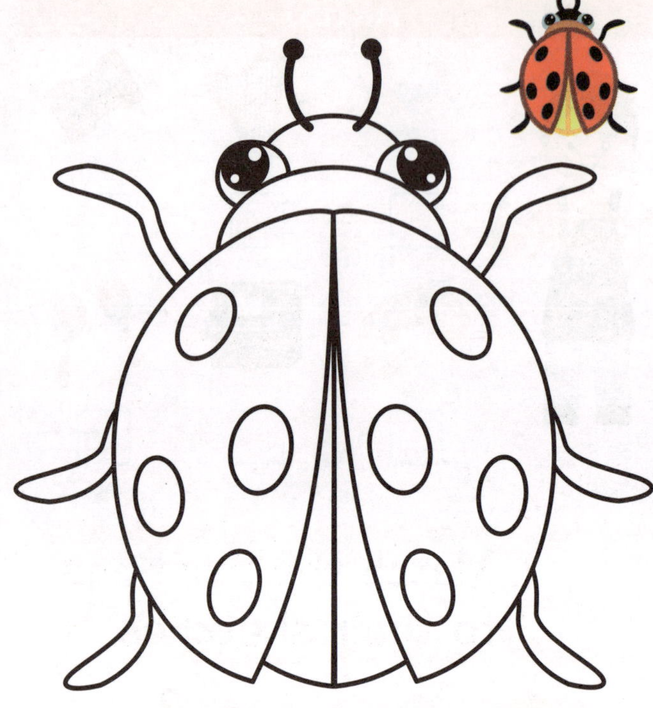

311 Match the picture with its name.

astronaut

moon

earth

satellite

saturn

comet

sun

rocket

312 Colour using the clue.

4

313 Solve the insect crossword.

314 Tick the things that a musician will use.

315 Copy the pattern.

316 Help the bee reach the honeycomb.

317 Colour the picture.

318 Colour by code.

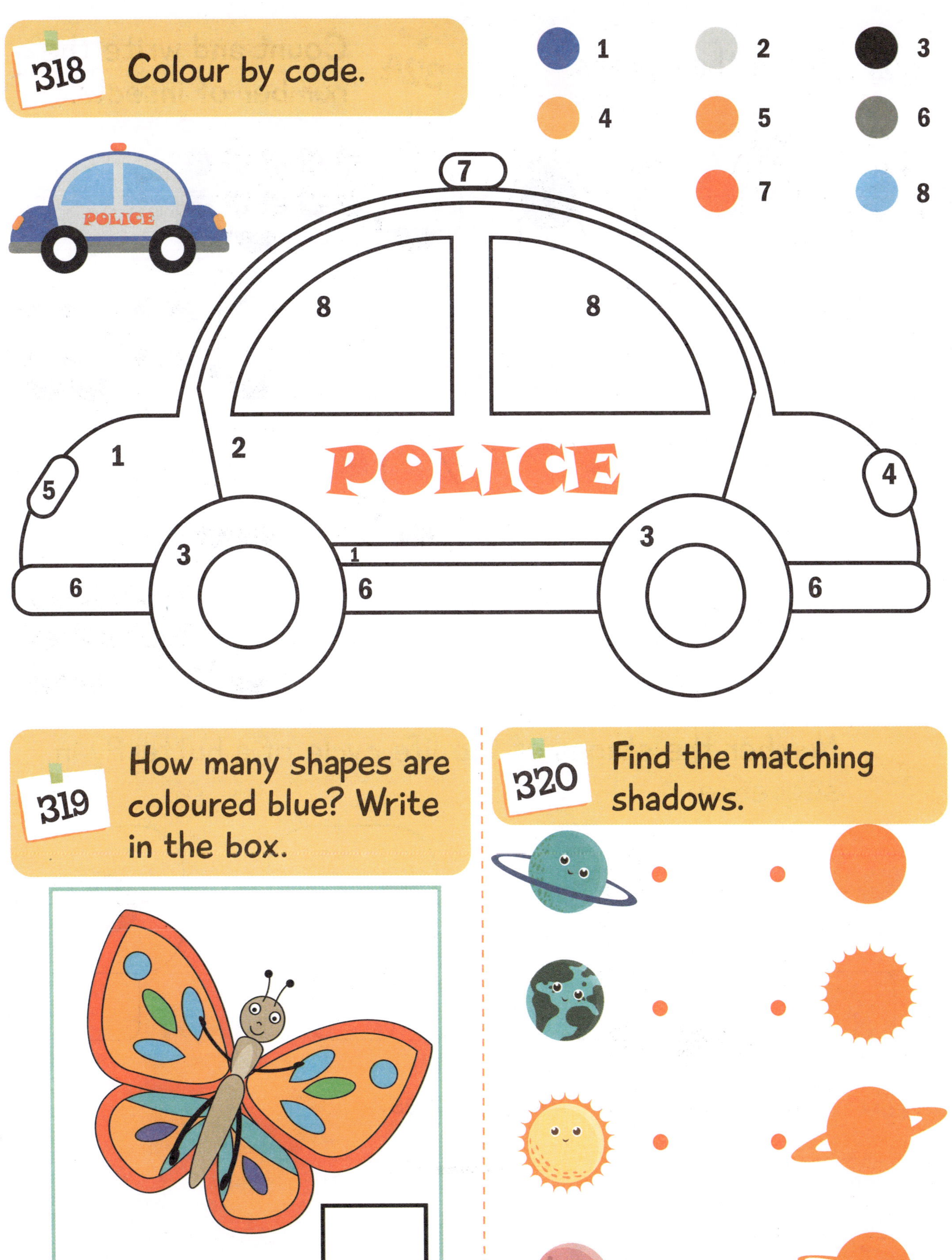

319 How many shapes are coloured blue? Write in the box.

320 Find the matching shadows.

321 Trace their paths.

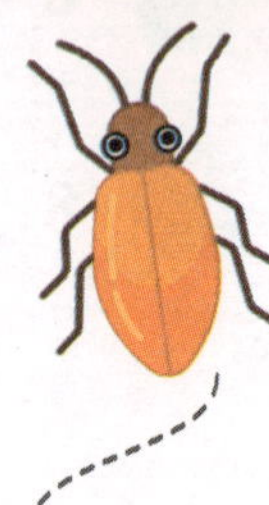

324 Count and write the number of insects.

322 Number the stages of the life cycle of a butterfly in sequence.

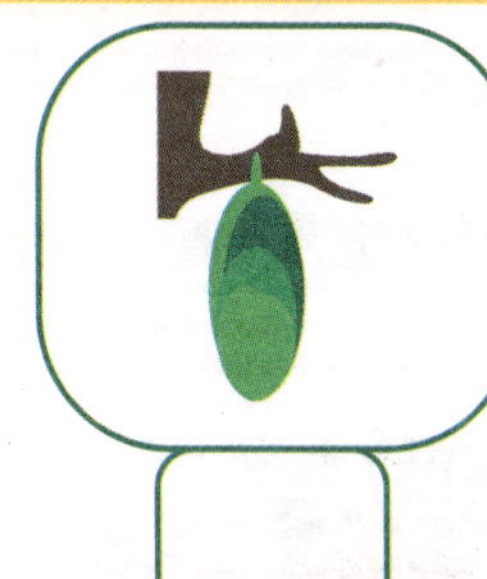

323 Trace and colour the pictures.

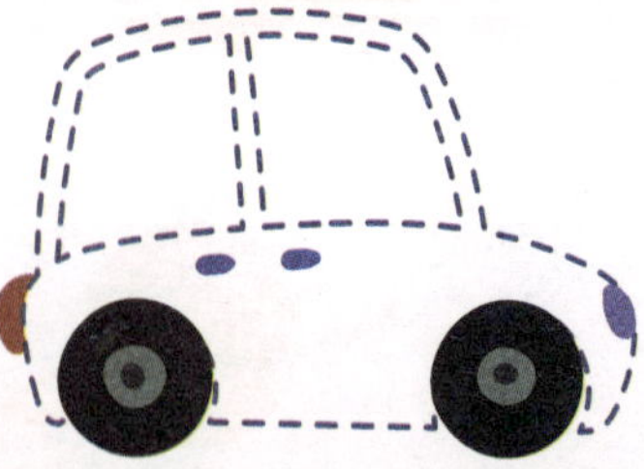
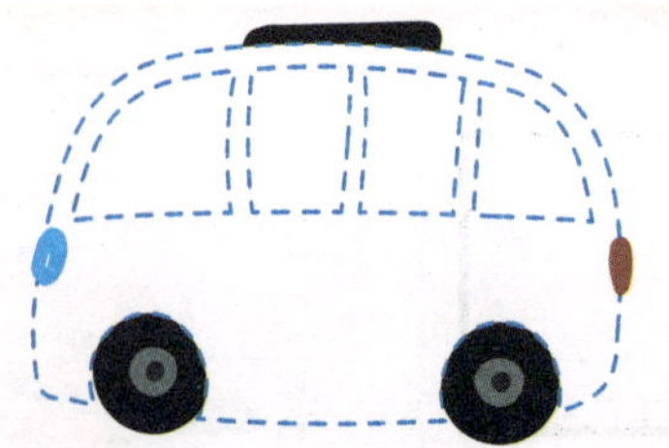
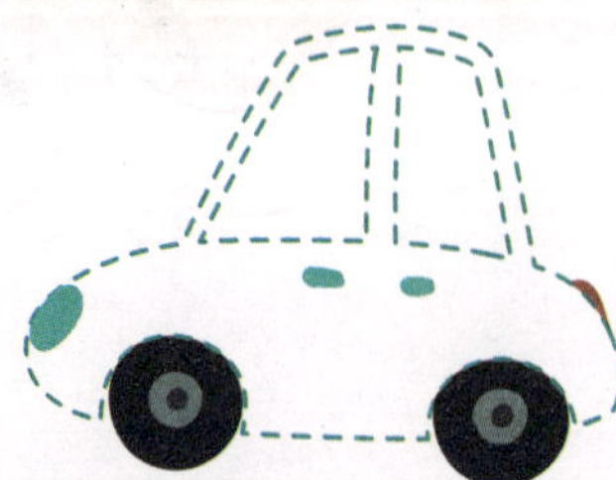

325 Which two planets look the same?

326 Match those things that go together.

327 Colour the picture.

328 Help the rocket reach a planet and colour the picture.

329 Join the dots to make a UFO and colour it.

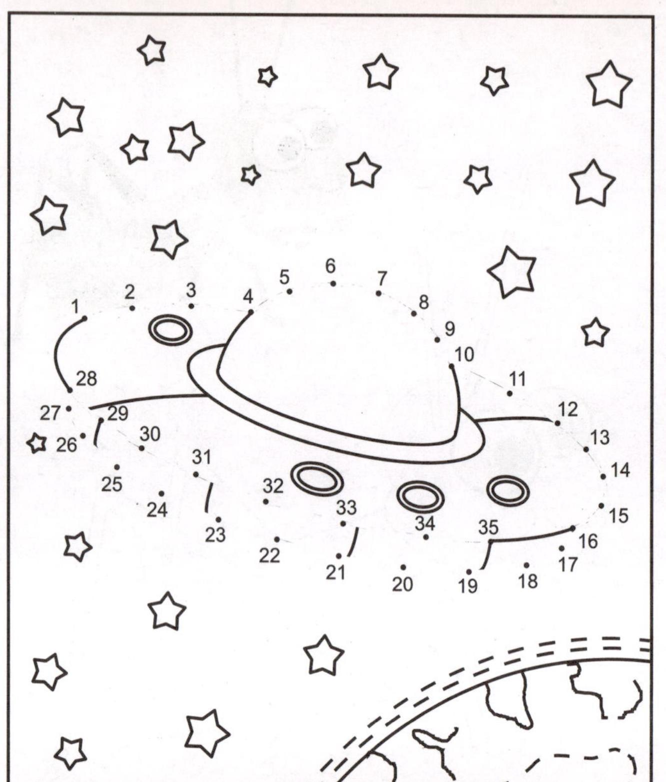

332 Tick the two spaceships that are identical.

330 Trace the various space routes.

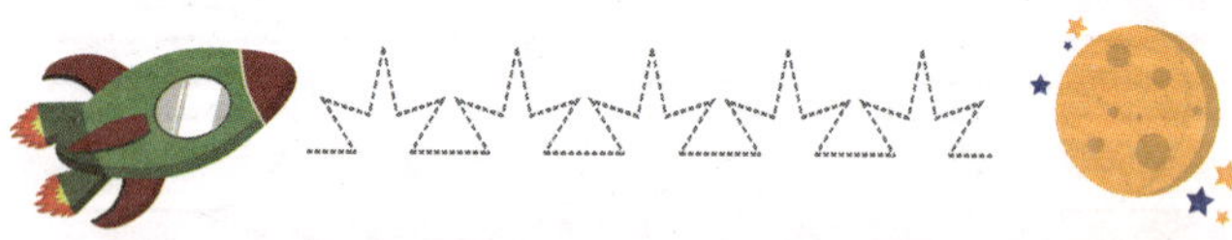

331 Unjumble the letters to find their names.

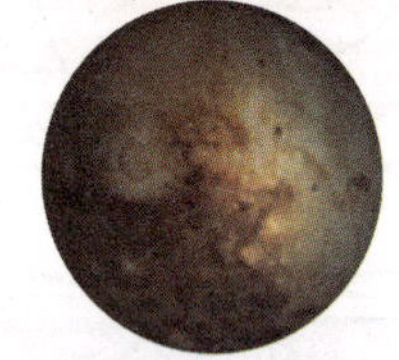

O L P T U

E N S V U

U R I P E J T

333 Trace and colour the picture.

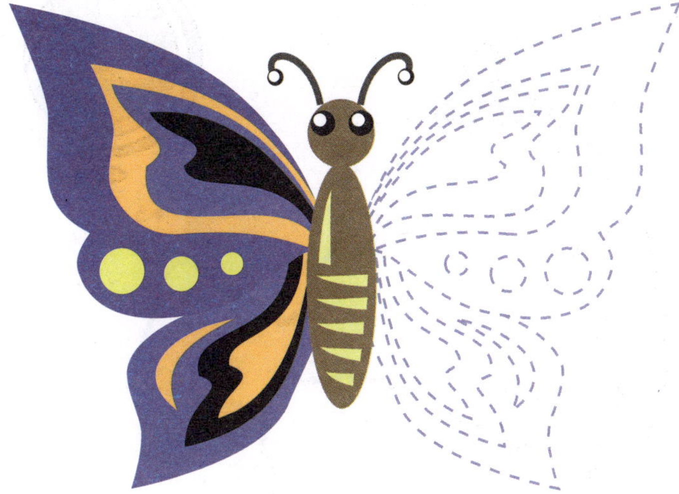

335 Tick the things that a builder will use.

334 Help the space dog reach planet Earth.

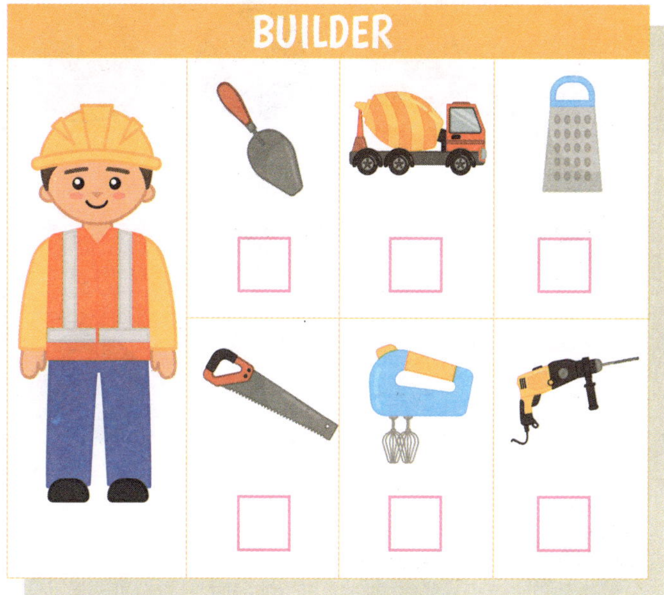

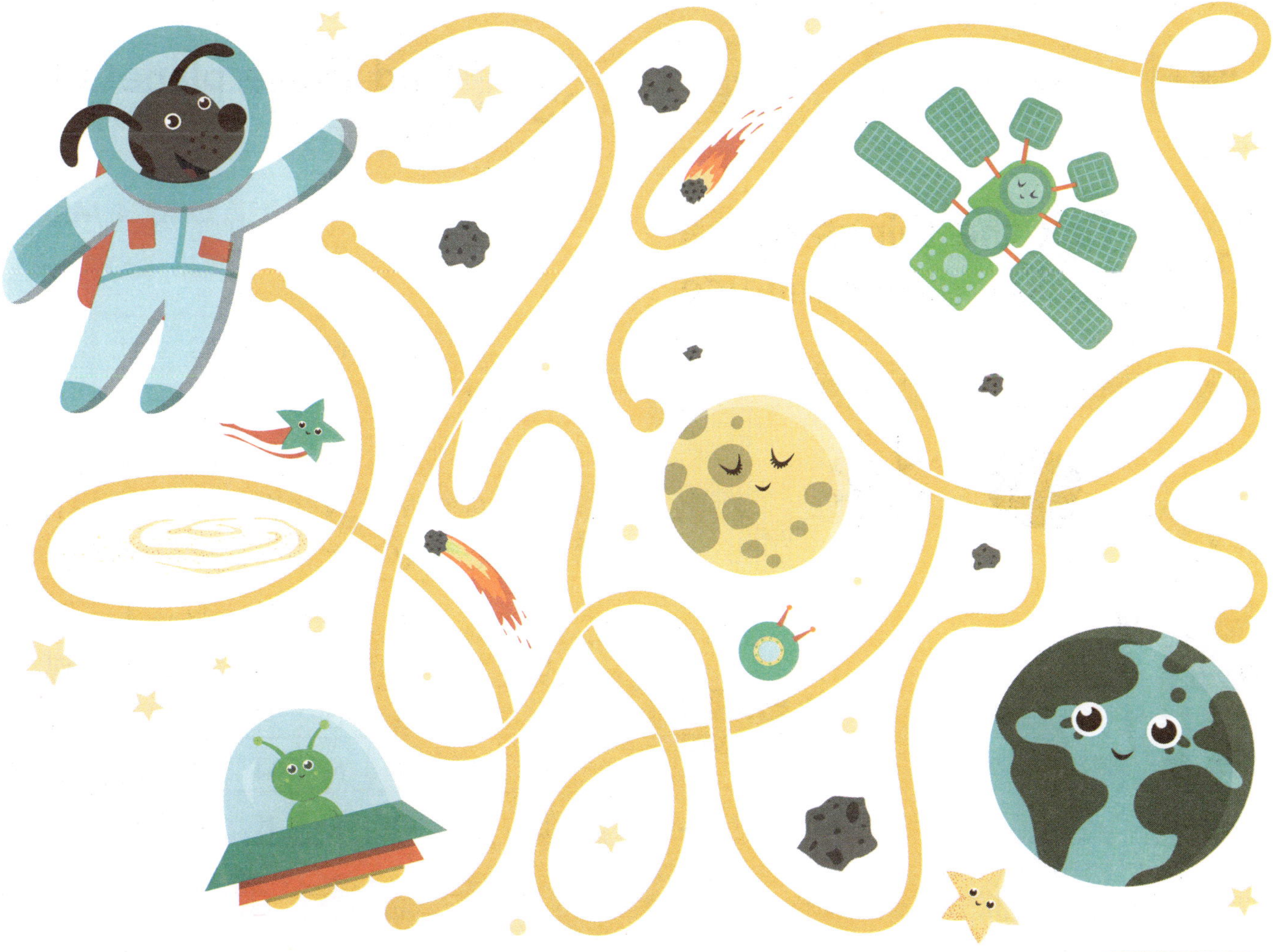

Solve the sudoku puzzle.

Tick the things that a hockey player will use.

338 Connect the dots and colour the picture.

339 Find these planets in the grid.

SUN, URANUS, NEPTUNE, EARTH, MARS, MERCURY, JUPITER, VENUS, SATURN

U	R	A	N	U	S	U	E
A	M	B	X	N	A	P	A
M	A	R	S	J	T	J	R
E	G	Y	N	P	U	U	T
R	C	V	E	T	R	P	H
C	V	E	P	U	N	I	E
U	I	N	T	W	H	T	W
R	U	U	U	F	J	E	S
Y	P	S	N	H	Q	R	U
L	Z	O	E	K	R	T	N

340 Count and write the answers in the boxes.

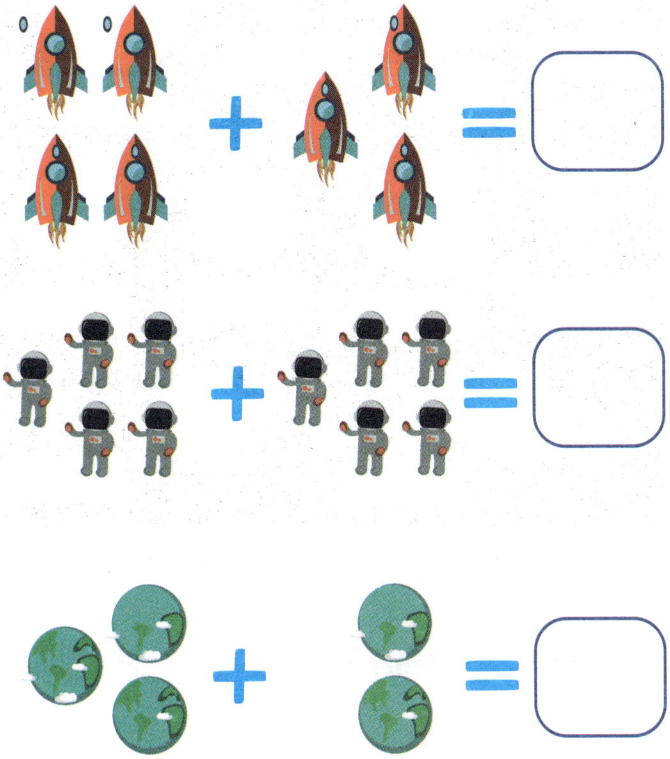

342 Solve the sums using addition and subtraction.

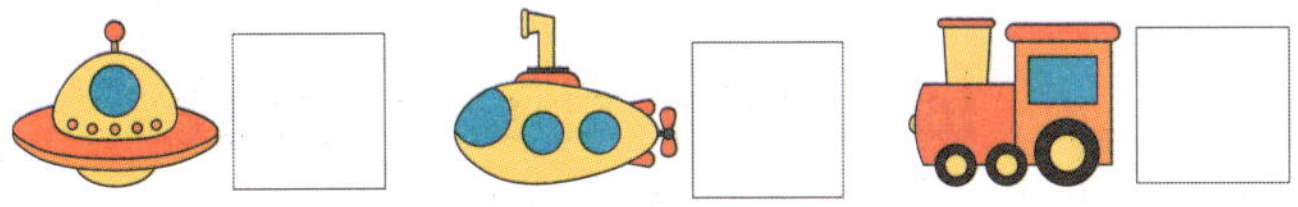

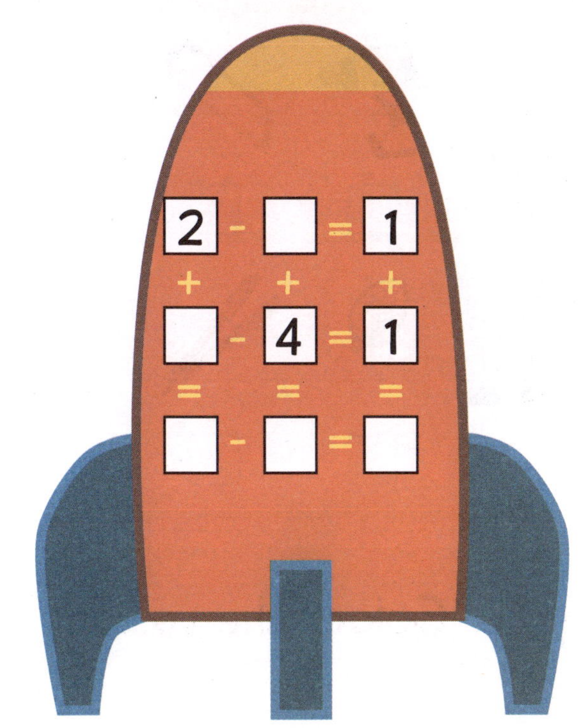

341 Add and write the answers in the boxes.

+ =

+ =

+ =

343 Trace and colour the rocket.

344 Tick the things that a repair man will use.

345 Colour the volcano.

346 Colour by numbers.

347 Identify the planets and write their names.

Jupiter	Mercury	Earth	Venus
Uranus	Saturn	Moon	Neptune
	Mars	Sun	

348 Match the correct letter to complete each name.

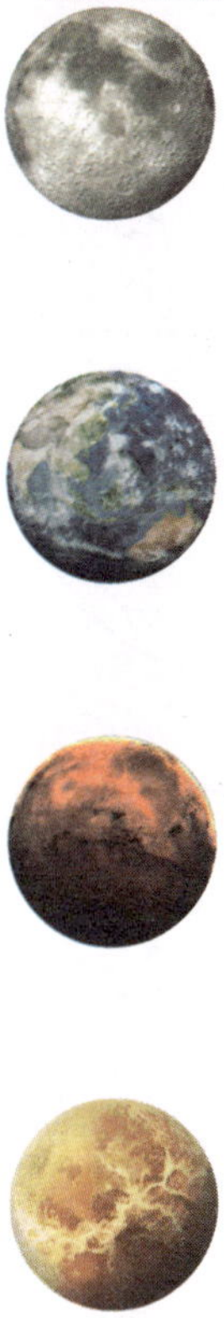

Mo__n u

Ear__h o

__enus t

Merc__ry V

349 Trace the lines.

350 Trace and colour the picture.

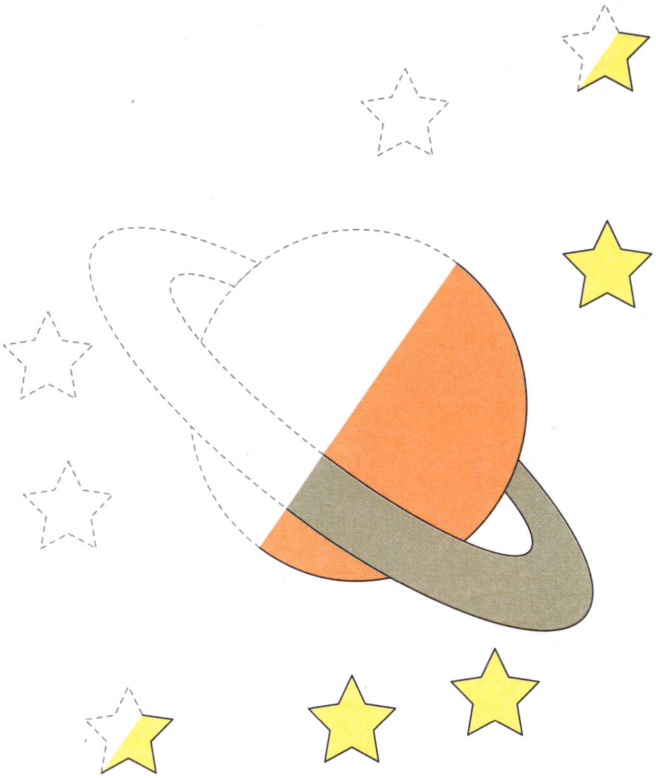

351 Find the matching shadow.

352 Match the image with its shadow.

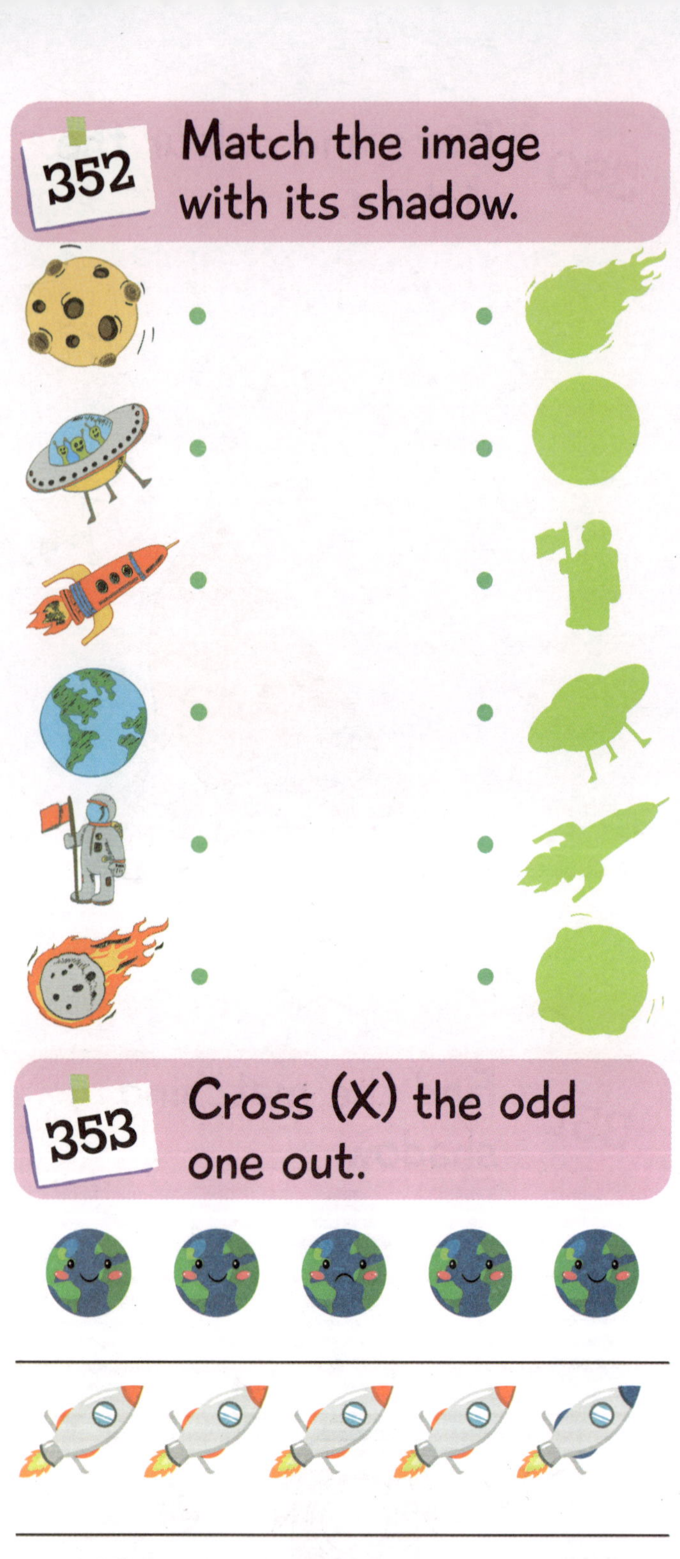

353 Cross (X) the odd one out.

354 Colour the picture.

355 Count and circle the answers.

356 Tick the things that a librarian will use.

357 Find the aliens that look alike.

358 Count the shapes.

359 Count the number of stars for each colour.

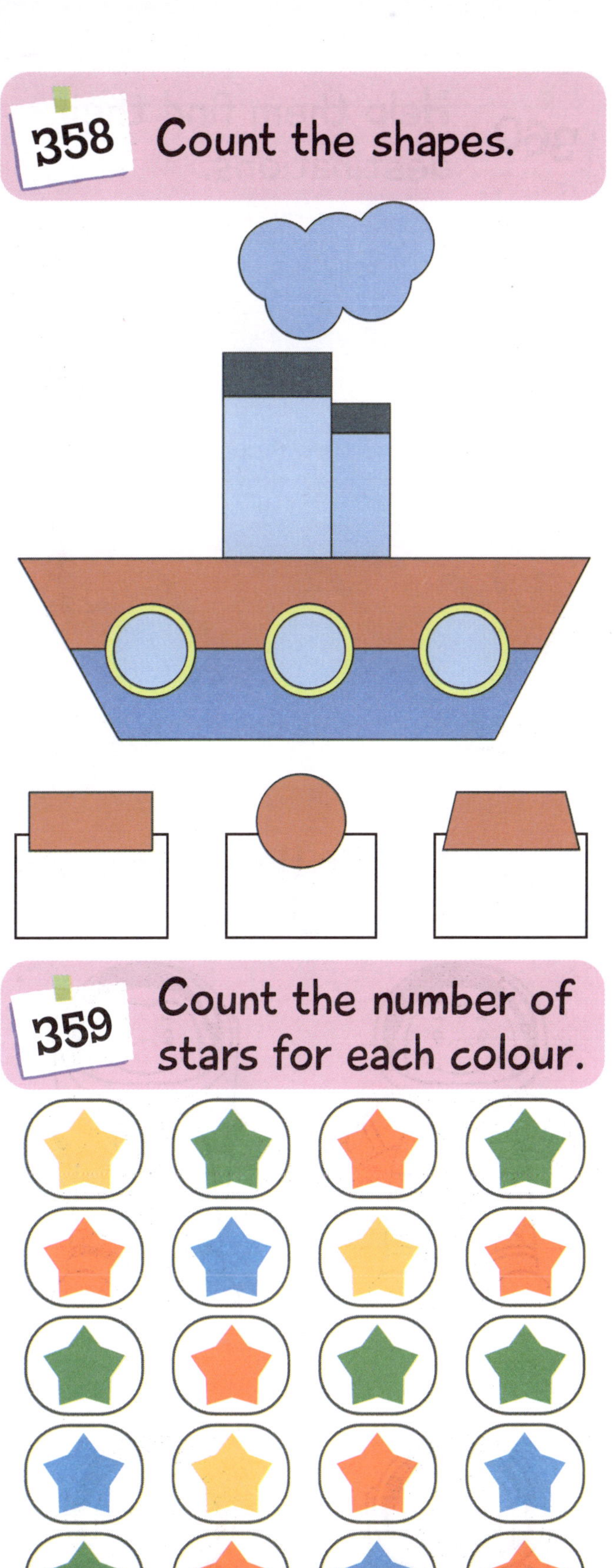

360 Help them find their destinations.

361 Colour the astronauts that look alike.

362 Match the insects with their shadows.

363 What will a carpenter use? Tick the correct options.

364 Help them find their other half.

366 Cross (X) the odd one out.

365 Join the dots and colour the picture.

1
2
3
4
5
6
7
8
9
10

367 Continue the colour patterns.

368 Add and match the answer with the UFO of the same number.

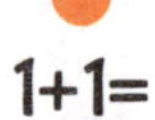
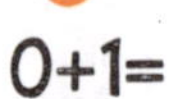

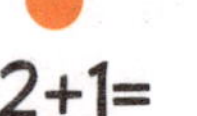

1+1= 0+1= 3+2= 2+1= 2+2=

369 Trace and colour the picture.

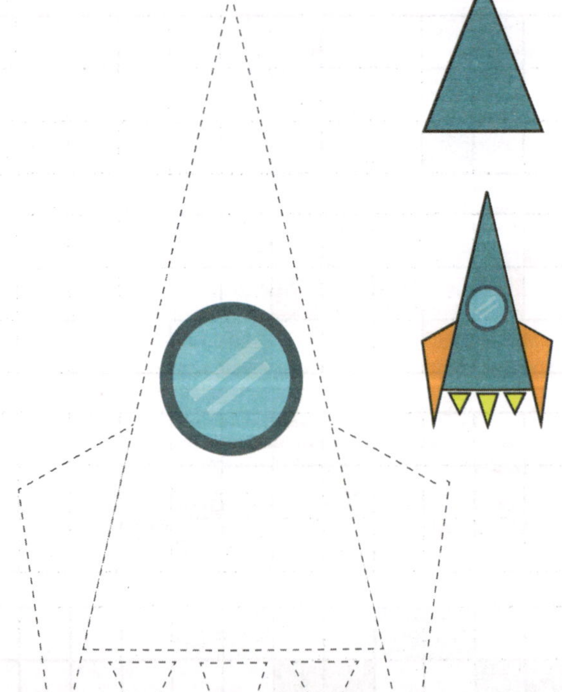

370 Colour by numbers.

1 2 3 4 5 6

371 Add and find the sum.

= 1 = 2 = 3 = 4 = 5

= 6 = 7 = 8 = 9

= ☐ = ☐

= ☐ = ☐

= ☐ = ☐

372 How many look to the left and how many look to the right?

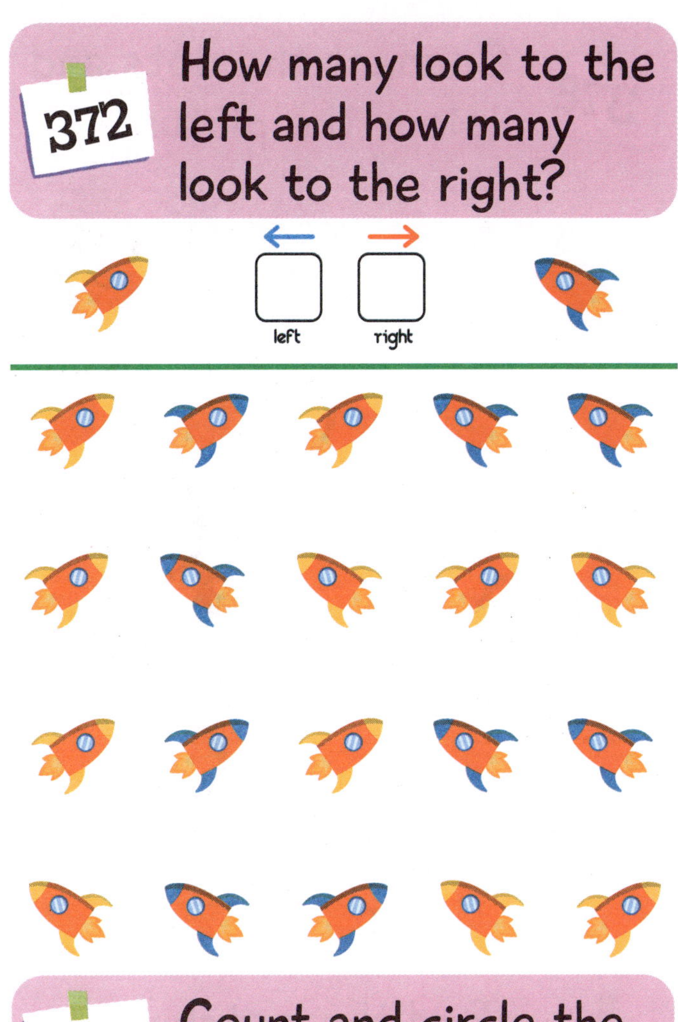

373 Count and circle the answer.

4
5
3
2

7
4
5
6

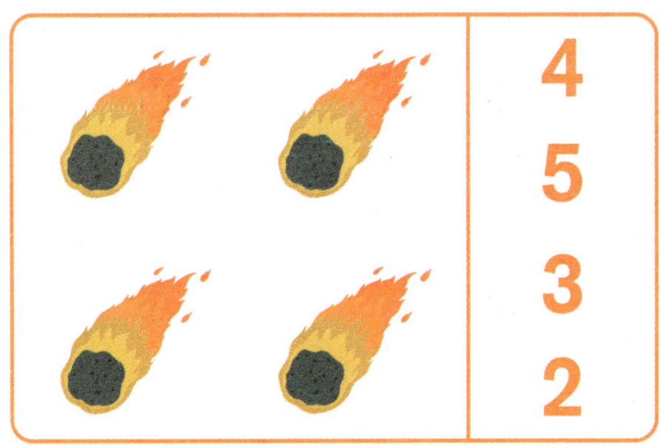

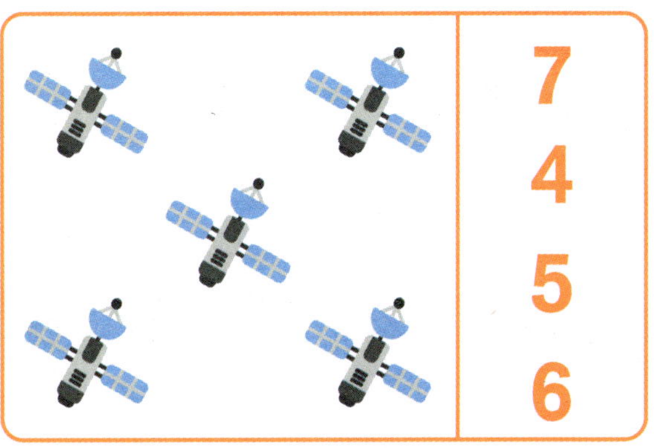

374 Which suits whom?

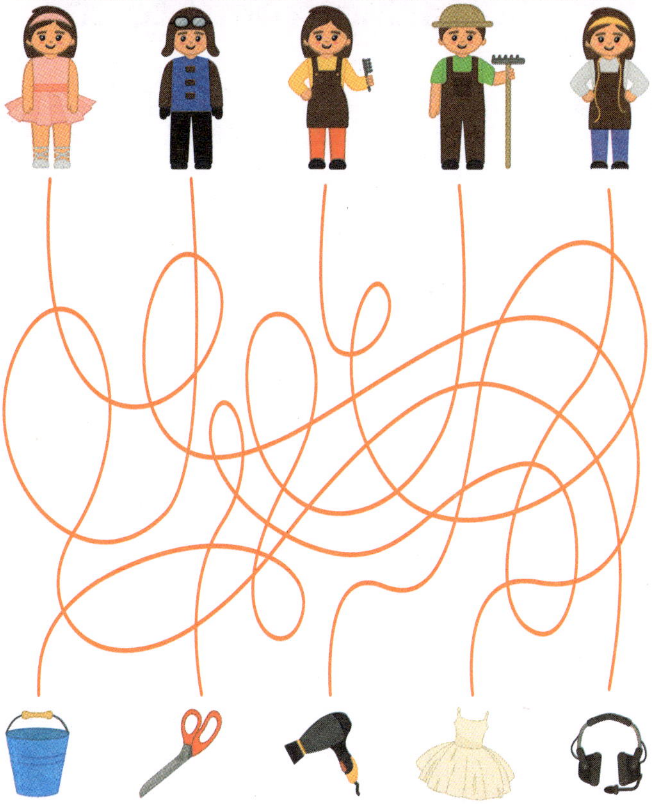

375 Find the matching shadow.

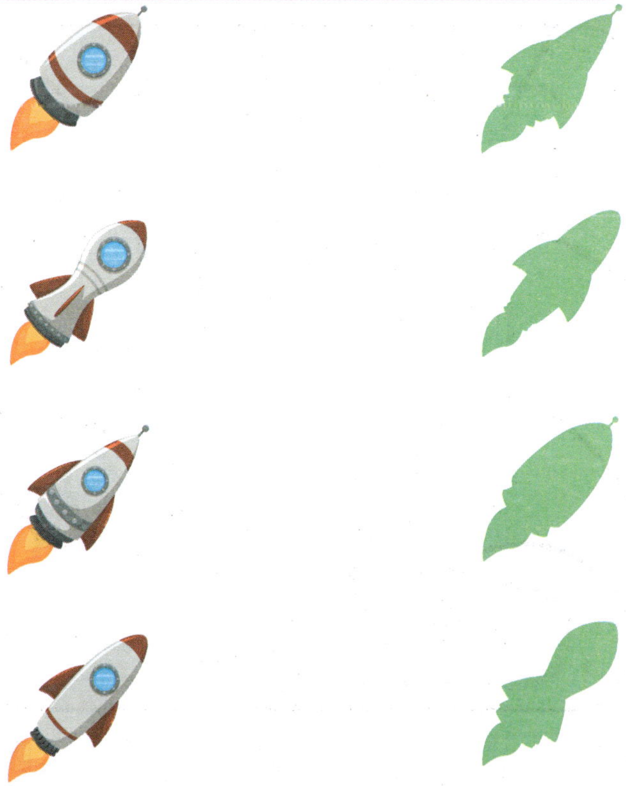

376 Help the astronaut reach the rocket by trailing from 1 to 16.

		1	2	4	5	7
		→	1	2	7	8
5	7	8	5	3	4	9
7	10	9	5	4	6	5
0	5	7	6	11	14	10
4	9	8	10	12	13	9
12	10	11	14	18	19	17
15	14	12	15	16		
11	16	13	14	↓		

377 Colour by numbers.

1  2  3 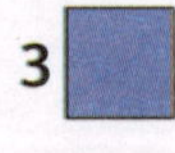 4 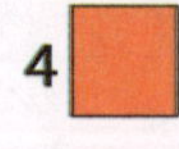 5  6 

378 Connect the dots and colour the picture.

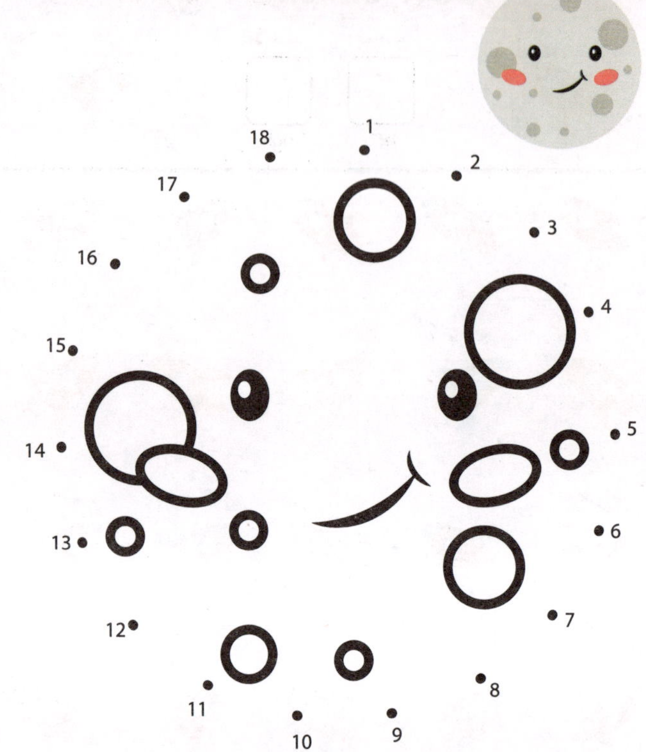

379 Find the matching shadow.

380 Circle the crescent shape of the moon.

381 What will a miner use? Tick the correct options.

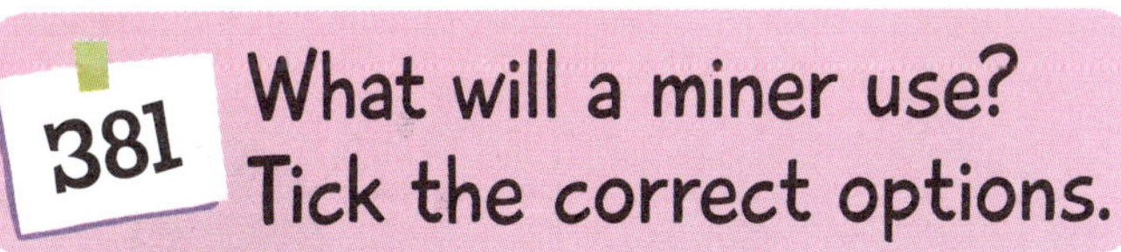

382 How many red shapes are there? Count and write.?

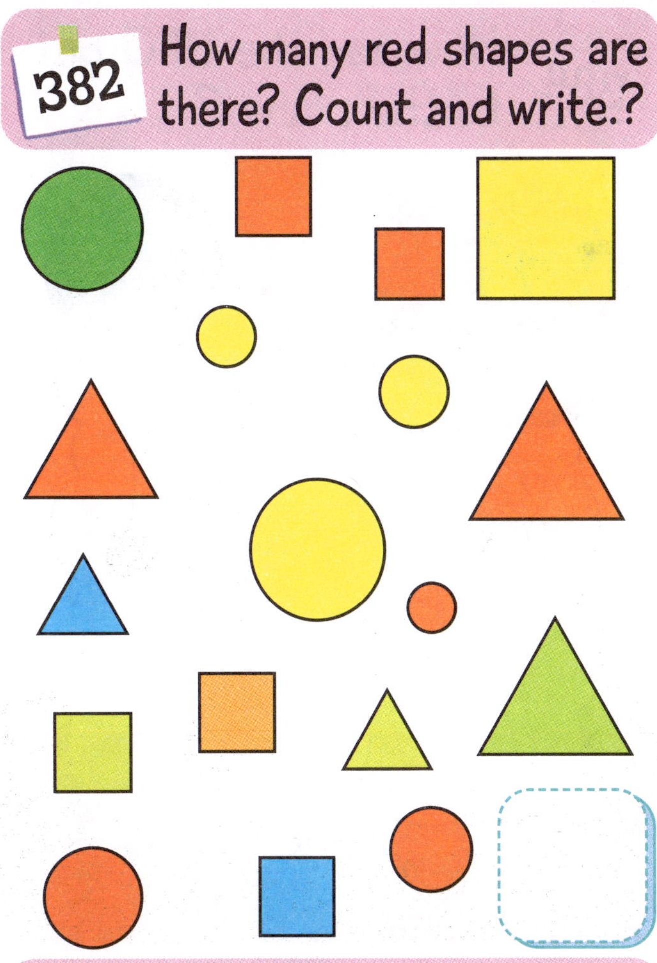

383 Help the air hostess board the plane.

384 How can the UFO get to the planet?

385 Solve the sudoku puzzle.

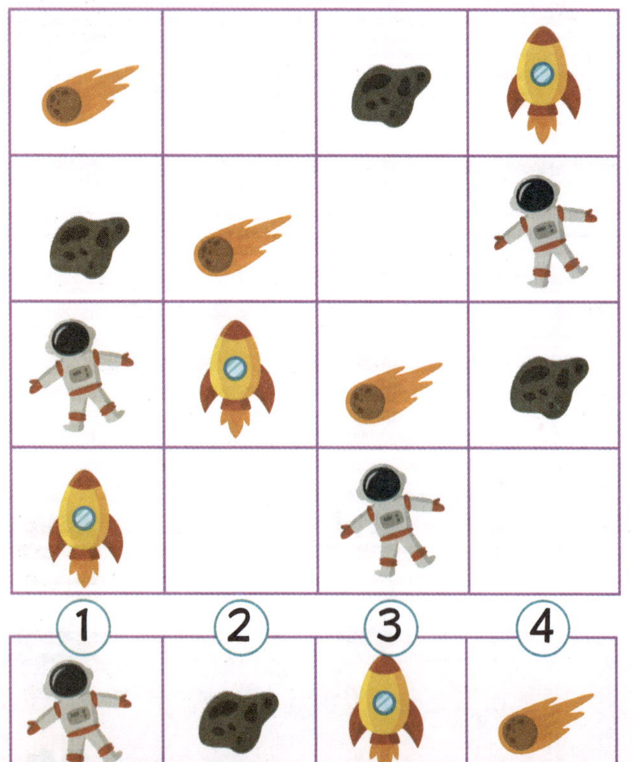

386 Match the ships to the directions they are headed in.

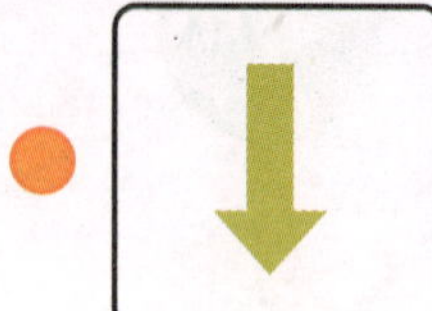

387 Trace and colour the picture.

388 Colour by numbers.

1
2
3
4
5
6
7

389 Count and write.

390 Count and circle the answer.

4
5
7
6

1
5
3
2

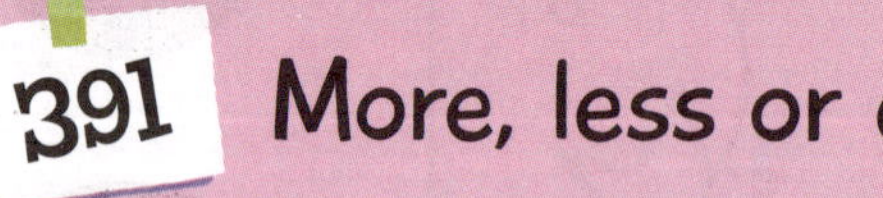

391 More, less or equal?

392 Match with the initial letter of the name of each picture.

A

393 Find the identical vehicles.

394 Help the kid reach the moon and colour the picture.

396 How many eggs are there of each colour?

395 Count and write.

397 Find the matching shadow.

398 Trace and colour.

400 Fill in the circles.

399 Colour the pictures.

401 Find 10 differences.

403 Where should each vehicle go?

402 Join and colour the picture.

404 Which does not fit? Circle the answer.

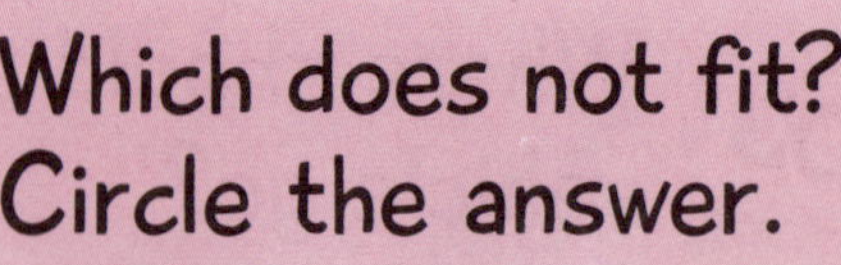

405 Choo-choo! Colour me.

406 Find 7 differences.

407 Where are they driven? Match accordingly.

408 Trace the dotted lines and colour the picture.

410 Find the identical three.

409 Solve the puzzle.

♥ + ♥ + ♥ = 6

⬢ + ♥ + ♥ = 8

⬢ + ▲ + ♥ = 9

▲ = ☐

7 3 5 1

411 Which group has more, less or equal?

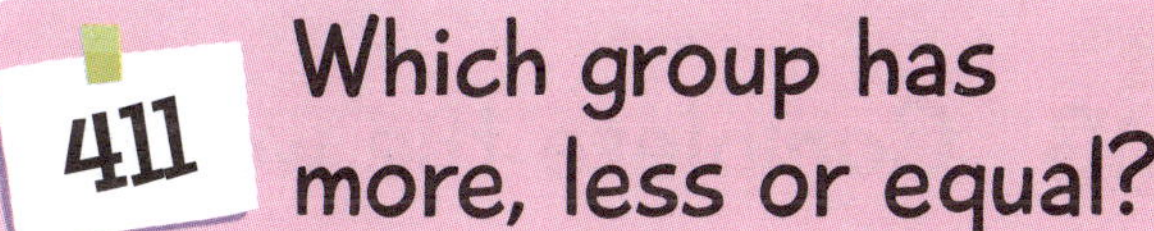

< = >

412 Connect the dots and colour.

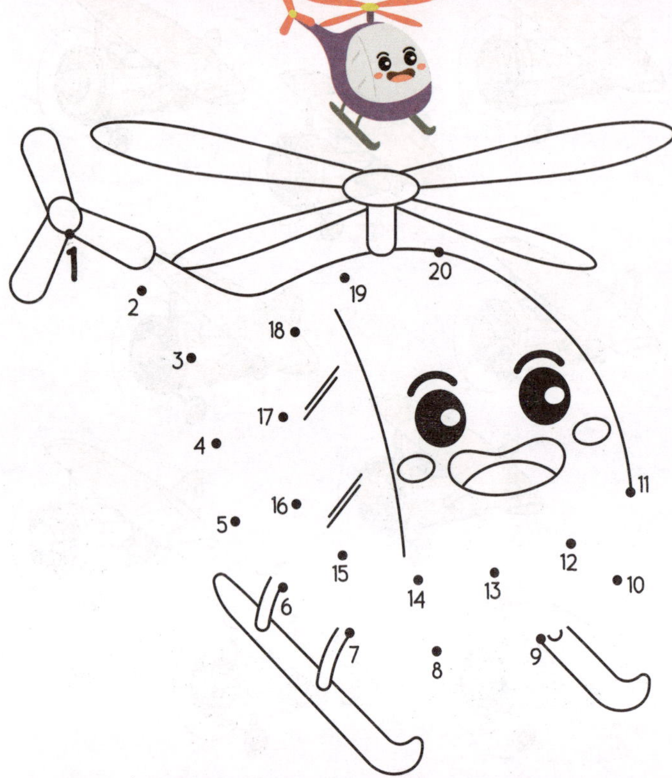

414 Match the sounds with the pictures.

I hear with my ears.

Hiss 

Roar 

Quack 

Buzz 

413 Complete the words.

	o		

s			

r			

s		

					o	

415 Find the identical two.

416 Colour the school bus.

417 Match to complete the image.

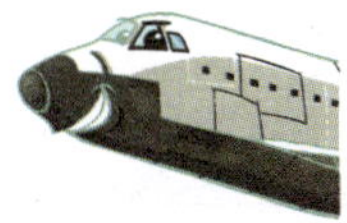

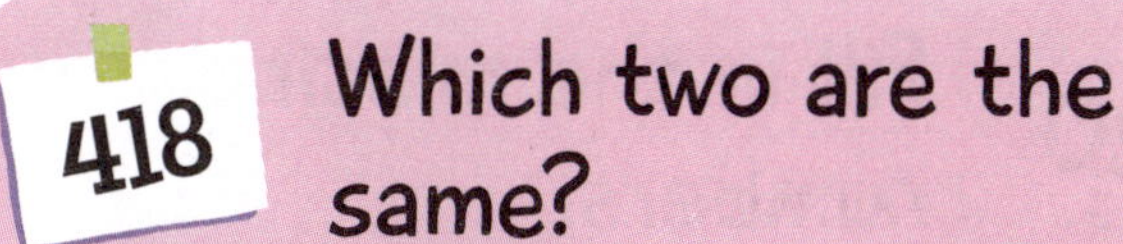

418 Which two are the same?

419 Unjumble the letters to find my name.

420 Fill in the missing numbers.

421 How many look to the left and how many look to the right?

left right

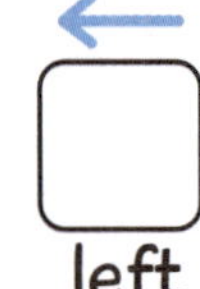

422 Find 5 differences.

423 Find the matching shadows.

424 Trace and colour the picture.

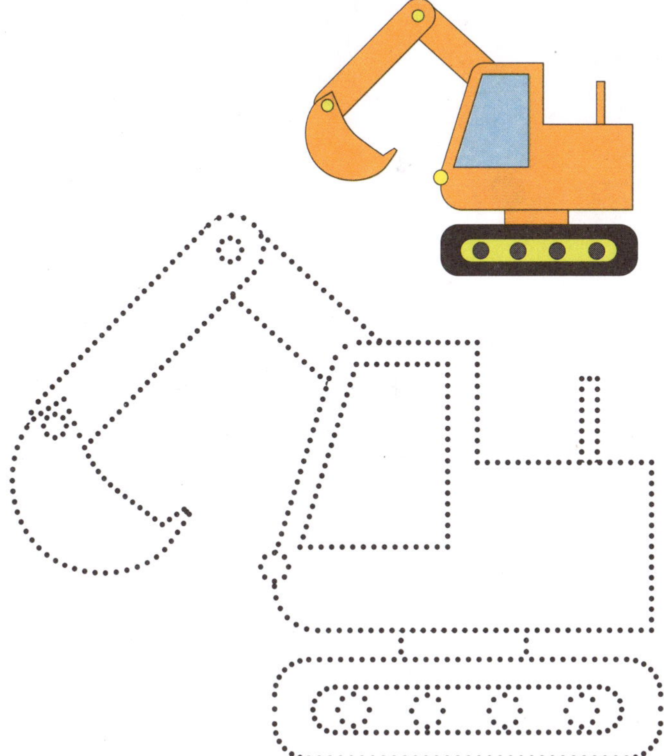

425 Draw the other half and colour.

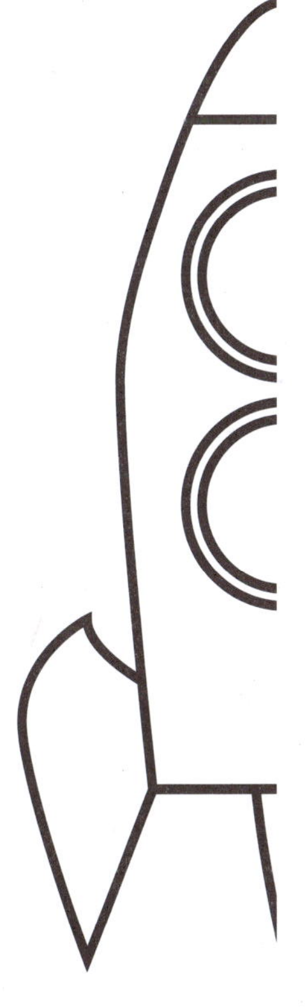

426 More, less or equal?

427 Colour the picture.

428 Trace and colour.

430 Count and write.

429 Find 5 differences.

431 Find the matching shadows.

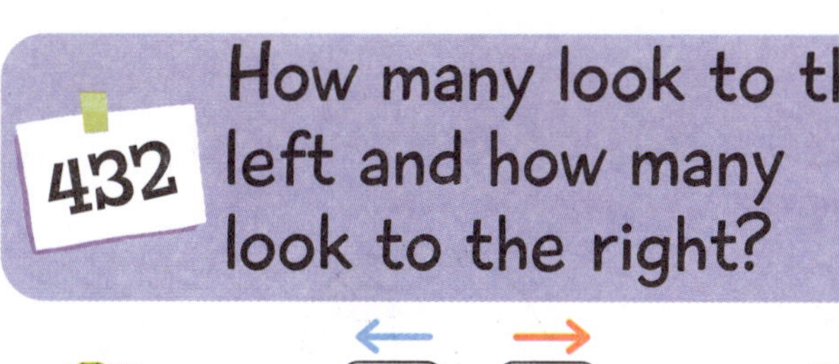

432 How many look to the left and how many look to the right?

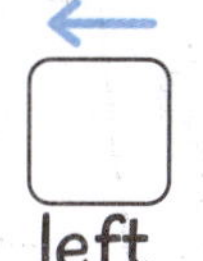

left right

433 Add and subtract to solve the sum.

434 Fill in the missing numbers.

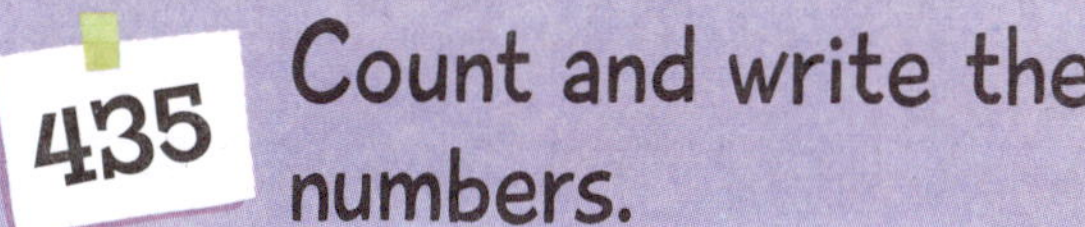

435 Count and write the numbers.

436 How many objects can you see here? Spot the odd one out.

439 Find 5 differences.

437 Which has two wheels? Circle the answers.

438 Copy the pattern.

Colour the picture.

Subtract and write the answer in the box.

6 - 3 =

Solve the alphabet sudoku.

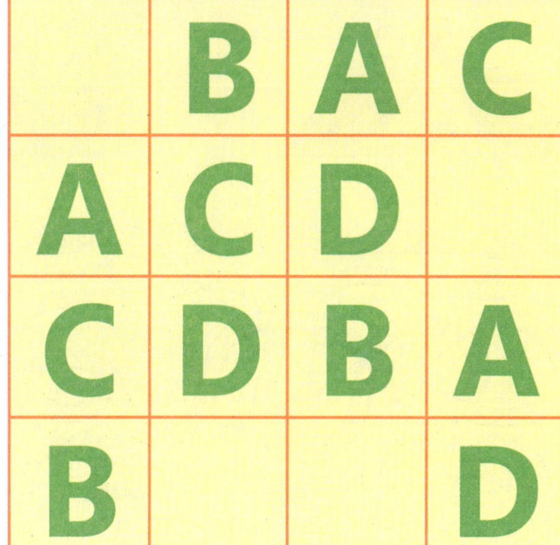

	B	A	C
A	C	D	
C	D	B	A
B			D

Decode the word.

a	b	c	d	e	f	g	h	i	j	k	l	m
1	2	3	4	5	6	7	8	9	10	11	12	13

n	o	p	q	r	s	t	u	v	w	x	y	z
14	15	16	17	18	19	20	21	22	23	24	25	26

444 Help the school bus find its way to the school.

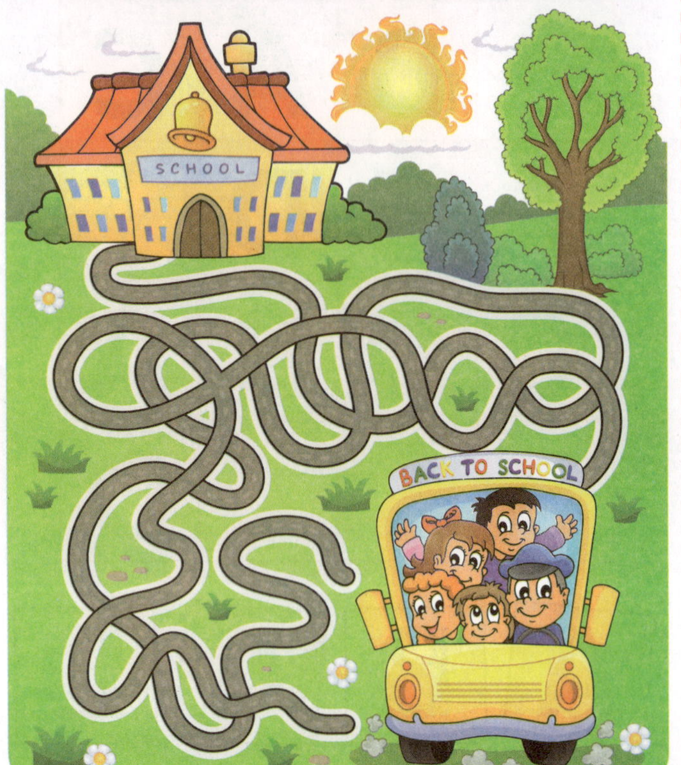

446 Count and match.

445 Motor crossword.

447 More, less or equal?

448 Count and write.

449 Trace and colour the picture.

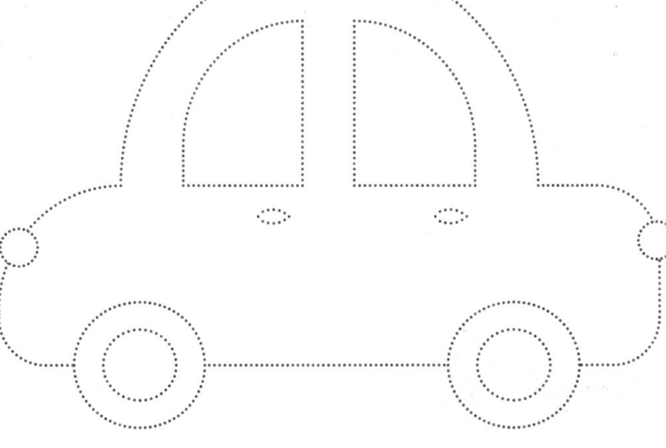

450 Sort the transport by type.

WATER		ROAD	

451 Spot the odd one out. Circle the answer.

454 Write the first letter of each thing to make a new word.

452 What time is it?

453 Add and write the answers in the box.

2 + 6 = ☐

1 + 5 = ☐

Trace and colour the picture.

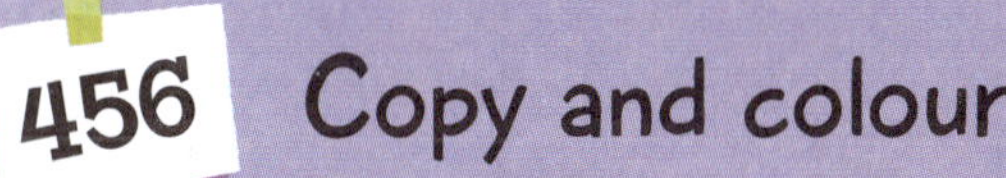

Copy and colour.

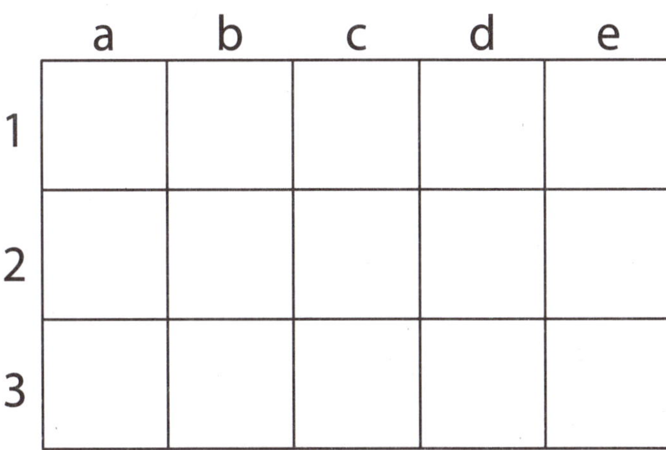

Complete the names.

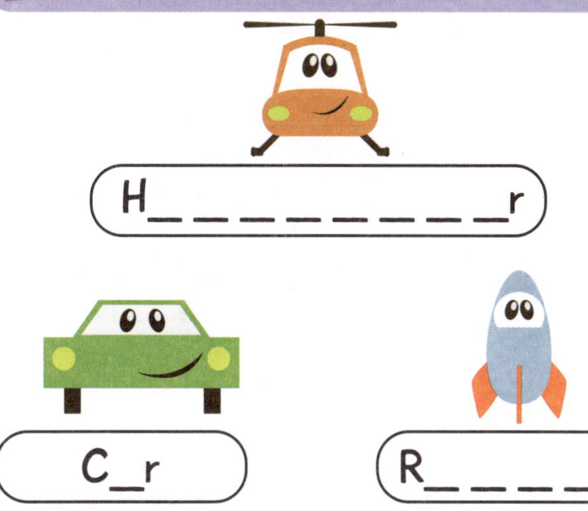

T_ _ _n

Taxi

C_b

458 Write the first letter of each thing to make a new word. Colour the picture.

459 Trace and colour.

460 Trace the dotted lines and colour the picture.

462 Write the first letter of each thing to make a new word. Colour the picture.

461 Add and write the sum in the box.

463 Find 10 differences.

464 Join to colour the picture.

465 Find the correct shadow.

466 Match the initials.

S • 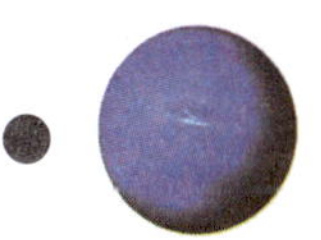

N • 

V • 

M • 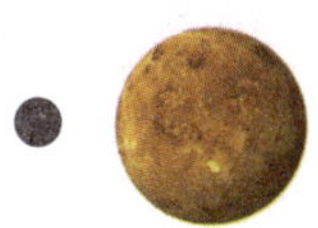

E • 

467 Mark these means of transport in the grid.

P	L	T	N	E	B	L	D	F	S	P
L	P	R	L	E	A	P	R	A	U	Y
A	B	U	L	L	B	V	O	P	B	R
N	E	C	A	C	I	J	C	Y	M	A
E	H	K	O	B	C	T	K	T	A	M
P	O	M	S	C	Y	C	E	R	R	S
Z	J	B	M	K	C	Y	T	T	I	D
Z	N	A	R	I	L	R	U	C	N	S
L	Y	H	O	T	E	A	E	S	E	H
F	I	R	E	E	N	G	I	N	E	I
E	P	O	L	I	C	E	C	A	R	P

469 Copy and colour.

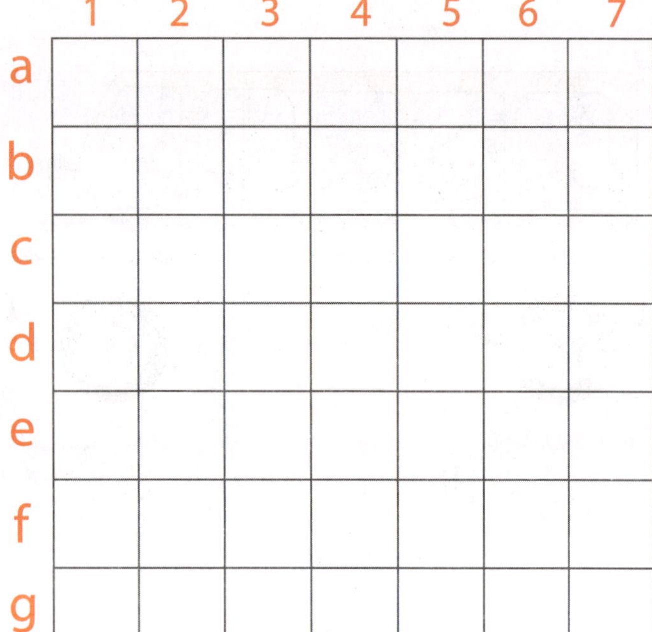

468 Join the dots and colour the picture.

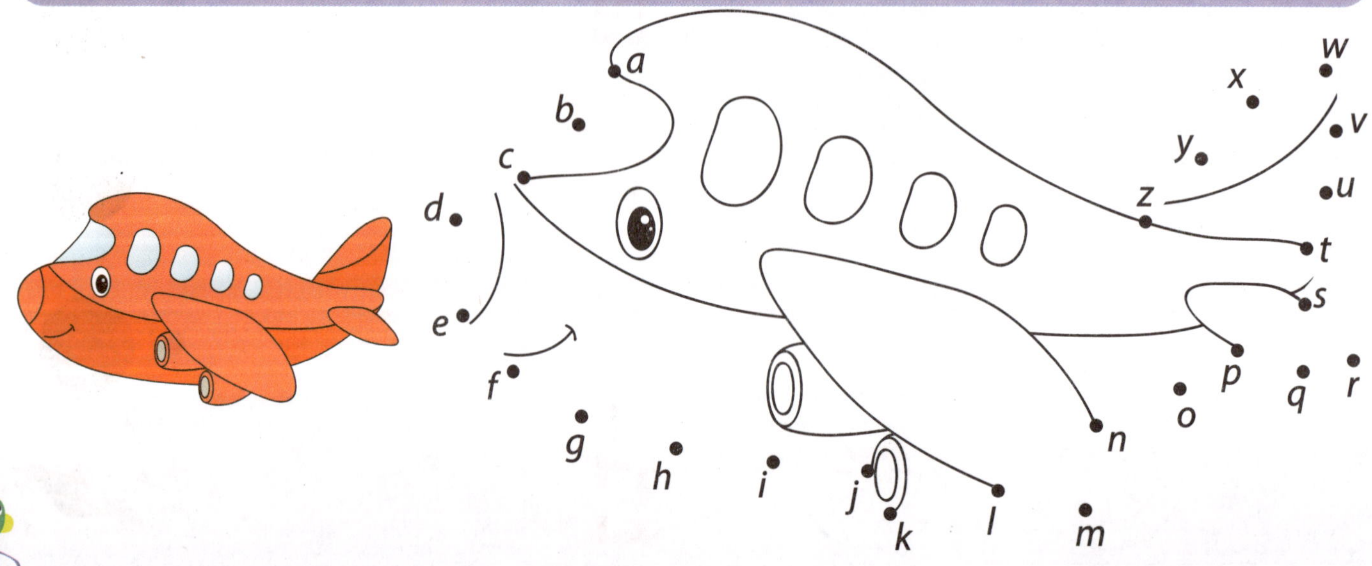

470 Solve the puzzle.

472 Colour the picture.

471 Count the trailers.

473 Sort the means of transport by type.

474 Write the first letter of each thing to make a new word. Colour the picture.

475 Which does not fit? Tick the answer.

476 Calculate and match the sum.

477 Sort the transport by the direction they are moving in.

478 Colour the picture.

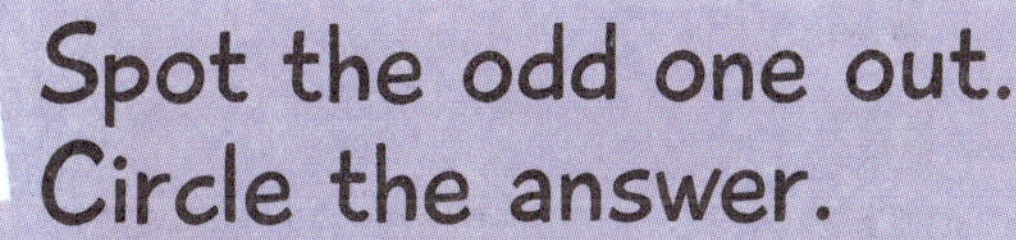

479 Spot the odd one out. Circle the answer.

480 Match with the correct shadows.

481 Solve the sudoku puzzle.

1	2	3	4
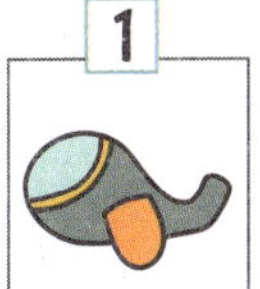	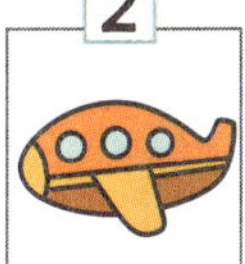		

482 Help the ambulance reach the hospital quickly.

483 Find the correct shadow.

484 Who will drive what?

485 Count and write.

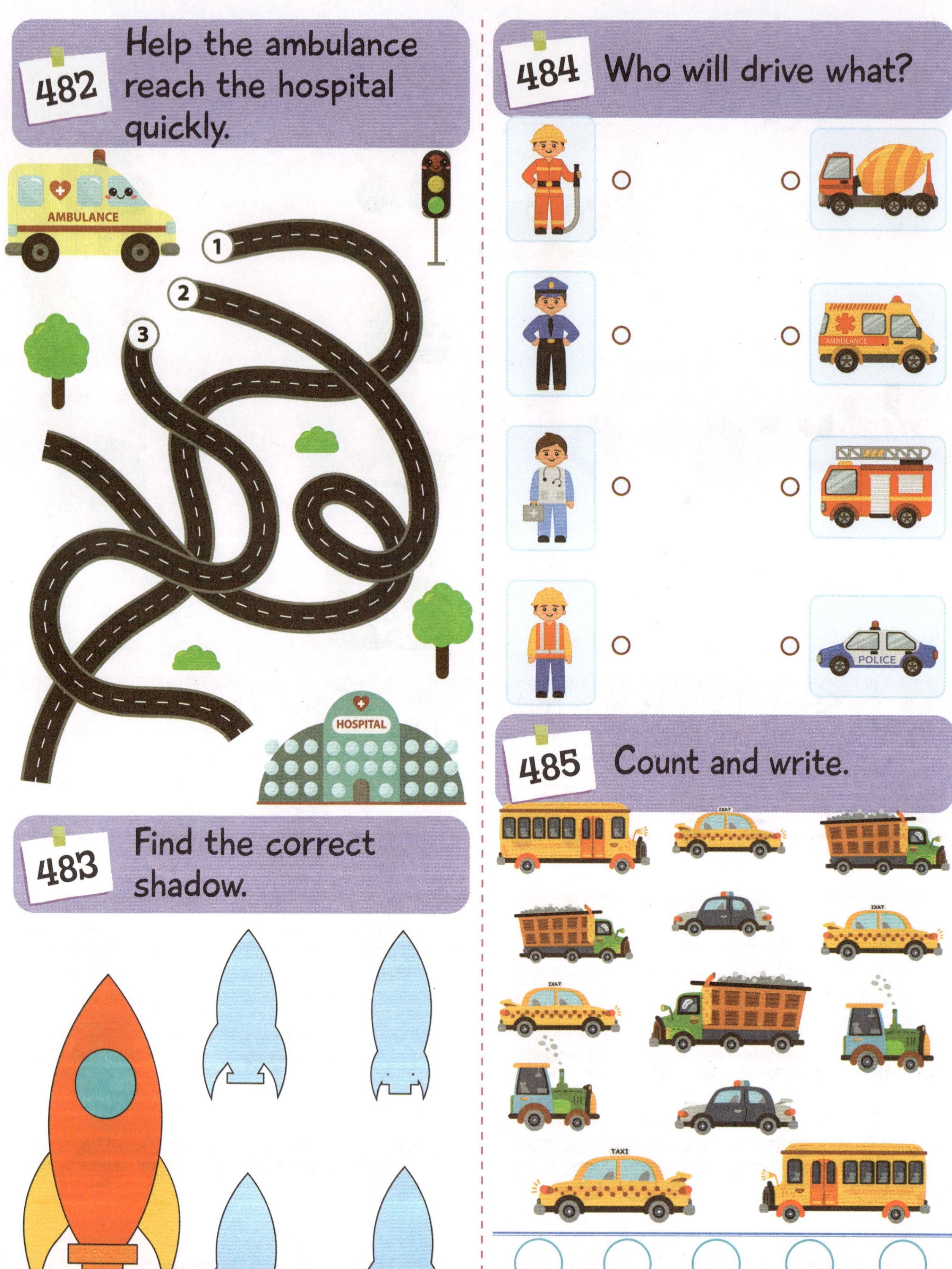

486 Write the first letter of each thing to make a new word. Then, colour the picture.

487 How many each?

488 Trace and colour the picture.

Spot the odd one out.

Count and circle the right answer.

3
5
6

4
5
3

490 Trace and colour.

492 Match the parts.

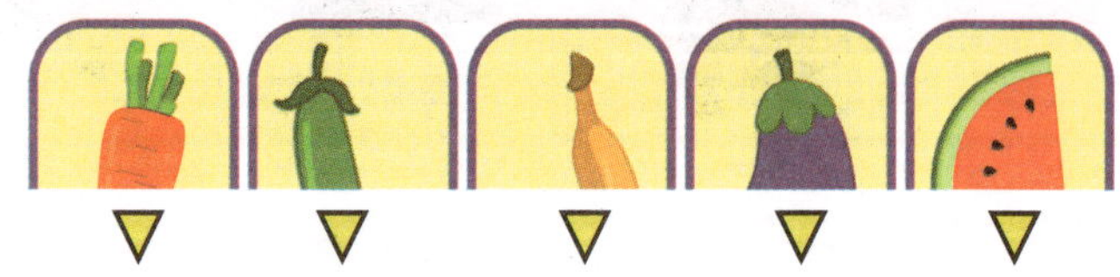

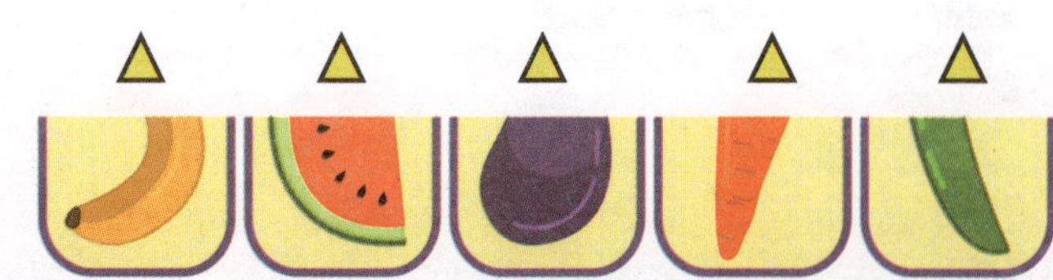

493 Colour by numbers.

495 Trace the lines.

494 Space crossword.

496 Fill in the missing letters.

BI_D

BANA_A

ORAN_E

TRACT_R

497 Which direction are they headed in?

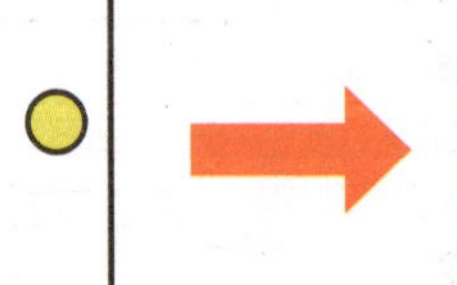

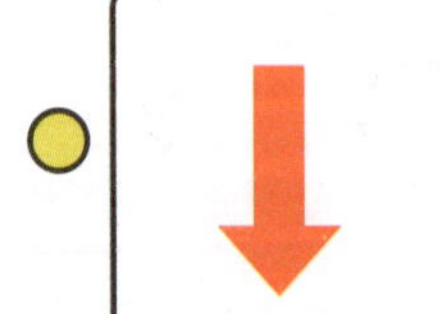

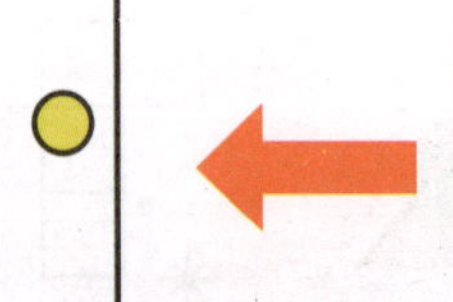

498 Connect the numbers and colour the picture.

499 Join to colour the picture.

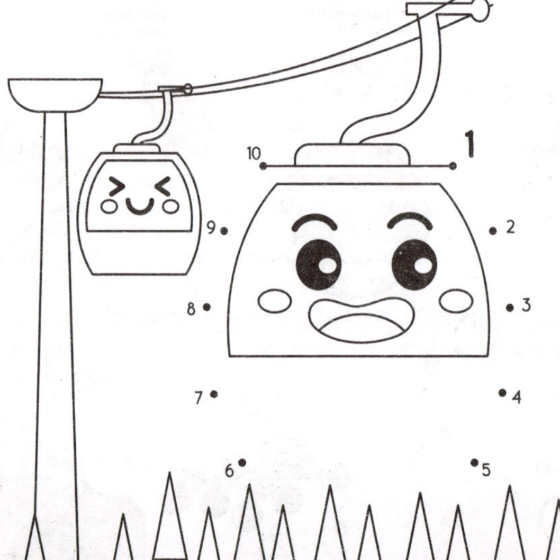

500 Find 7 differences.

501 Match with the correct shadow.

502 If big is 1, bigger is 2 and biggest is 3, then add and find their sums.

503 Trace the dotted lines and colour the picture.

504 Solve the sums and colour by answer.

505 How many vehicles? Count and write.

506 Trace the lines.

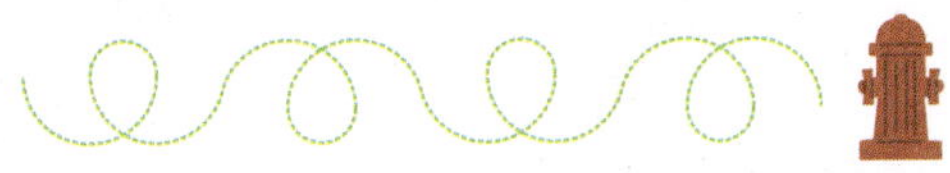

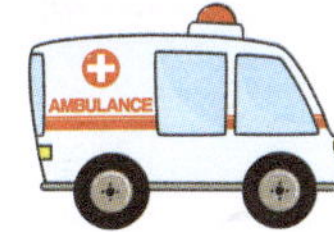

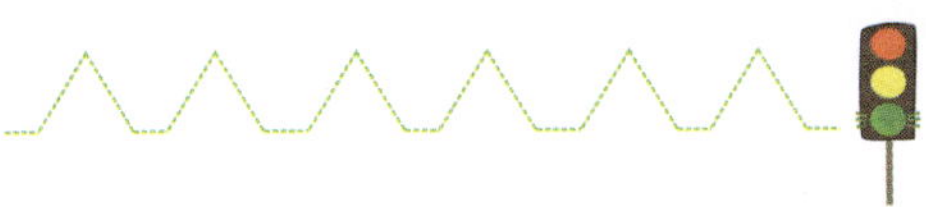

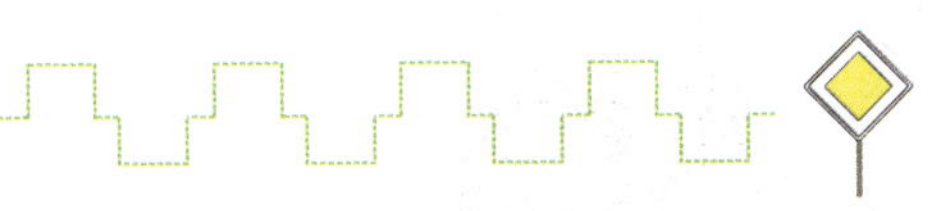

509 Match the shadow with its image.

507 Join the dots and colour the picture.

508 Which two are the same?

510 Trace the lines.

511 What are these pieces of?

512 Find the matching shadow.

513 Write the first letter of each thing to make a new word. Colour the picture.

514 Join the dots and colour.

515 Repeat and colour.

Which does not fit? Tick the answer.

Count and circle the right answer.

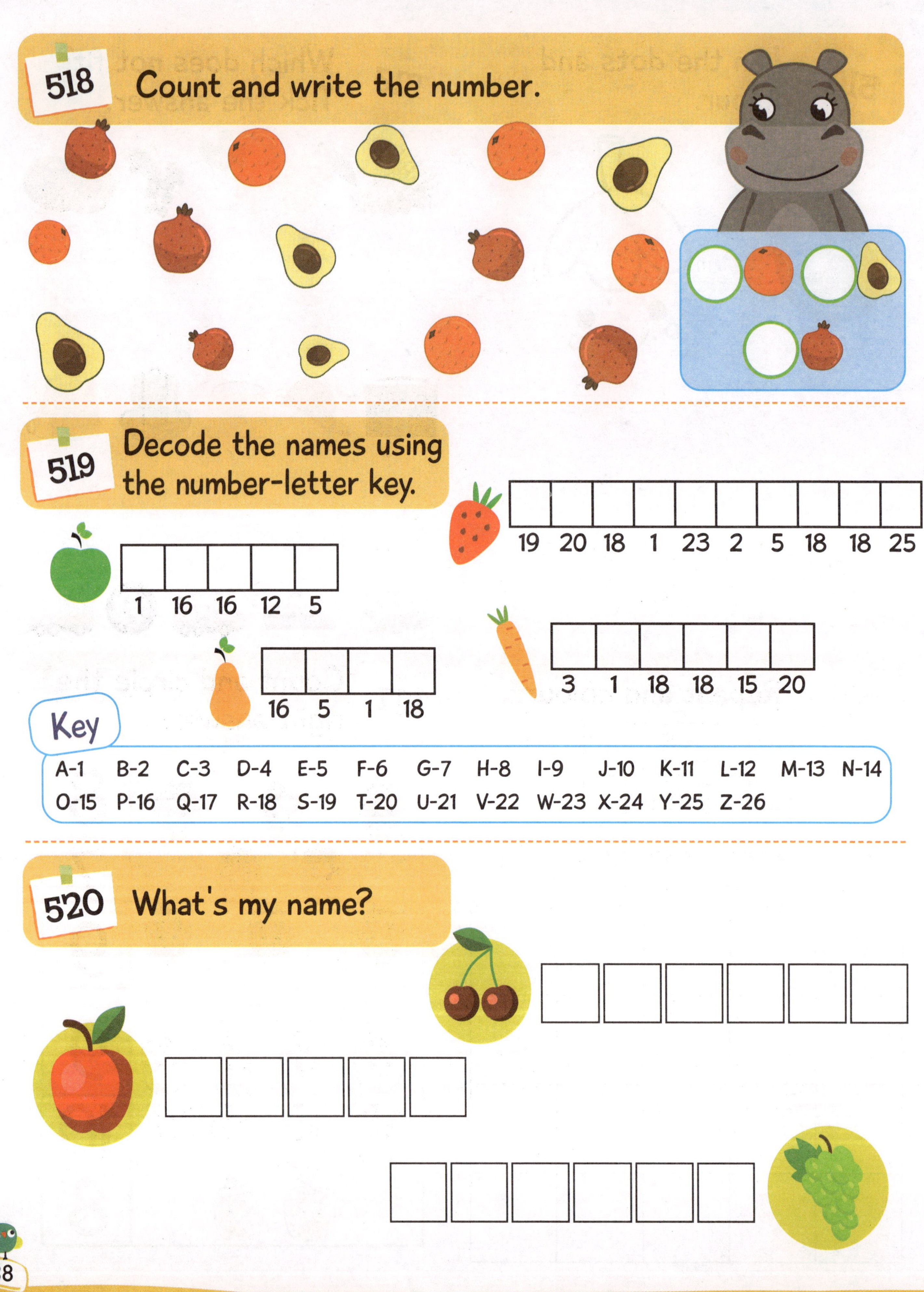

518 Count and write the number.

519 Decode the names using the number-letter key.

1	16	16	12	5

19	20	18	1	23	2	5	18	18	25

16	5	1	18

3	1	18	18	15	20

Key

A-1 B-2 C-3 D-4 E-5 F-6 G-7 H-8 I-9 J-10 K-11 L-12 M-13 N-14
O-15 P-16 Q-17 R-18 S-19 T-20 U-21 V-22 W-23 X-24 Y-25 Z-26

520 What's my name?

521 Spot the odd one out.

522 Match the parts to the correct fruit or vegetable.

523 Join to colour.

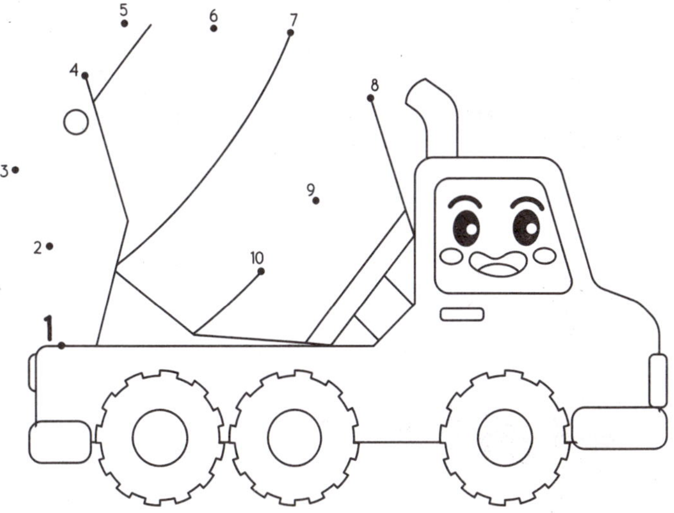

524 Count and match.

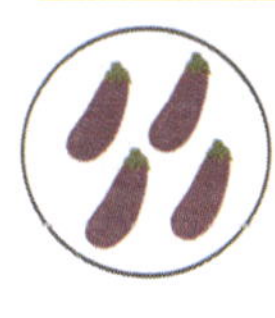

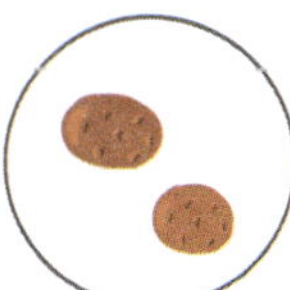

525 Find the matching shadow.

527 Finish the pattern.

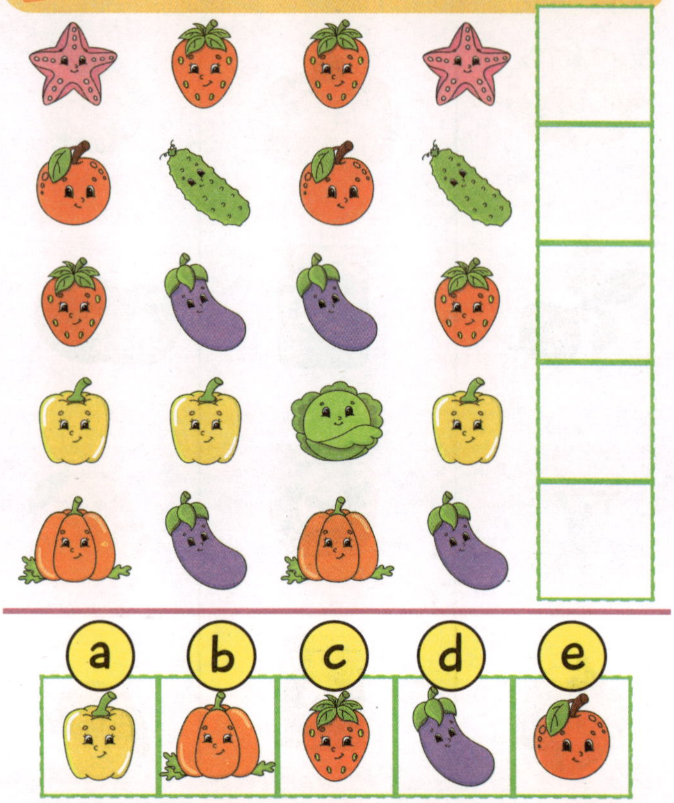

a b c d e

526 Count and match the answer.

2

5

1

4

3

528 Trace the lines.

529 Subtract and write the answer in the box.

531 Spot the odd one out.

530 Count and circle the answer.

532 Match to complete the pictures.

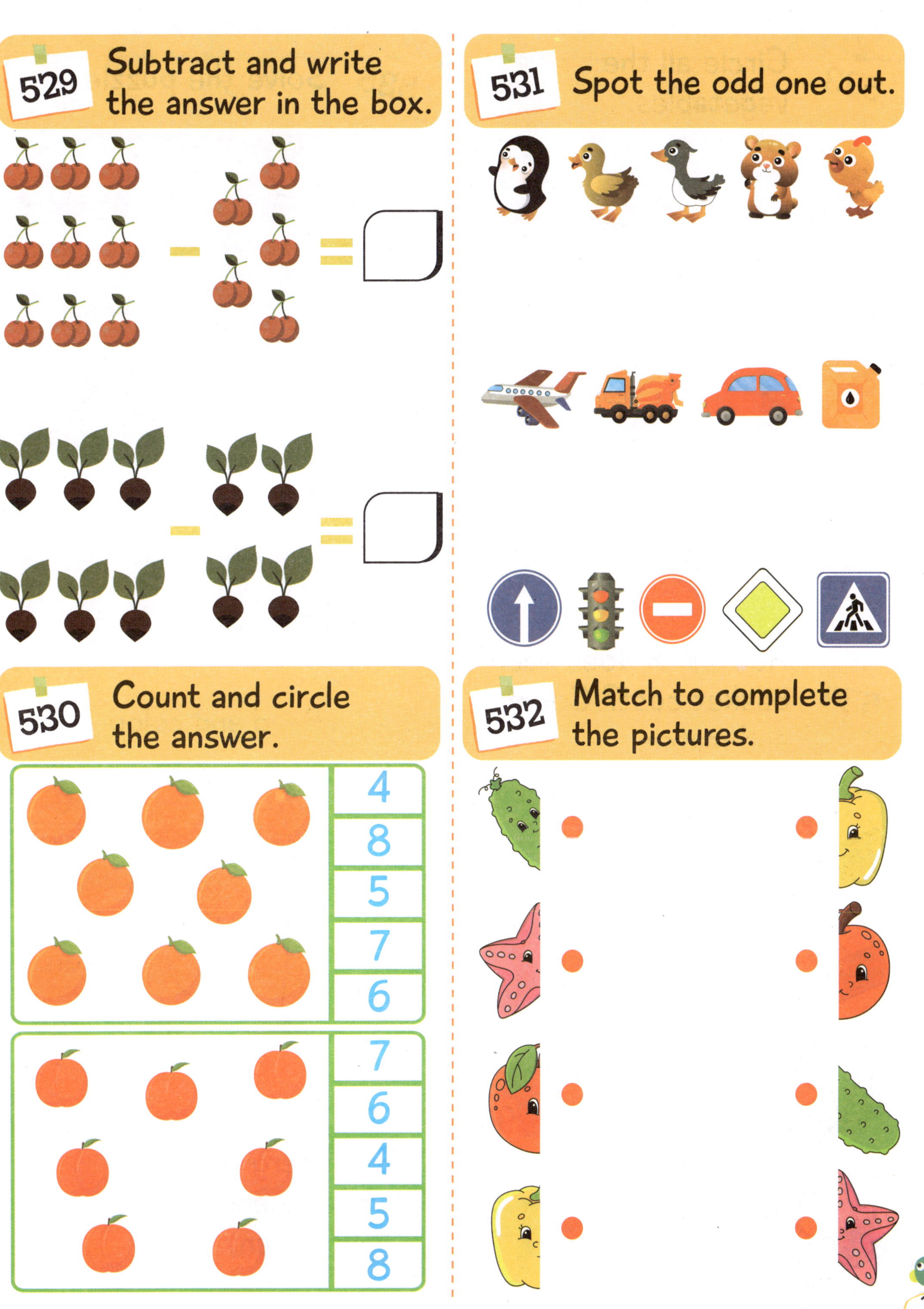

533 Circle all the vegetables.

535 Solve the puzzle.

534 How much does each basket cost? Count and match.

536 Read and colour.

537 Subtract and write.

539 Add and write.

10 + 3 + 3 =

2 + 8 + 10 =

538 Solve the sudoku puzzle.

A B C D

540 Trace the lines.

541 Tick (✓) the smaller group.

542 Colour the spinach.

543 Trace the lines.

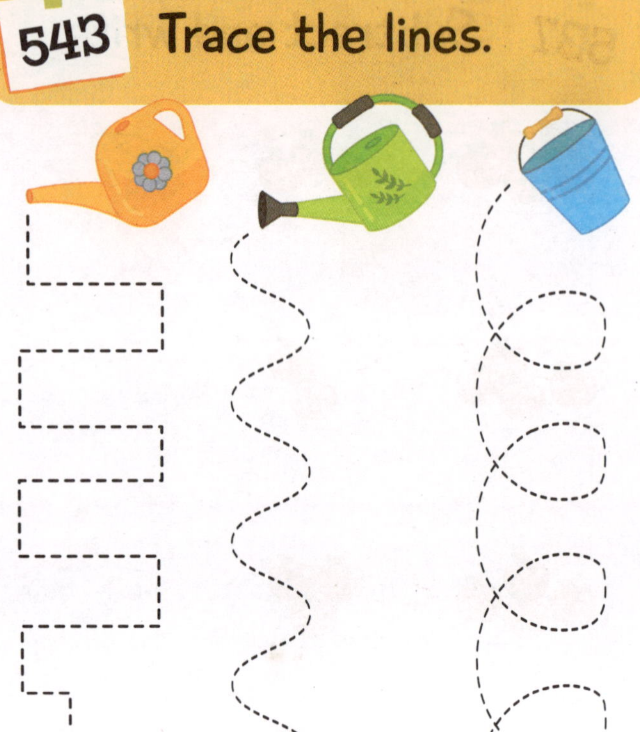

544 What are they known as?

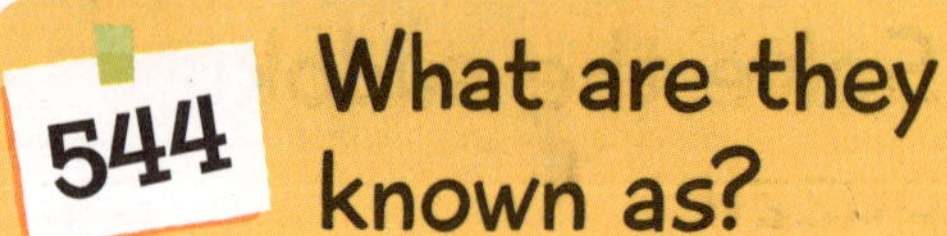

Lettuce

Cauliflower

Cucumber

Apple

Onion

Broccoli

545 Colour by numbers.

1
2
3
4
5
6
7

546 Connect my dots and colour me!

547 Add and match to their sums.

 + 

9

548 Trace the path.

549 Find the matching shadow.

550 Connect my dots and colour me!

551 Match by size.

552 Repeat and colour.

553 Count and write.

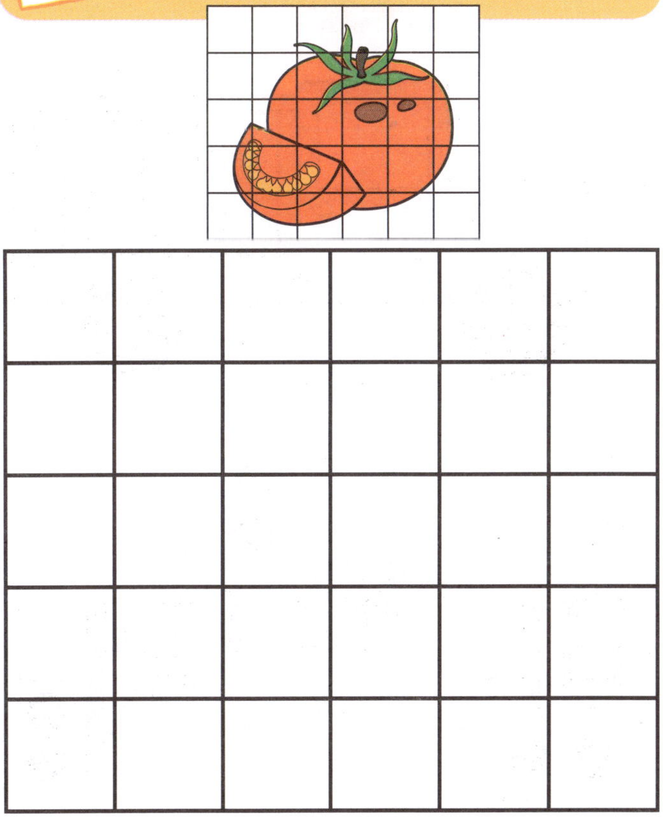

554 Find twin cats.

555 Colour the onion.

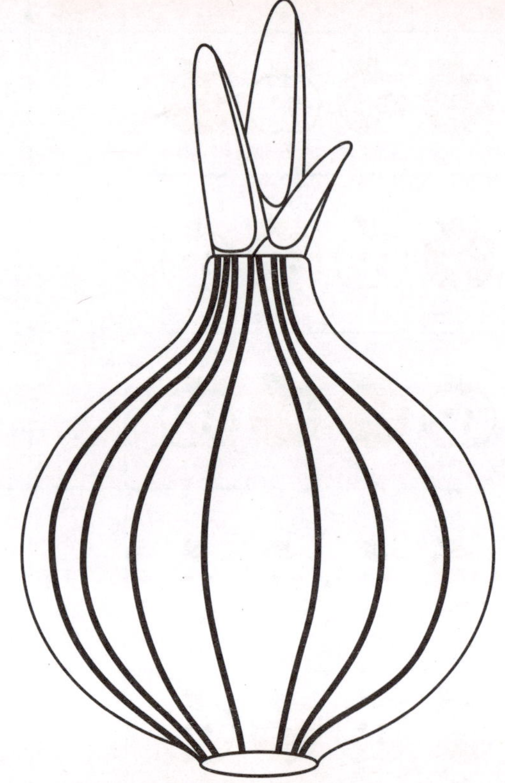

556 Find the matching shadow.

557 Count and circle the right answer.

558 Tick (✓) the right set.

559 Repeat and colour.

561 Draw and colour.

560 Colour the picture.

562 Put the bouquets in the matching vases.

563 Count and write.

564 Look at the picture and colour the rainbow.

565 Write the missing letters.

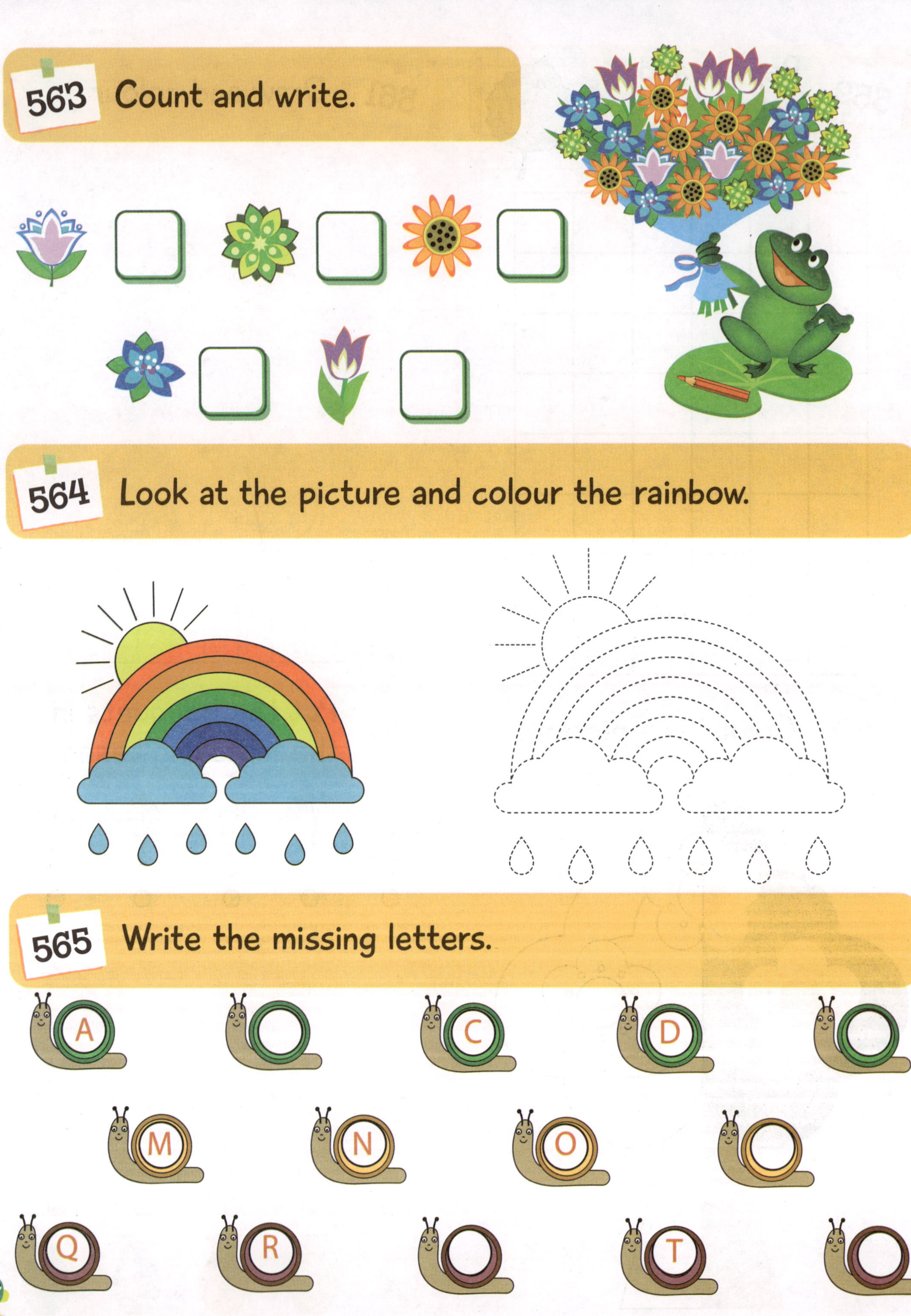

566 Count and write.

568 Colour by numbers.

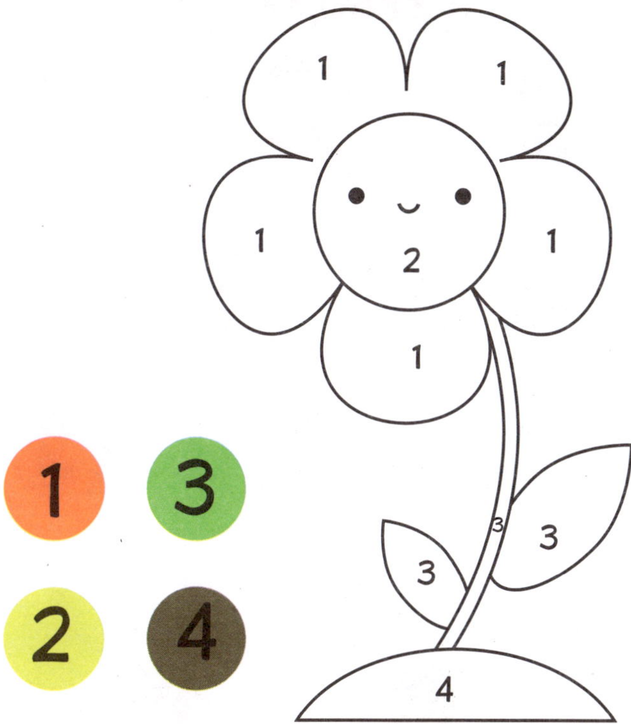

567 Count the flowers and write the sum in the box.

569 Help the bee reach the flower. Trace a path from 1 to 16.

570 Help the bunny and the bear fill up their baskets.

Fruits

Vegetables

571 Trace and colour.

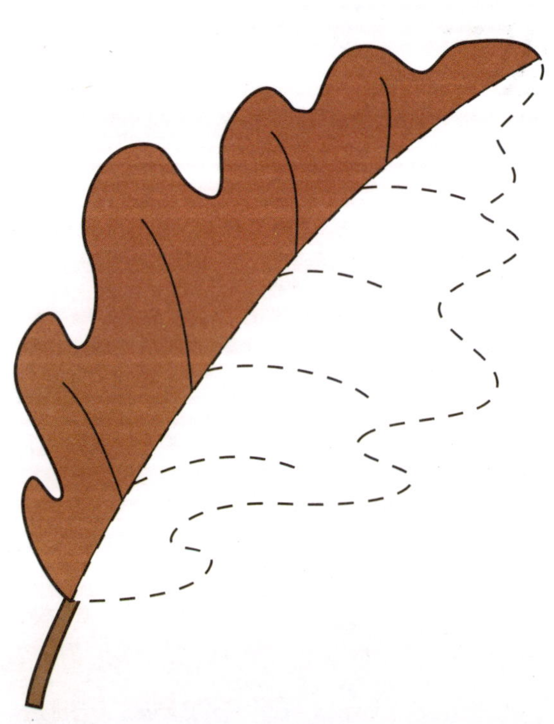

572 Count the gifts.

573 Count and write.

574 Identify and match.

EAR

HAIR

EYE

NECK

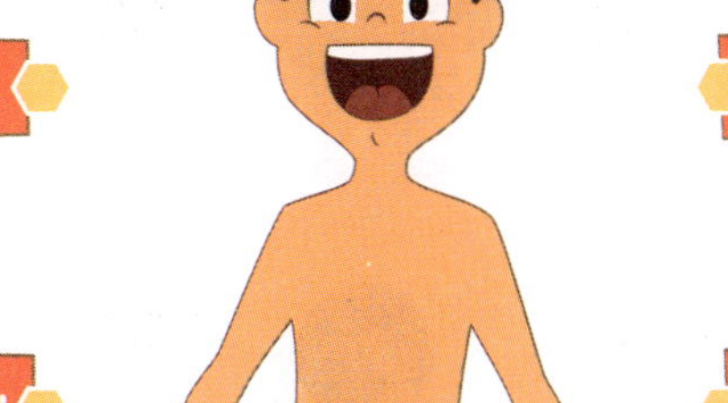

MOUTH

NOSE

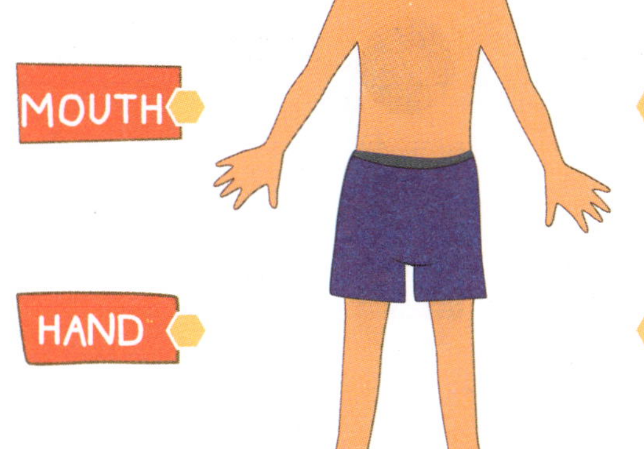

HAND

ARM

LEG

FOOT

575 Count and write.

576 Subtract and write the answer in the box.

3 - 1 = 2

3 - 2 =

4 - 1 =

4 - 2 =

3 - 1 =

4 - 3 =

577 Colour the picture.

Find the matching shadow.

Solve to help Santa reach the christmas tree.

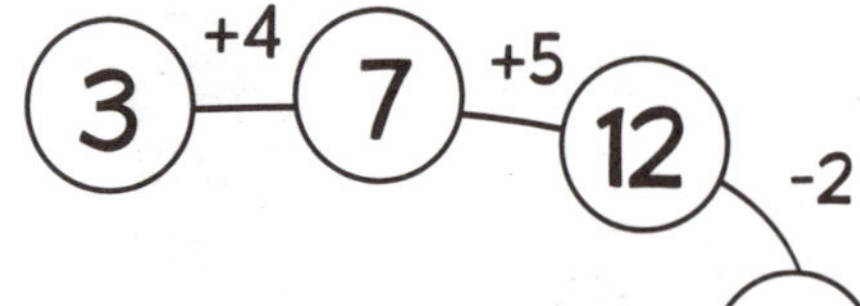

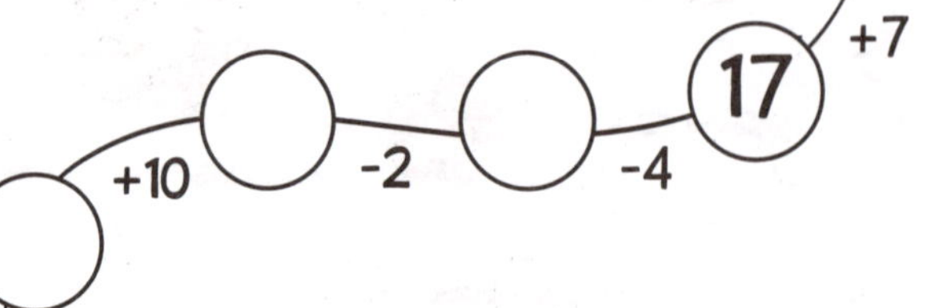

-6

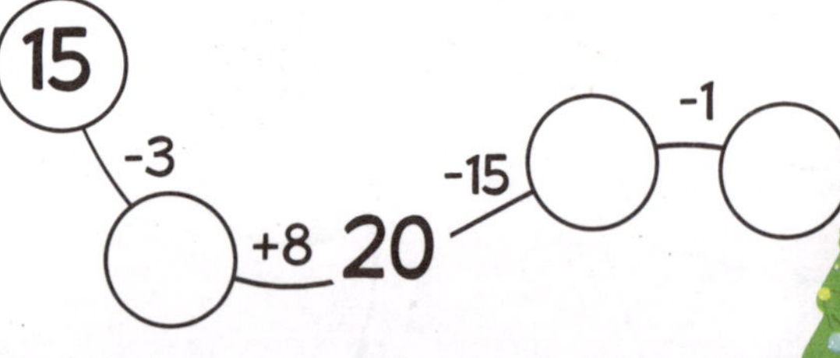

Add and write.

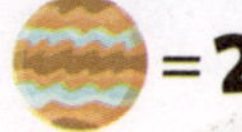 = 1  = 2  = 3 = 4

 +  = 

   =

   =

 +  =

581

Trace and colour.

582 Name the body part.

583 Match the pairs.

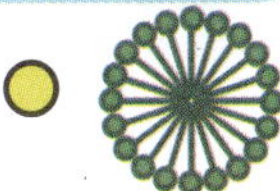

584 Find the total.

585 Complete and colour the snowman.

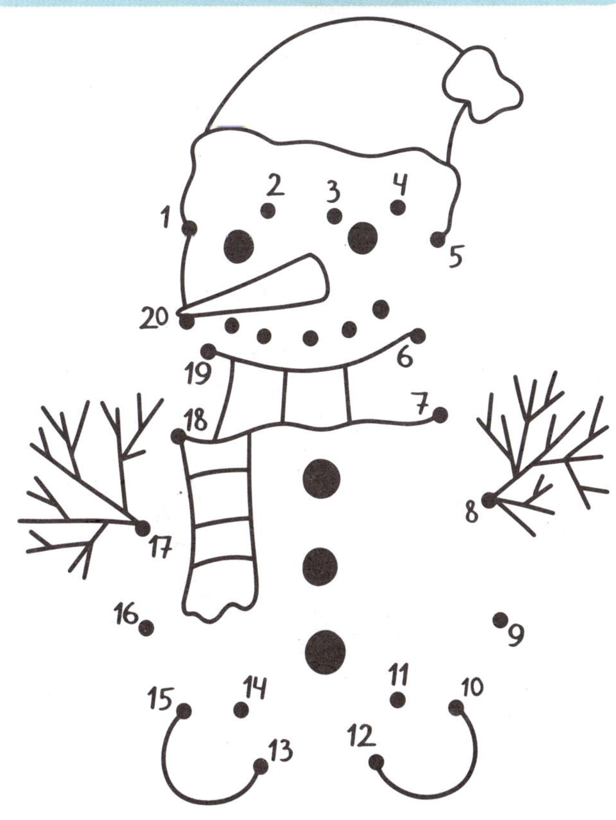

586 Trace the lines and colour the picture.

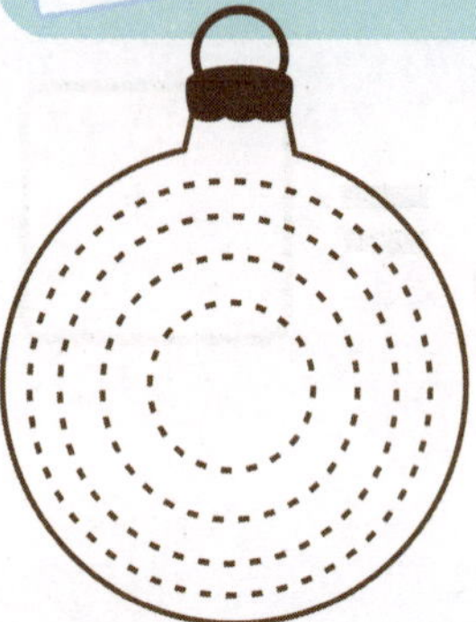
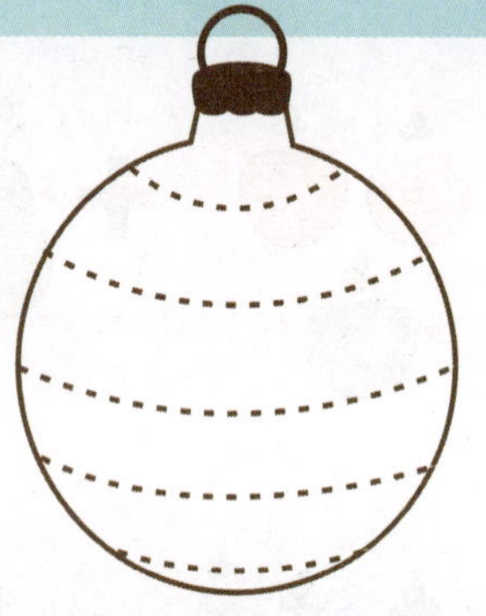
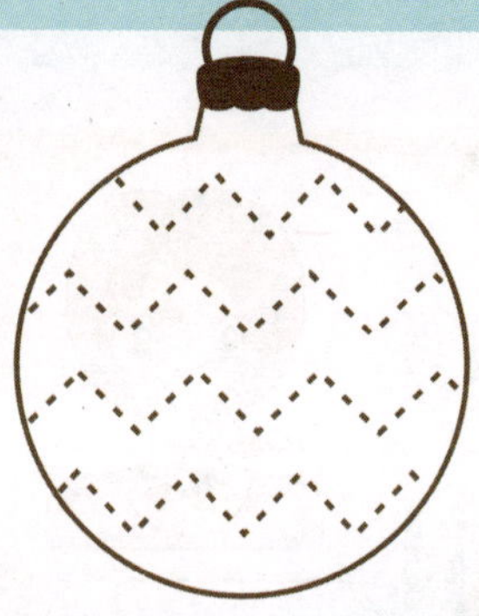
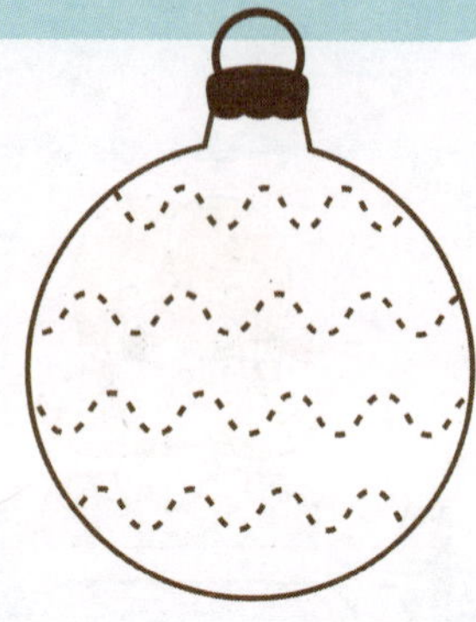

587 Find 10 differences.

588 Complete colouring his muffler.

589 Count and write.

590 Where will they be worn?

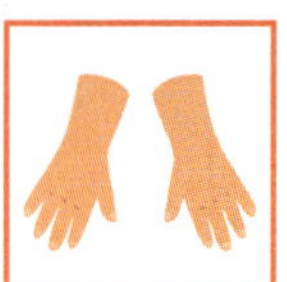

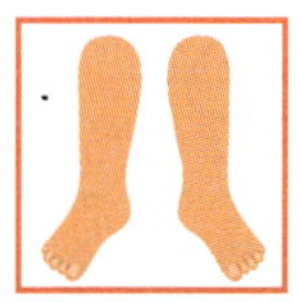

591 Colour the skating shoe.

592 Count and write.

593 Match the socks to the washing machine of the same colour.

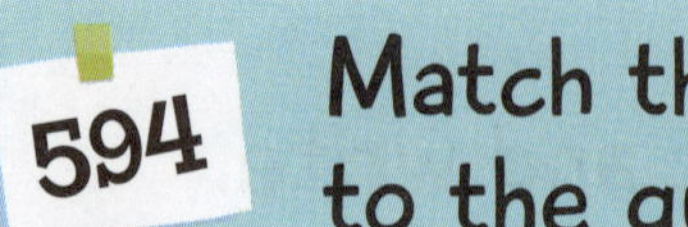

594 Match the umbrellas to the gumboots.

596 Colour the park.

595 Colour the sweater in Christmas theme.

597 Sort according to the seasons.

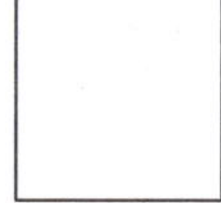

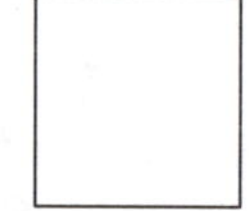

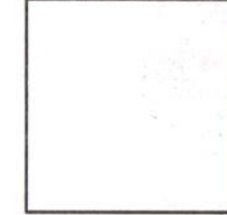

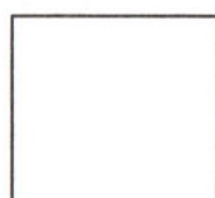
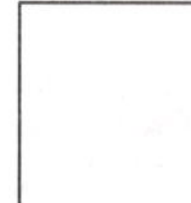
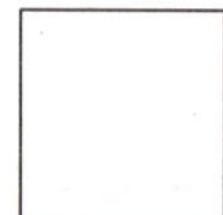

1 2 3 4 5 6

7 8 9 10 11 12

598 Find the identical two.

599 Match the pairs.

600 Trace and colour.

601 Which season is it?

602 Count and write.

603 Which season is it?

605 Match the body parts to their functions.

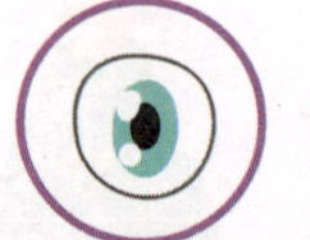

604 How many look to the left and how many look to the right?

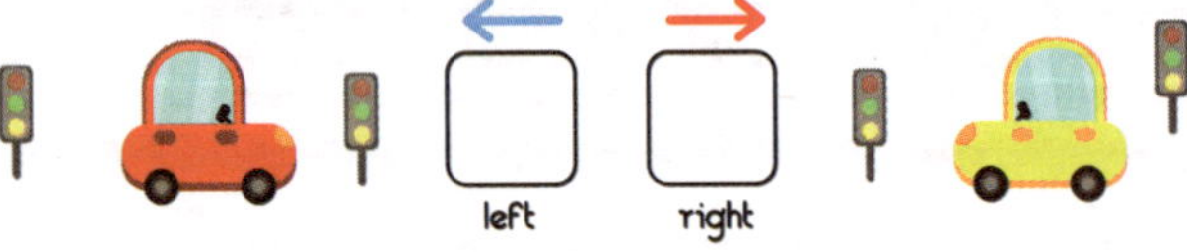

606 Find these body parts in the grid.

E	Y	E	A	F	G	A	A
I	P	C	O	E	A	R	B
R	B	E	H	I	C	M	I
C	A	F	A	R	D	I	M
A	L	O	N	B	E	D	O
H	E	A	D	I	G	C	U
O	G	C	E	F	O	O	T
P	S	I	D	O	B	F	H

607 Draw and colour.

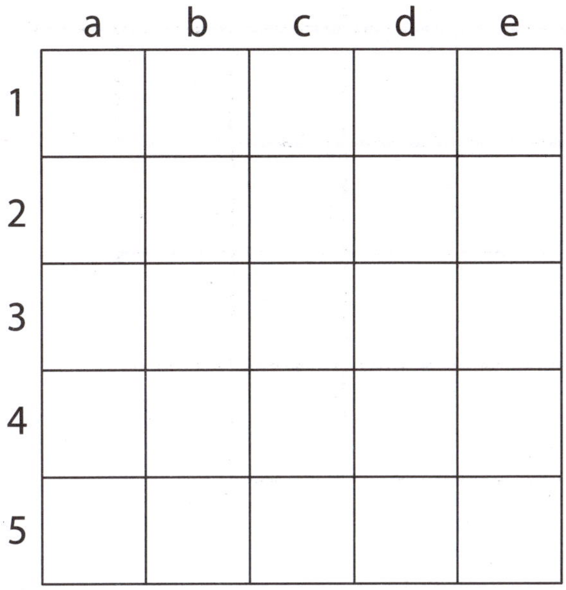

	a	b	c	d	e
1					
2					
3					
4					
5					

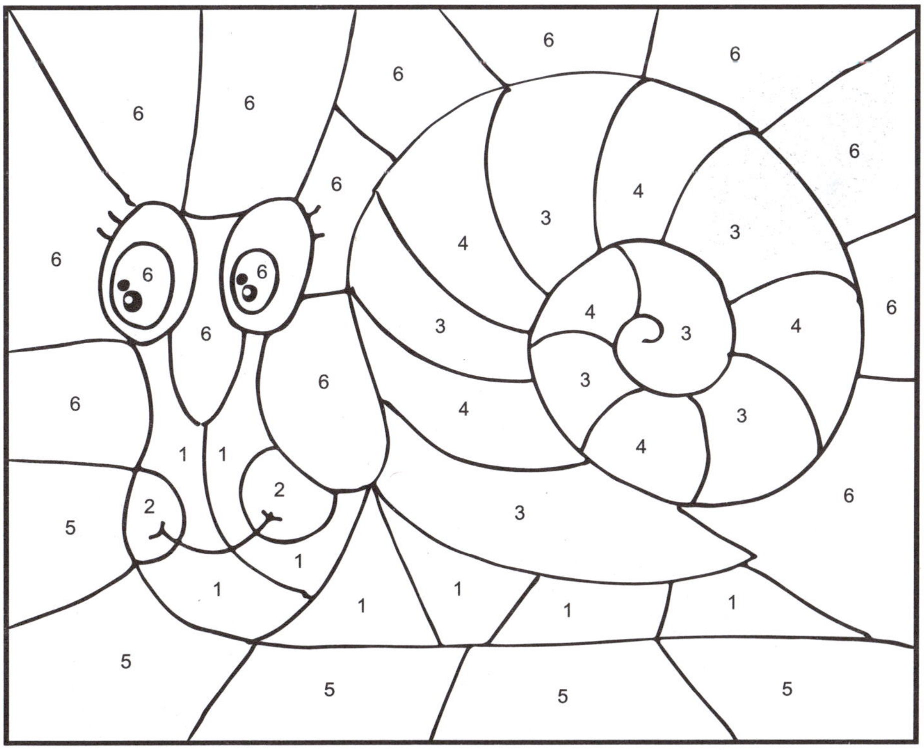

609 Circle the intestines.

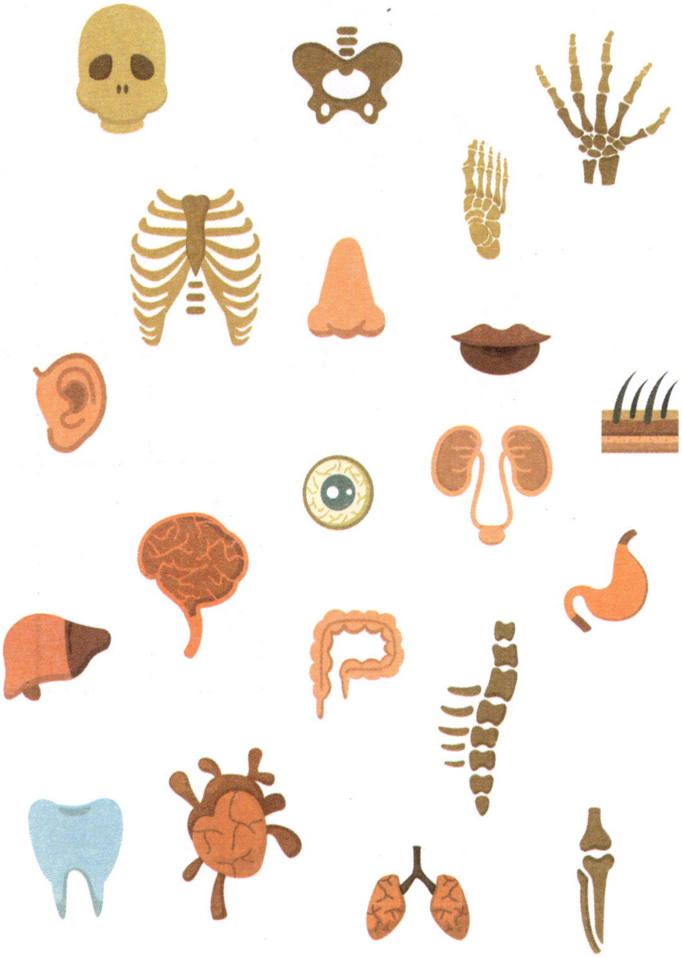

608 Colour by numbers.

3
4
2
6
5
1

610 Identify and solve the Easter crossword.

611 Join the dots and colour the picture.

612 Find the sum.

 =1 =2 =3 =4

 +  =

 +  =

 +  =

  +  = 

613 Match the body parts to their functions.

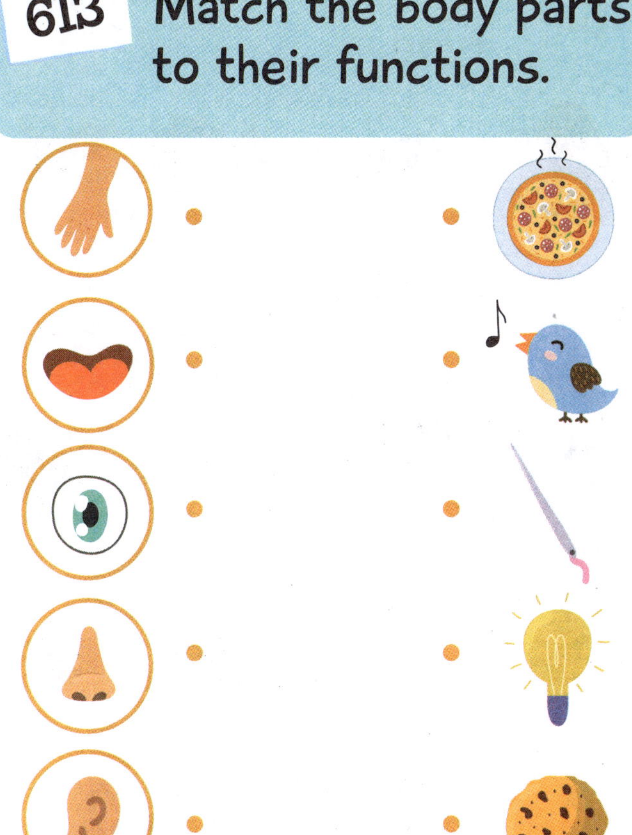

614 Match according to their descriptions.

I can see with my eyes.

I can hear with my ears.

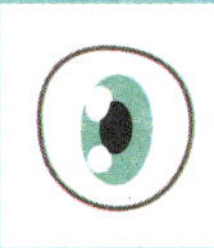

I can smell with my nose.

I can taste with my tongue.

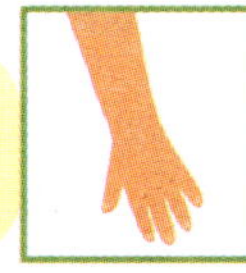

I can touch with my hands.

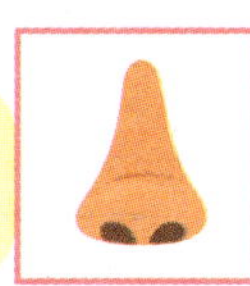

615 How many astronauts? Count and circle.

616 Match the smells with the pictures.

I smell with my nose.

Stinky

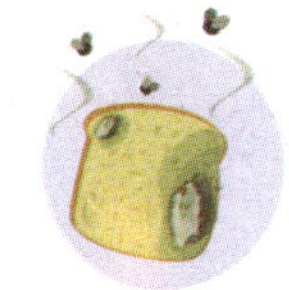

Musty

Putrid

Aromatic

617 Match the texture with the image.

I touch with my hands.

Soft	
Hot	
Hard	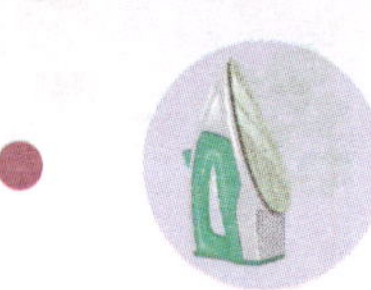
Slimy	

618 Trace the lines.

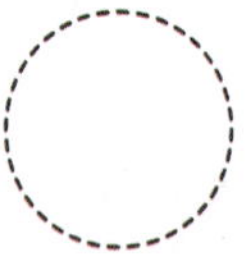

619 Count the heads by type.

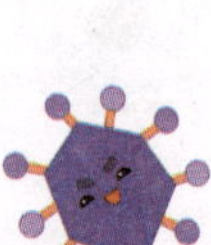

620 Fill in the correct numbers. You have:

_____ hands. 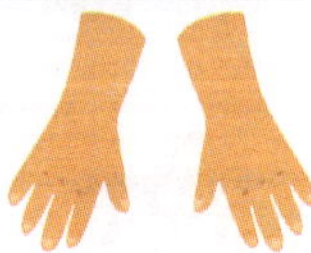

_____ eyes. 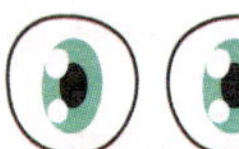

_____ ears. 

_____ mouth. 

_____ nose. 

_____ legs. 

621 Match according to the senses used.

622 Colour the picture.

623 <, > or =?

624 Label the fairy.

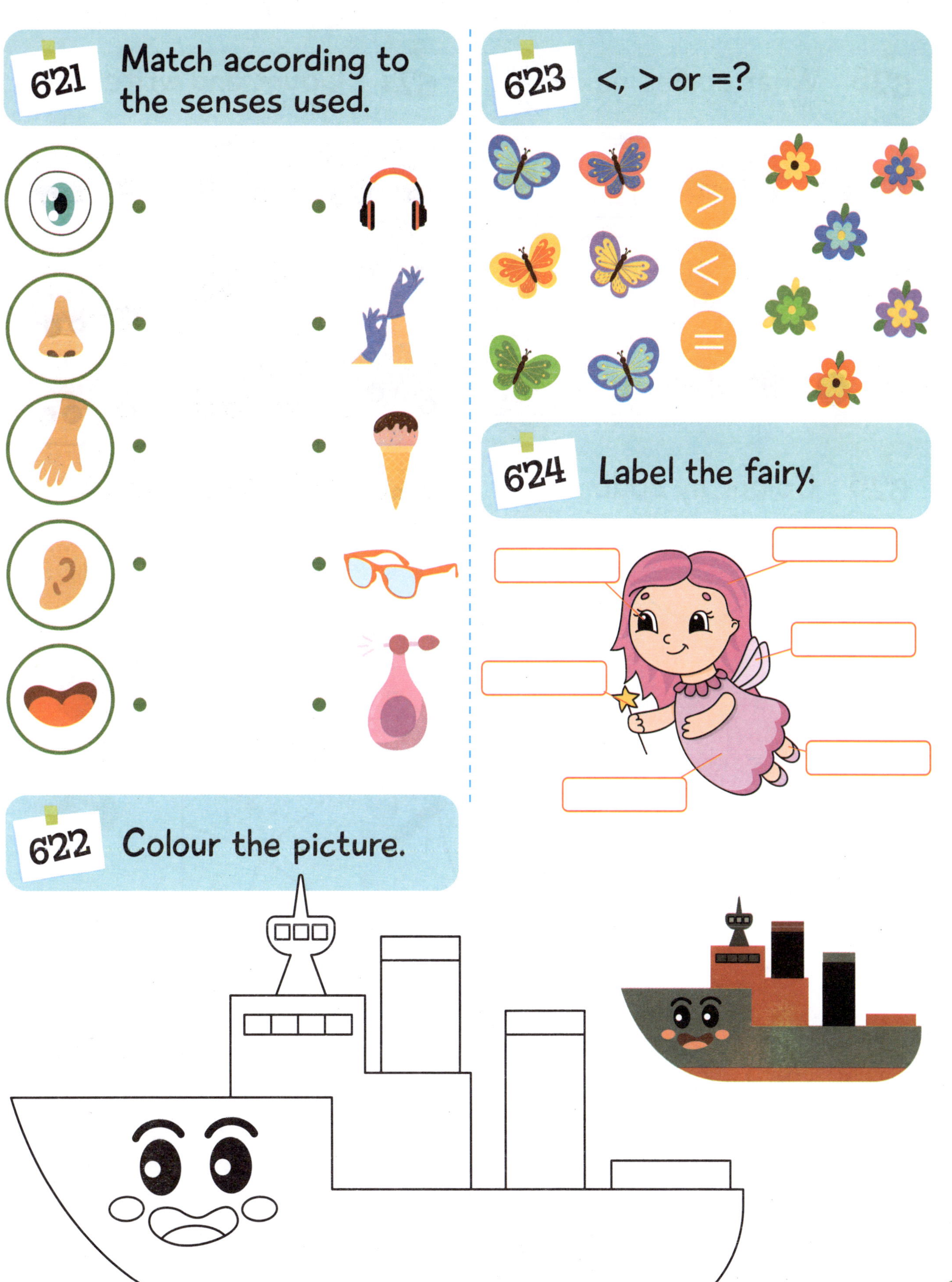

625 What comes next?

627 Count and write.

626 Colour by code.

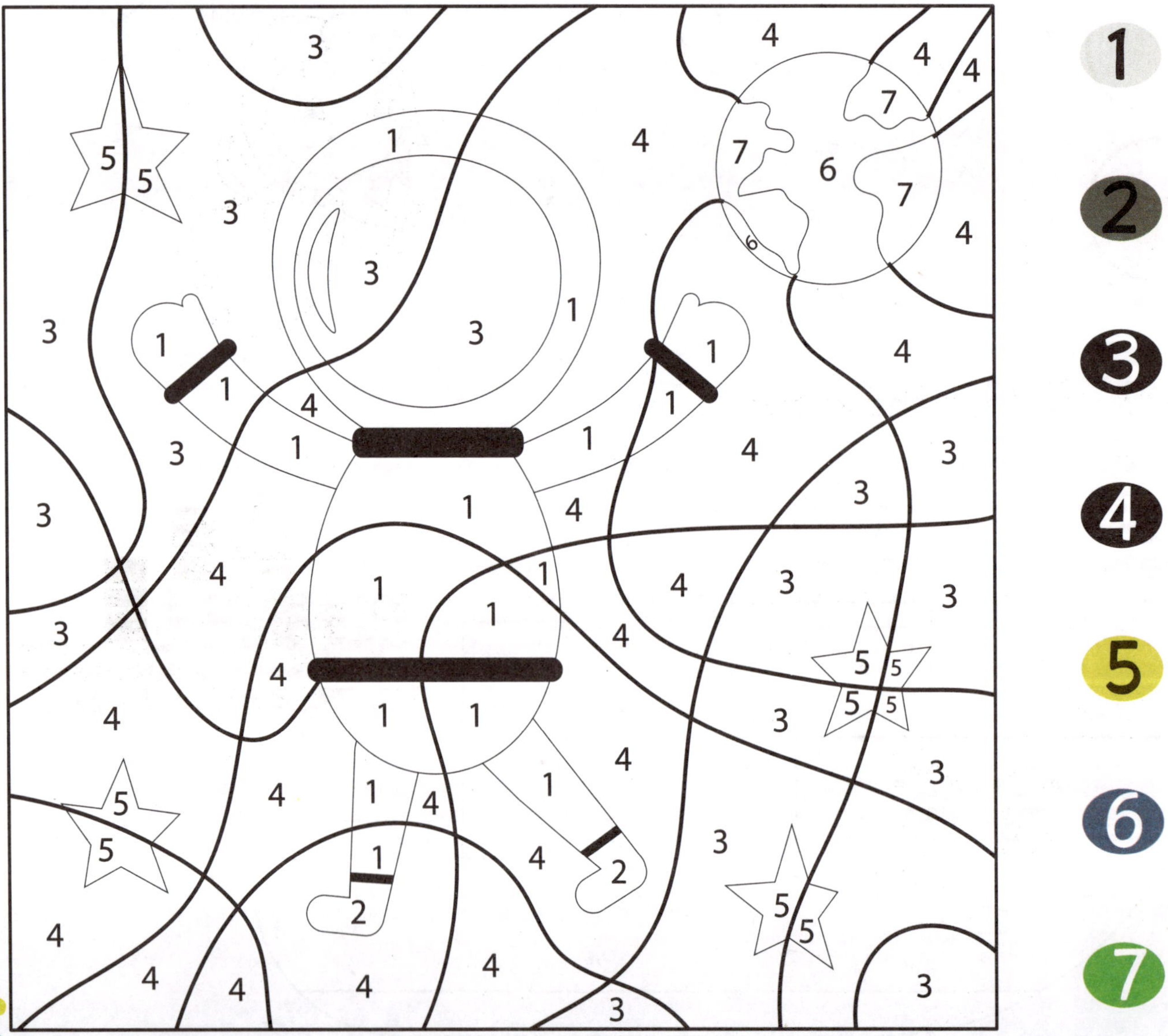

1 2 3 4 5 6 7

628 What are they known as? Write in the box.

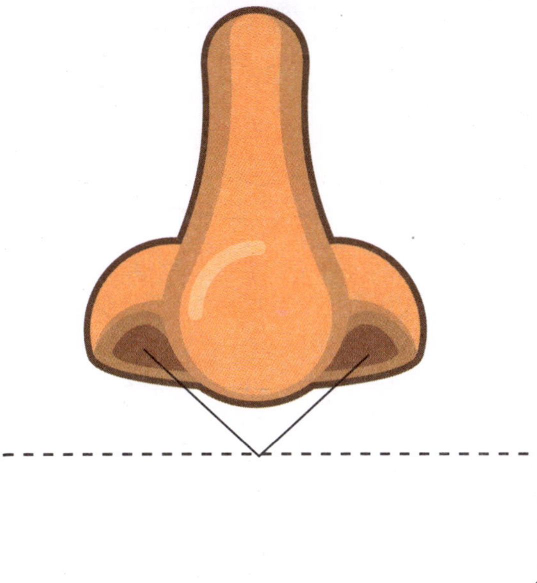

629 Label with the correct numbers.

1. Chin
2. Cheek
3. Jaw
4. Lip
5. Ear
6. Hair
7. Eye
8. Tongue
9. Tooth
10. Forehead
11. Nose
12. Eyebrow

630 What am I called?

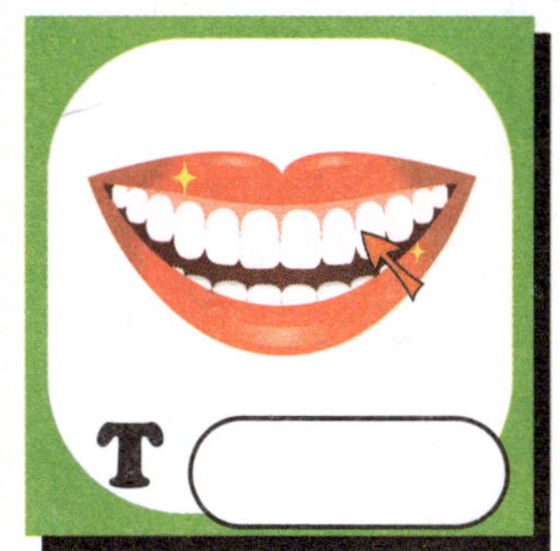

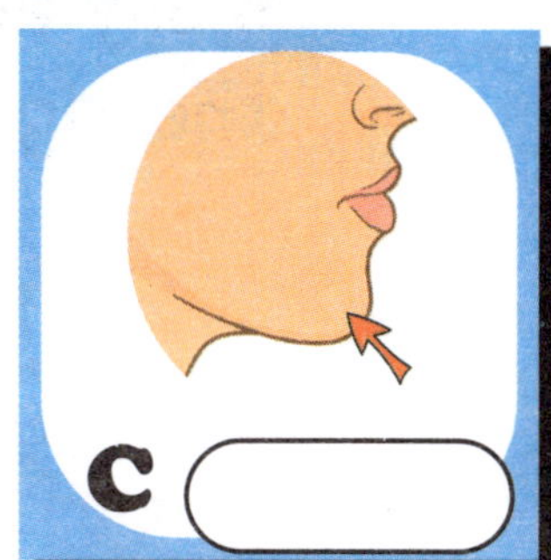

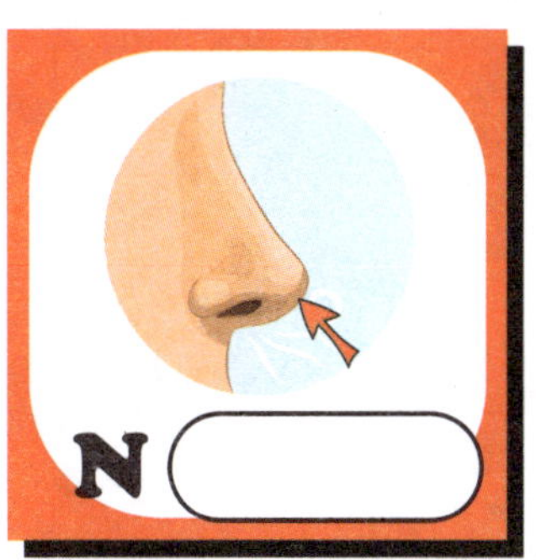

631 Trace and colour the picture.

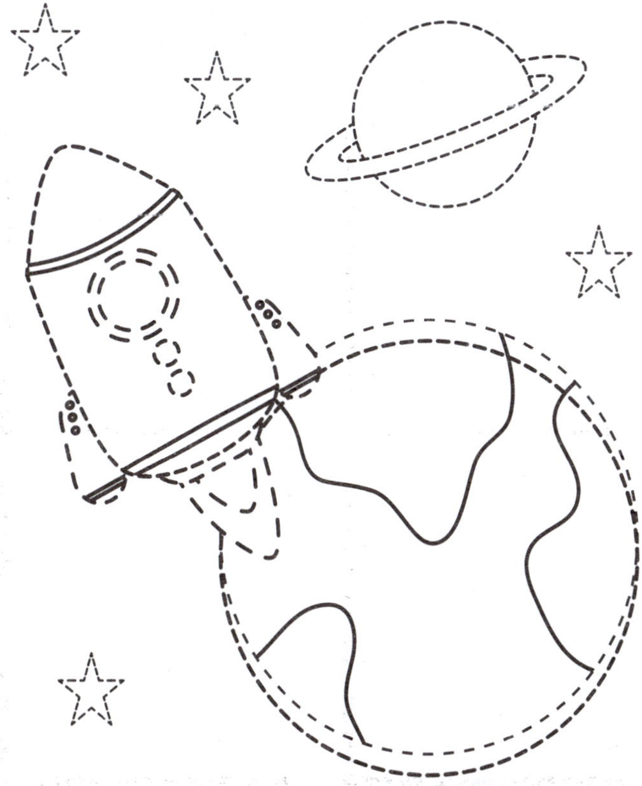

632 How many are running to the left and how many are running to the right?

633 What am I called?

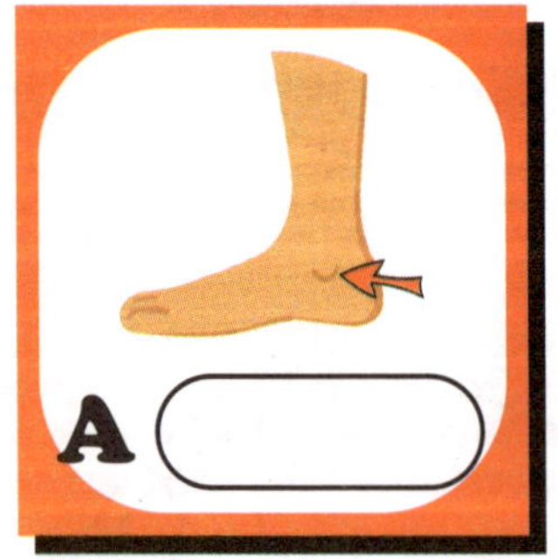

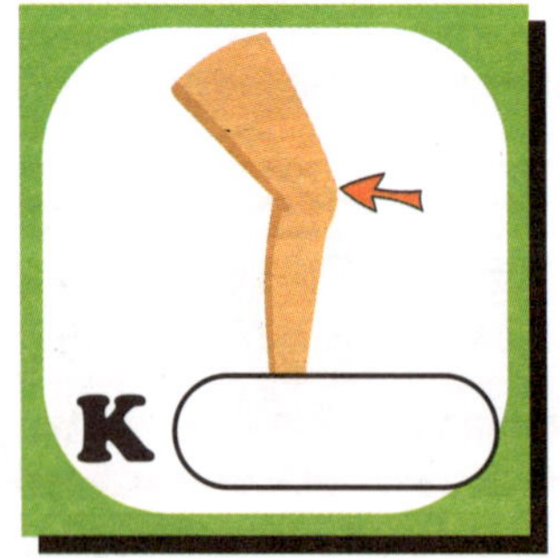

634 What are they known as? Write in the box.

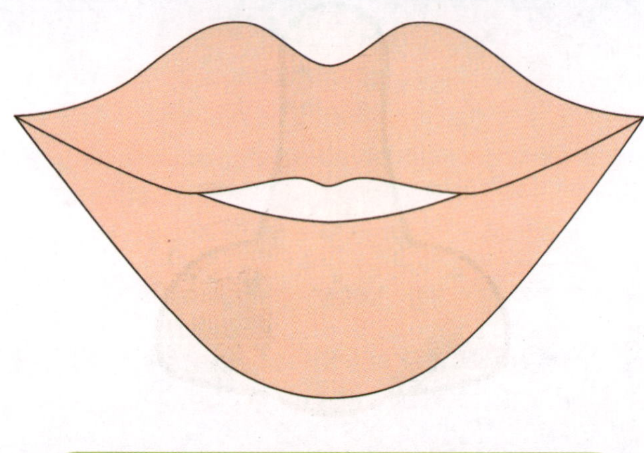

635 Does this look like a weak heart or a strong heart? Tick the correct option.

STRONG

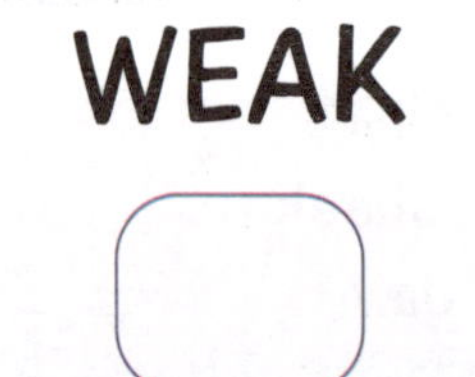

636 Add and write the sum.

2 + 5 = ◯

1 + 3 = ◯

8 + 9 = ◯

638 Colour the fairy.

637 Draw the other half and colour.

639 Mark the parts you see on this side of the face.

____

____

____

____

____

640 Trace and colour.

641 How many robots do you see?

642 What is it known as? Write in the box.

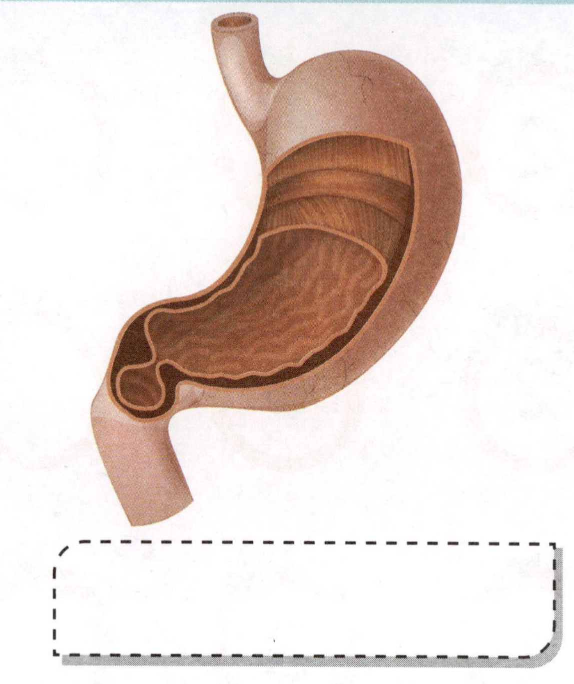

643 Identify and write.

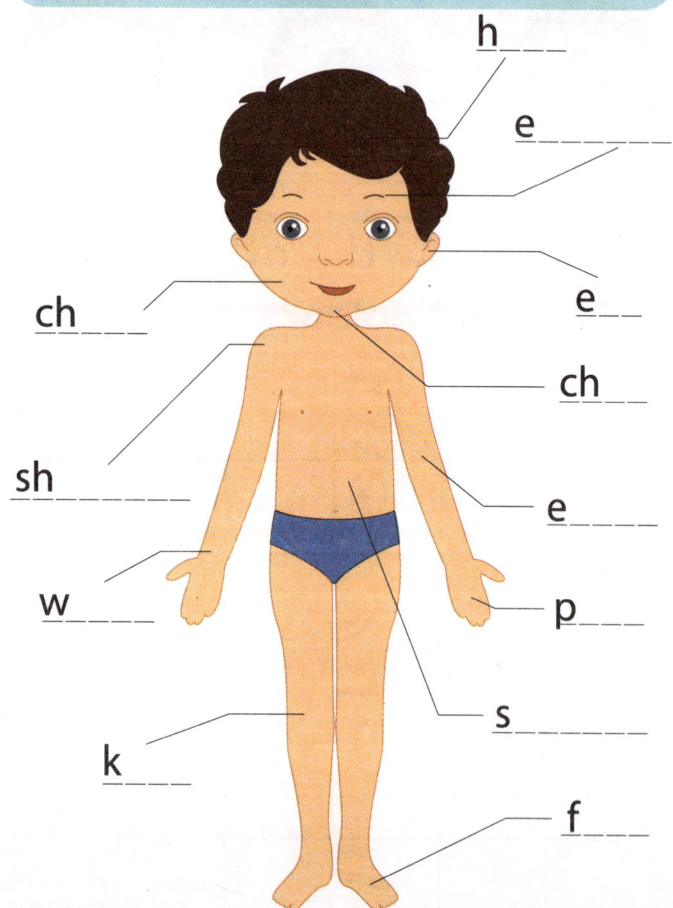

644 Match the view with the image.

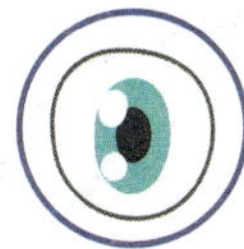

I see with my eyes.

Vibrant 

Ugly 

Shiny 

Spotty 

645 Circle the nervous system diagram.

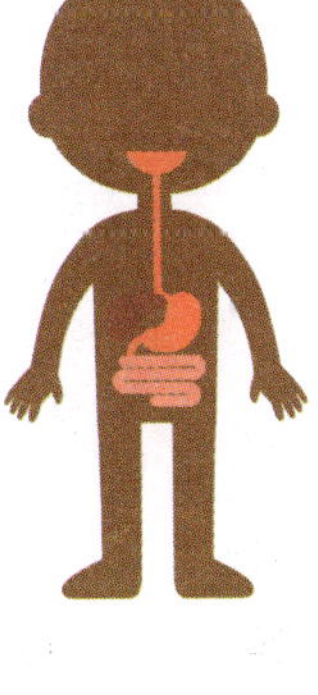

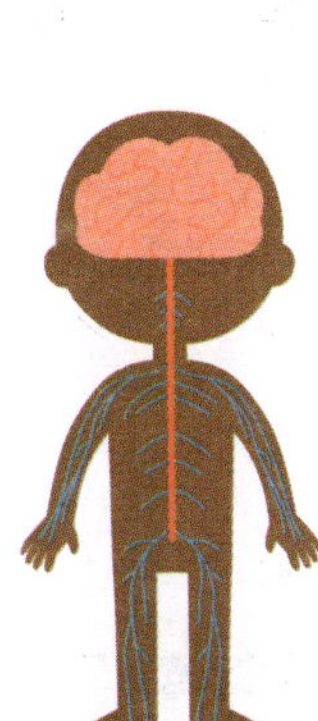

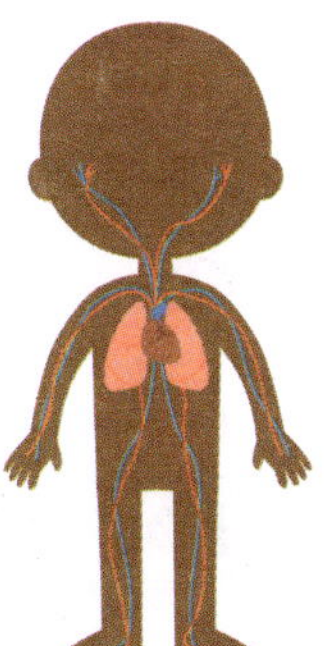

646 Match according to the senses used.

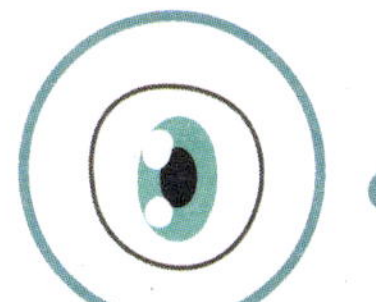 

647 Crack the maze.

648 Count as per shape and colour.

650 Colour the picture.

649 Colour by numbers.

651 Identify and match.

652 Find 7 differences.

653 Find the matching shadow.

654 Match the following.

655 Find two identical cars.

656 Trace and colour.

658 Find 5 differences.

657 Add and write the sum.

KEY

= 1 = 2 = 3 = 4

+ =

+ =

+ =

+ =

659 Copy and colour the picture.

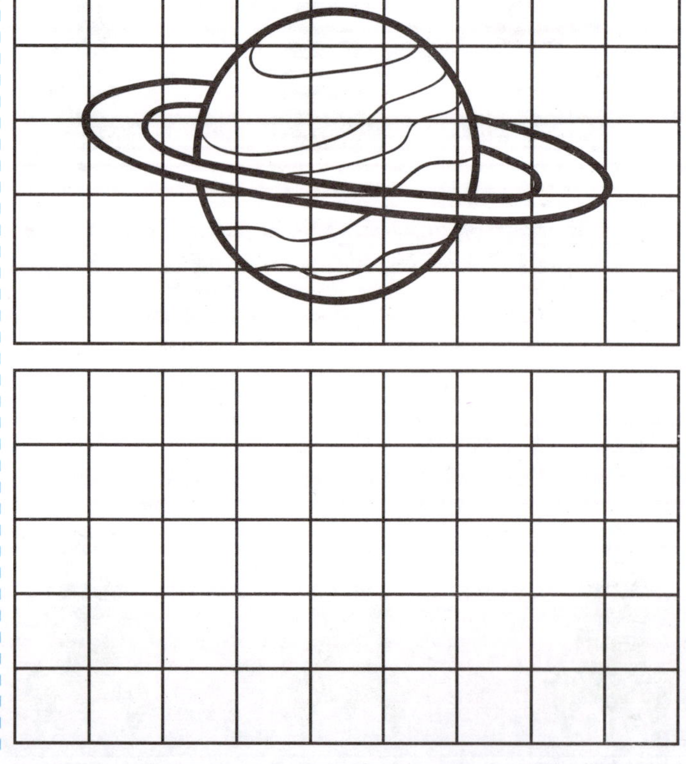

660 Circle the spine.

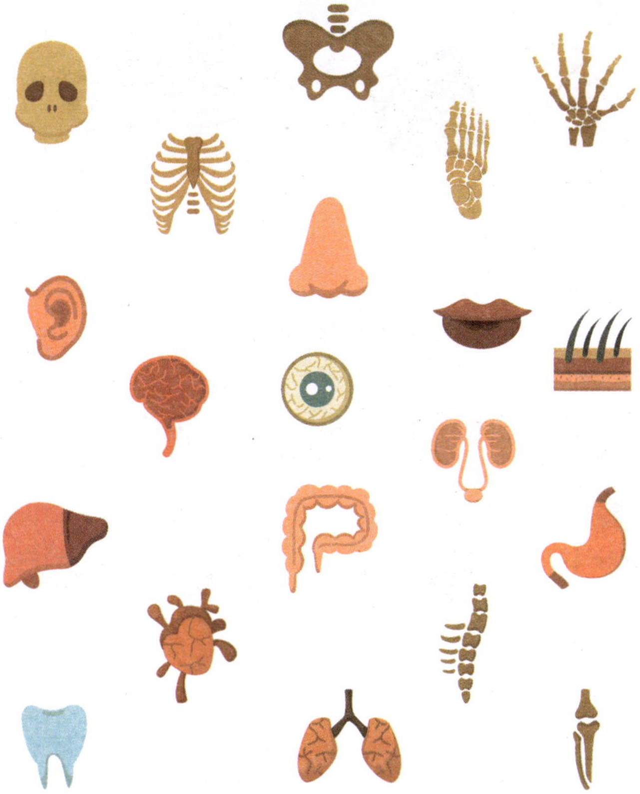

662 Help the apple reach the tummy.

661 Draw and colour.

663 Find the matching shadow.

664 How many look to the left and how many look to the right?
LEFT RIGHT
666 Tick (✓) the right preposition.
BELOW
NEAR
ABOVE
BETWEEN
IN
BETWEEN
BEHIND
NEAR
667 Add and match.
2+1=
1+3=
1+0=
1+1=
1
2
3
4
665 Trace the lines.
668 Which letter is missing?
V
M
N
_EPTUNE

669 Find 8 hidden objects in the picture.

670 Count and write.

671 Colour by numbers.

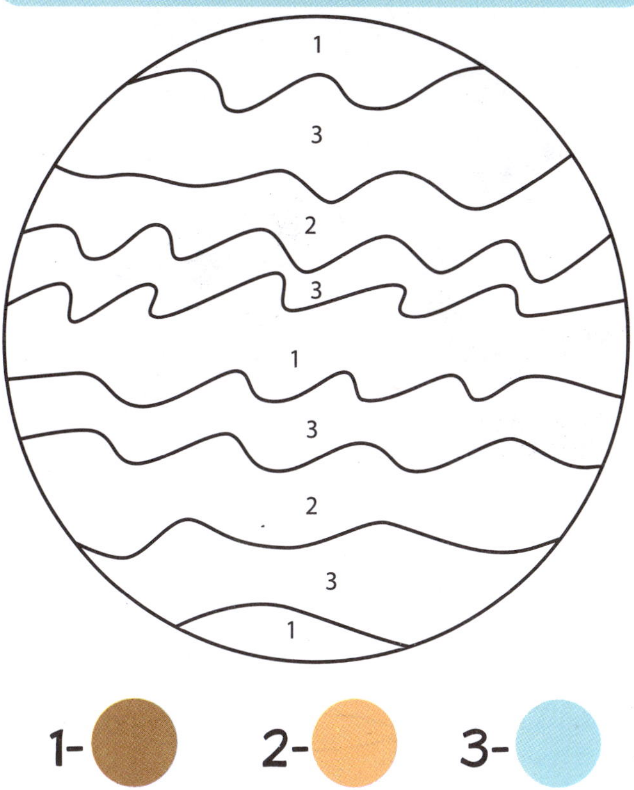

672 Find 5 differences.

673 Join the dots and colour.

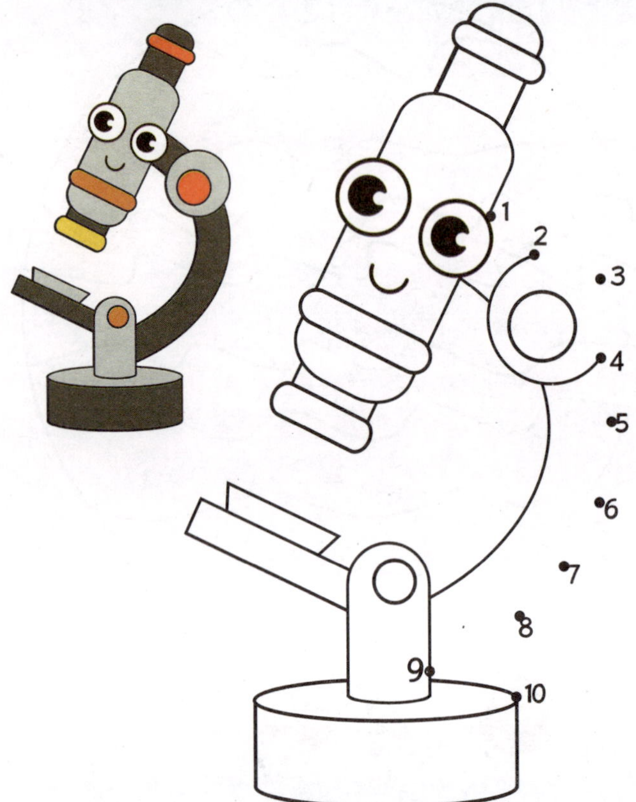

674 Find 10 hidden objects in the picture.

675 Count and write.

676 Colour by numbers.

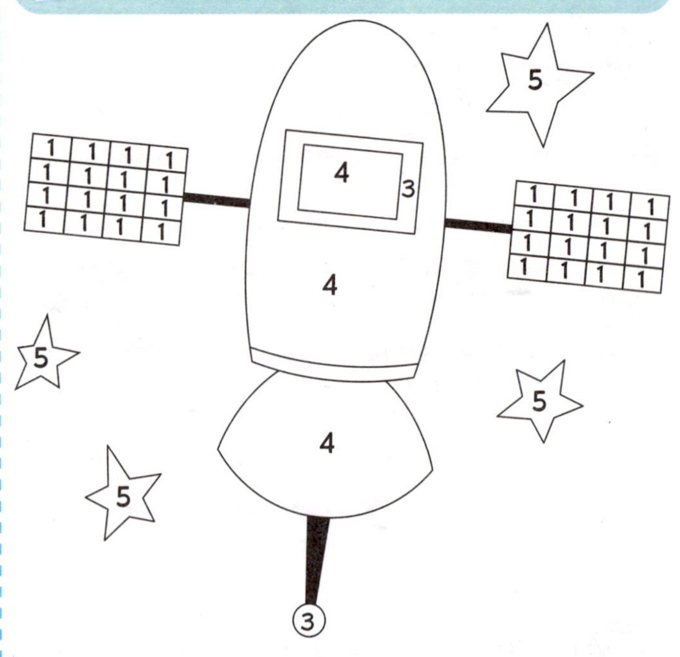

677 Colour by numbers.

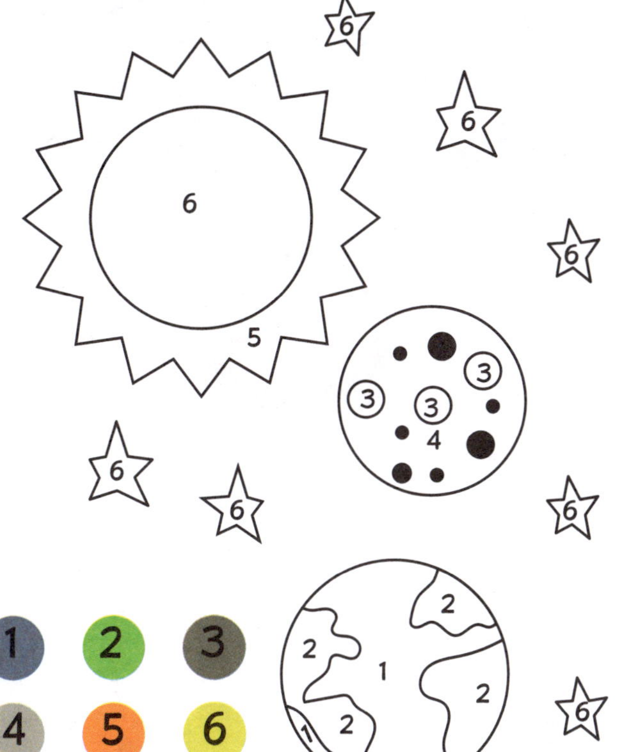

678 Count and circle the sum.

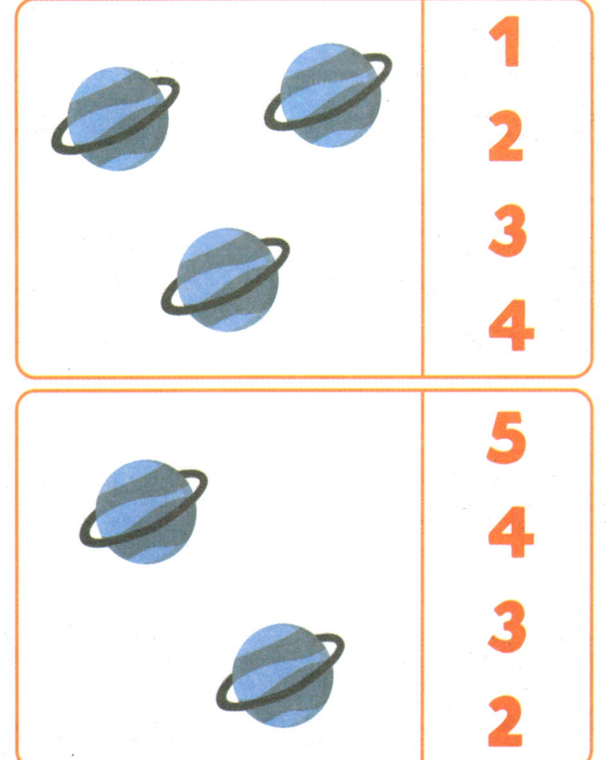

679 Match with seasons.

680 Draw the shapes next to the corresponding parts.

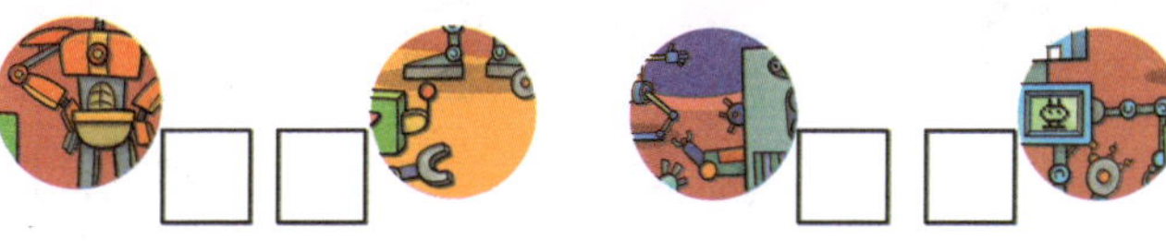

681 Count and circle the sum.

682 Guess the name.

R M S A

683 Match the patch.

684 <, > or = ?

685 Spot the odd one out.

686 Add and write the sum in the box.

+ =

+ =

+ =

+ =

2 5 4 3

687 Colour match.

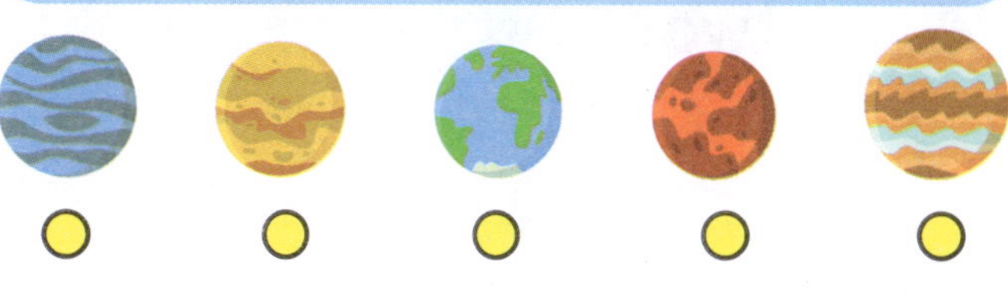

688 Subtract and write.

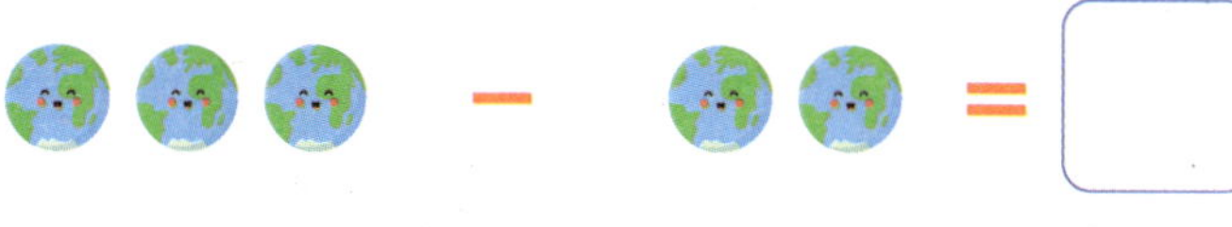

− =

− =

− =

689 Colour the lotus.

1 2 3

690 What colour will we get after mixing these two?

693 Colour the picture.

691 Which letter is missing?

692 Trace the lines to help them meet.

694 Trace and colour.

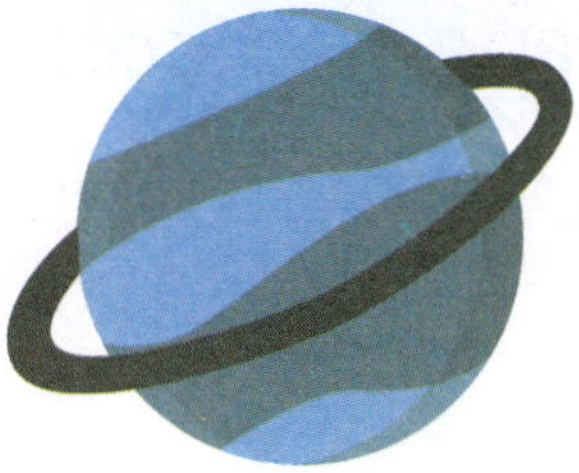

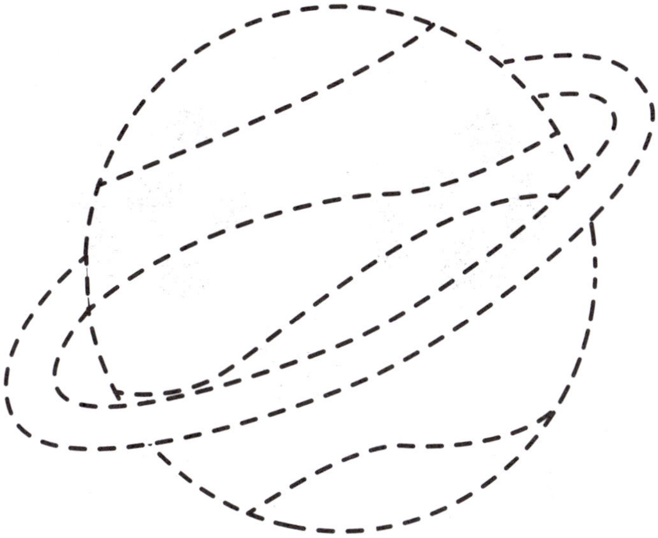

695 Write their names.

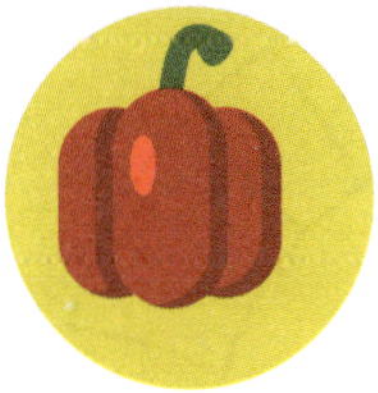

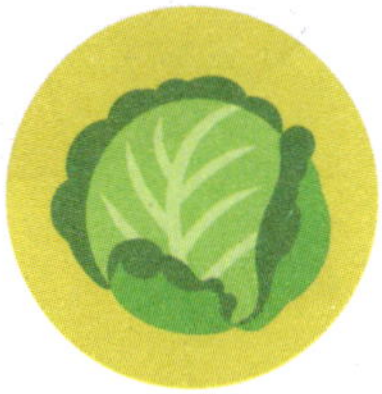

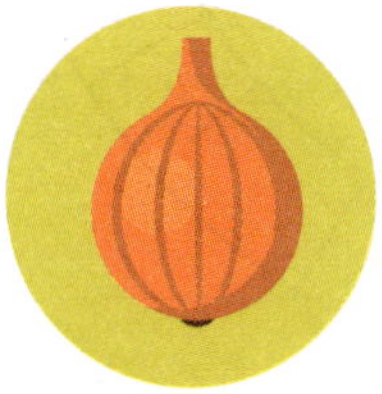

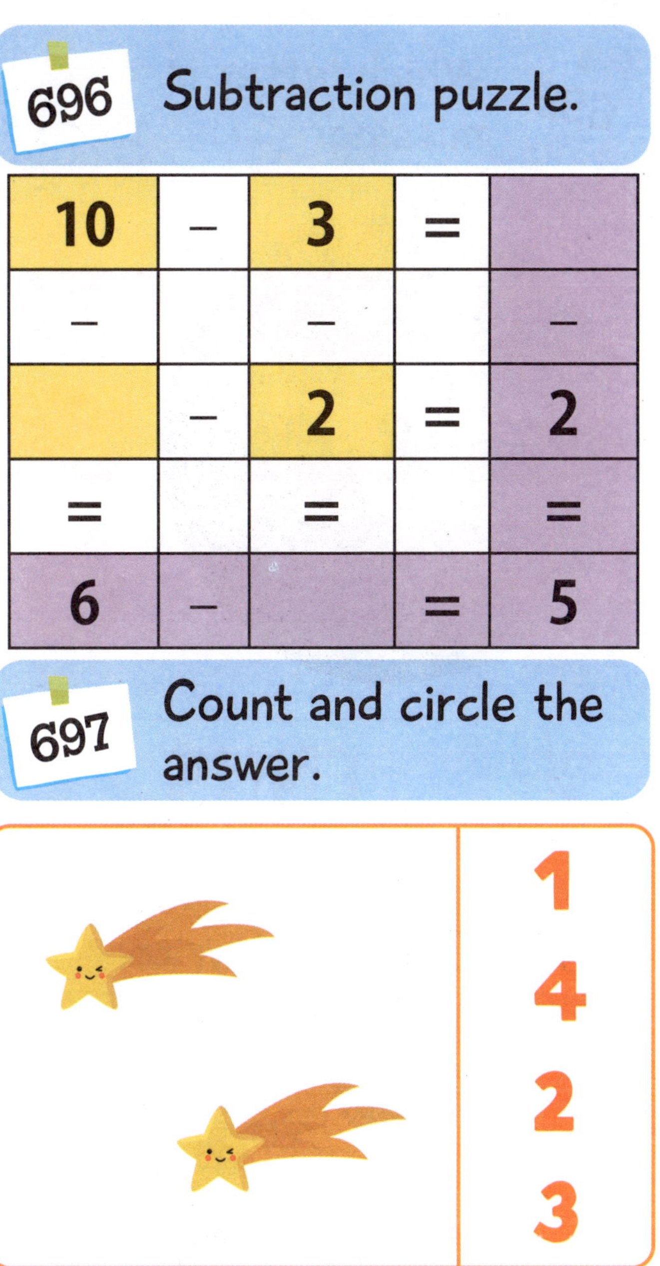

696 Subtraction puzzle.

10	–	3	=	
–		–		–
	–	2	=	2
=		=		=
6	–		=	5

697 Count and circle the answer.

1

4

2

3

698 Write the correct initial.

___ylophone

S C X

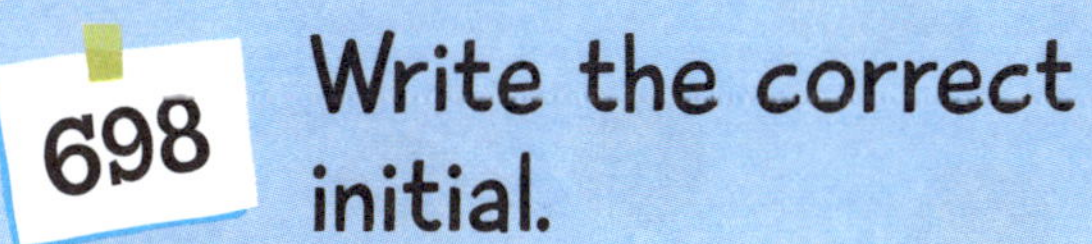

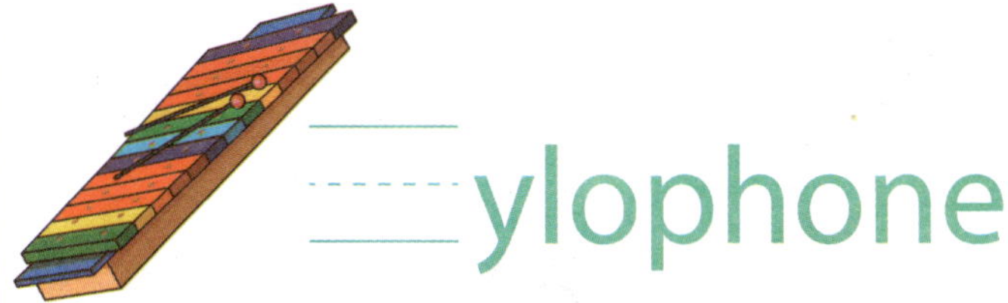

699 Which letter is missing?

_ENUS

700 Count and write.

701 Match the objects and paint cans by shape and colour.

702 Colour the scarf.

703 Find 6 differences.

704 Which number shows the exact shadow?

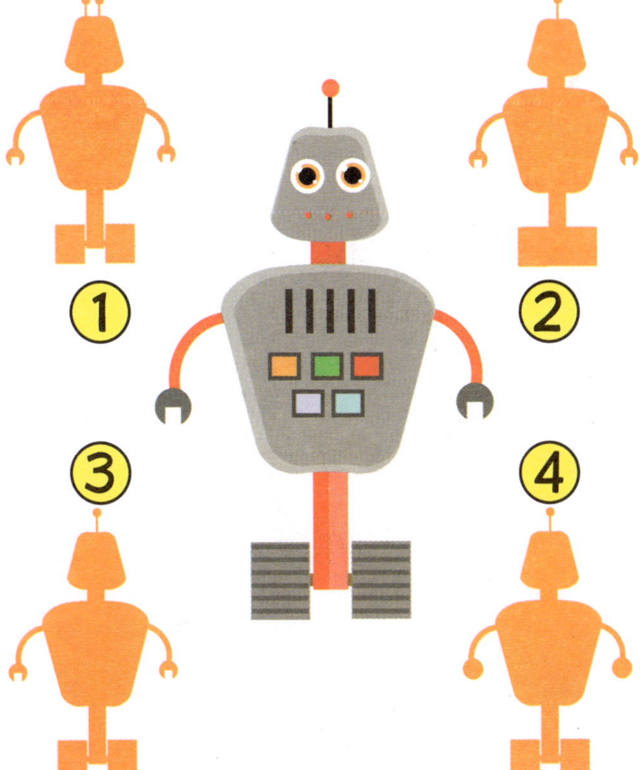

705 Count and circle the sum.

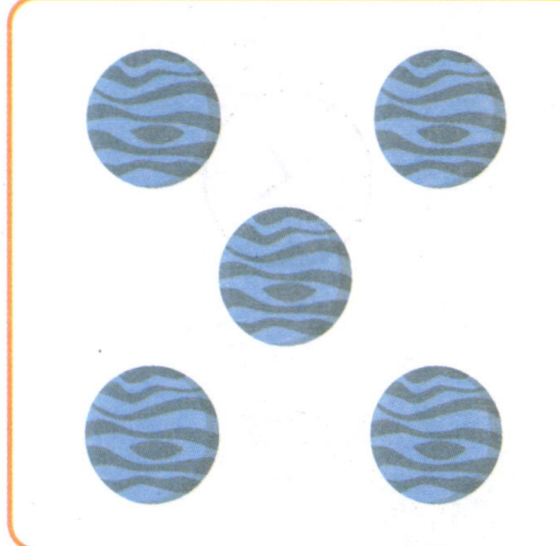

6
3
4
5

706 Trace the lines.

707 Count and circle the answer.

708 What time is it?

709 <, > or = ?

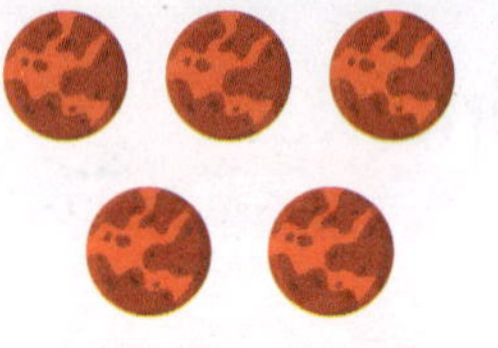

710 Draw and colour.

711 Colour the tin-man happy!

712 Find the matching shadow.

713 Count and write.

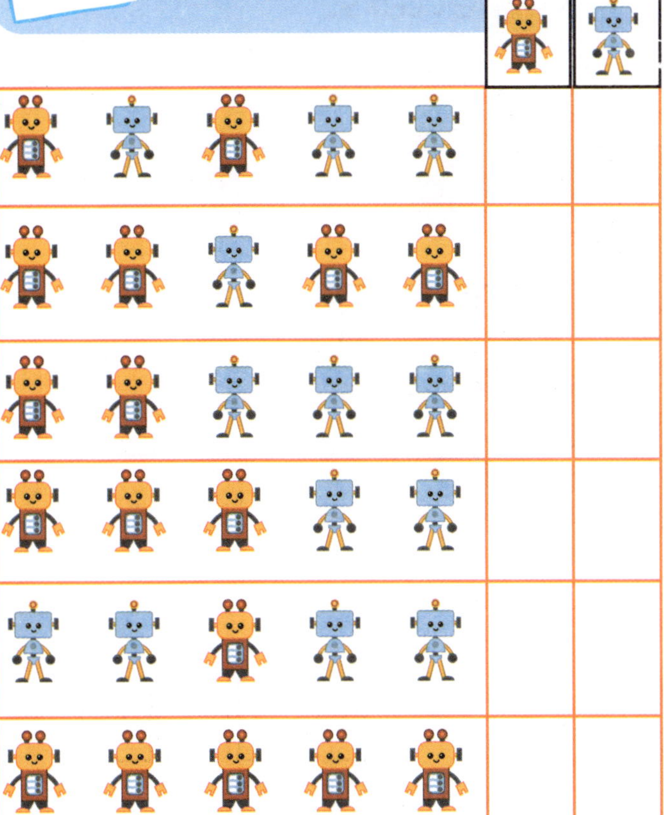

714 Connect the dots and colour.

715 Find 7 differences.

716 Count and circle the answer.

717 Which letter is missing?

__ATURN

718 Help each mama bird reach her nest.

719 Write the missing letters.

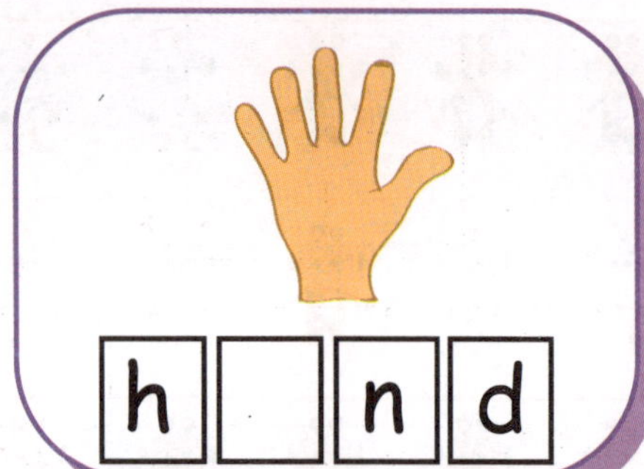

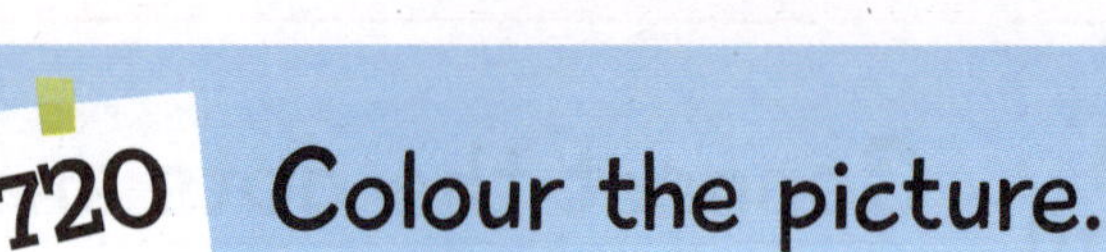

720 Colour the picture.

721 Decode and write.

722 Count and circle the sum.

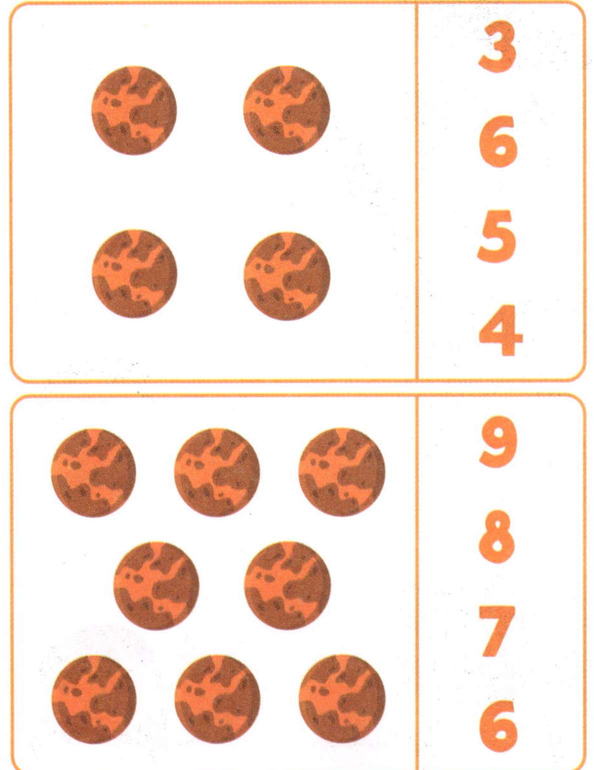

723 Find the duplicate.

724 Find the matching shadow.

725 Trace the lines.

726 Write the missing letter.

727 Count and circle the sum.

5
4
3
6

728 Find the odd one out.

729 Solve and match the solutions.

730 Solve the space sudoku.

A 
B 
C 
D 

731 Number the socks from shortest to longest.

732 Colour the picture.

733 Trace the lines.

734 Match the key with the lock.

736 Solve and match the uniforms.

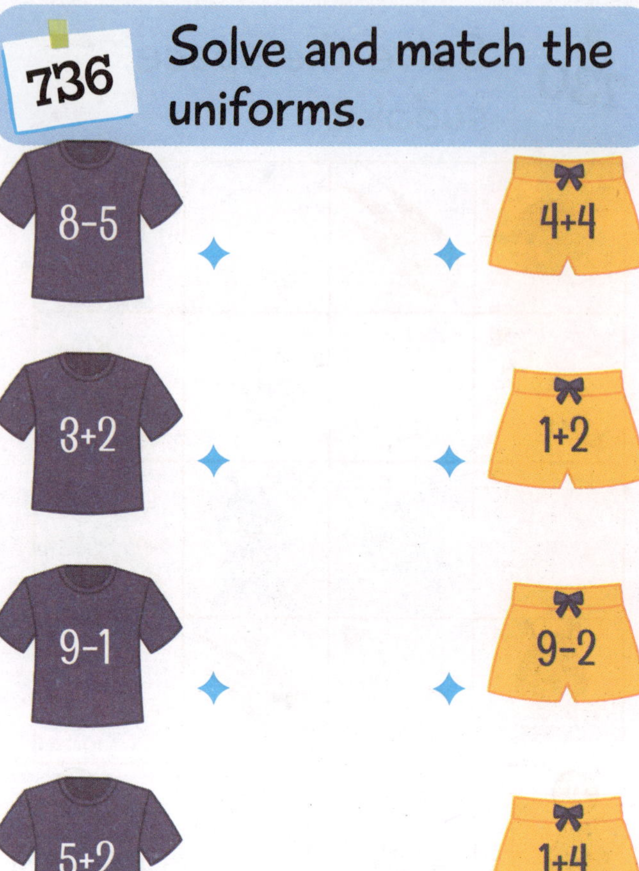

735 Which two pieces can be used to make the diamond?

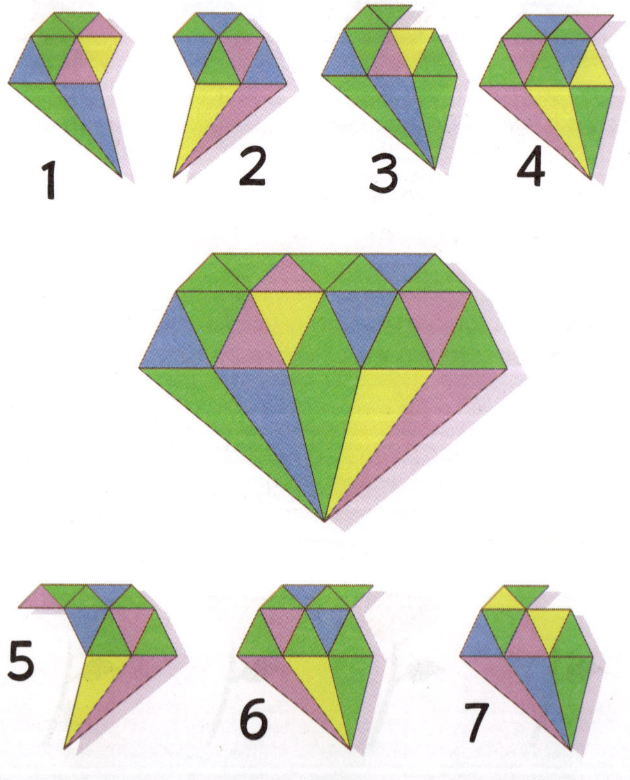

1 2 3 4

5 6 7

737 Colour the builder with the ladder.

738 Colour the picture.

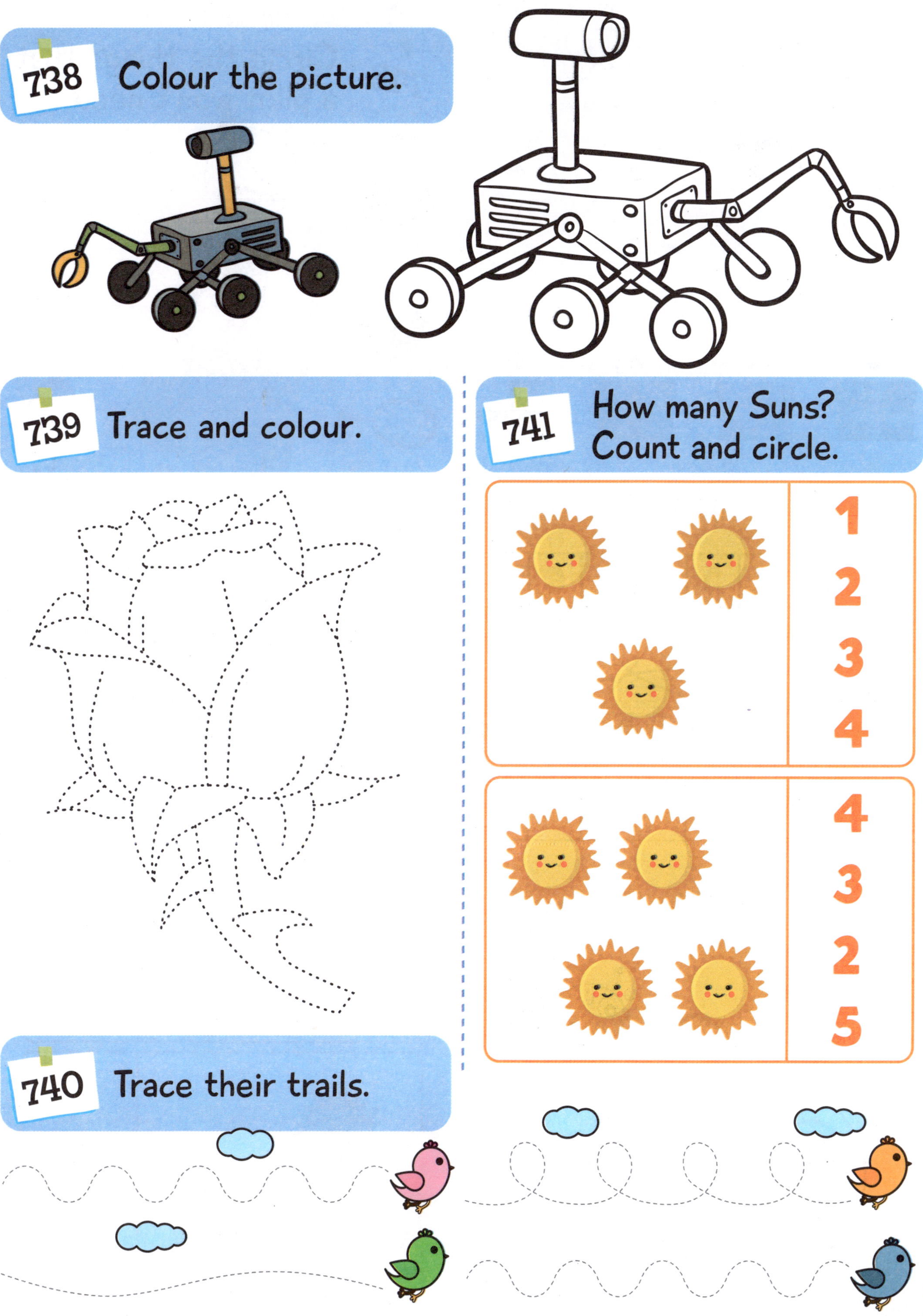

739 Trace and colour.

741 How many Suns? Count and circle.

1 2 3 4

4 3 2 5

740 Trace their trails.

742 Match the box with the bow.

743 Solve the word puzzle.

744 Colour the picture.

745 Circle the things that a pilot won't need.

746 Count and circle the sum.

747 Match objects and paint cans by shape and colour.

749 Guide the cow back to the farm.

748 Match the cut-out shapes with the objects.

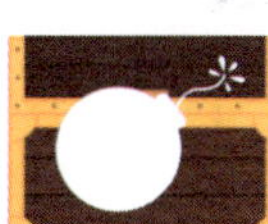

750 Count according to how they are shaped.

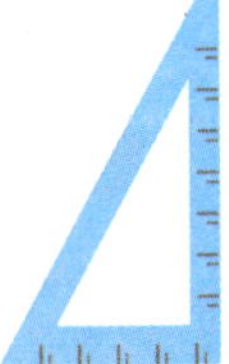

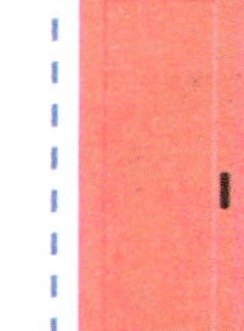

 ____

 ____

 ____

751 What is under the lid?

752 Help the farmer find his way to the barn.

753 Trace and colour.

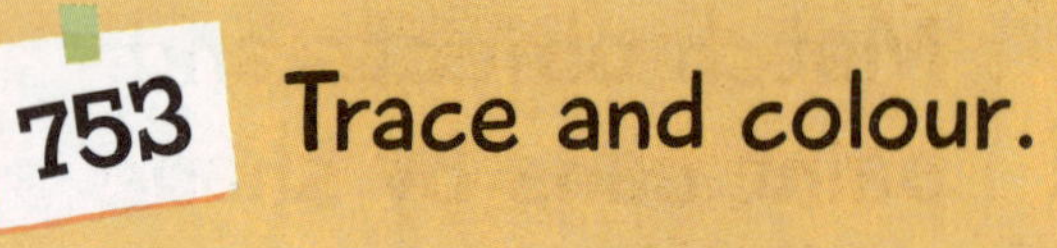

754 How many each?

755 Match capital and small letters.

R ◆	◆ x
V ◆	◆ w
S ◆	◆ z
X ◆	◆ s
Z ◆	◆ r
W ◆	◆ v

756 Trace a–z and finish.

757 Find 13 differences.

758 Spot and circle the birds.

759 Trace and colour.

760 Join the parts to make a word and match with the picture.

761 Circle all the small letters.

	H	I	A	M	P	D
n	D	R	A	L	a	h
S	J	c	R	Z	o	A
t	A	B	a	V	W	a
Y	b	a	u	h	A	K
R	a	w	A	N	m	E

762 Which way leads to the fort?

763 Count and circle the sum.

3
5
2
4

1
2
3
4

764 Match objects and paint cans by shape and colour.

765 Match the locks with the correct houses.

766 Which shapes make the given picture? Tick them.

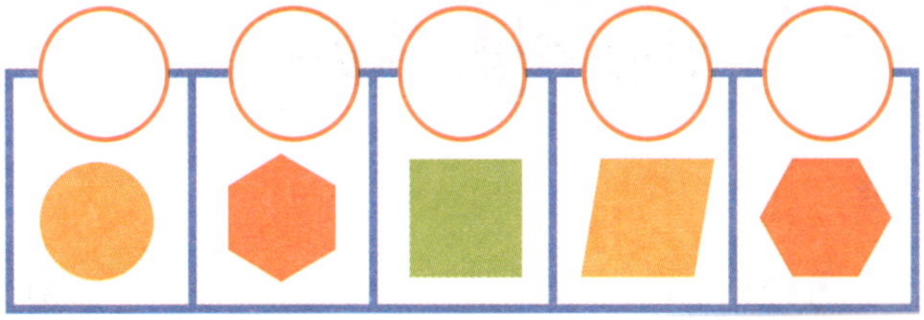

767 Number the objects from shortest to longest.

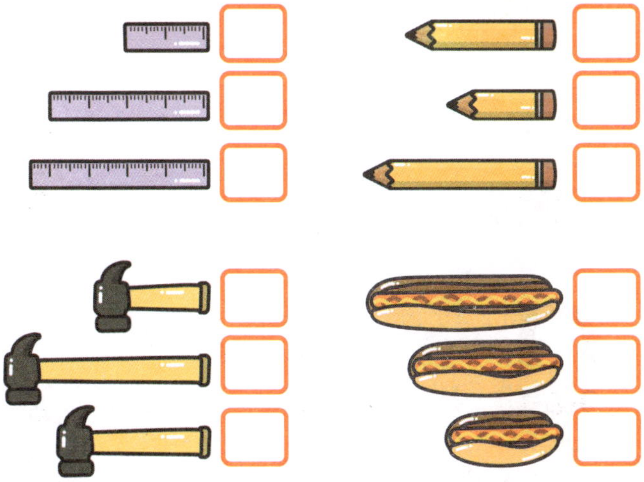

768 Join the numbers and colour the butterfly.

769 Solve and match with the right key.

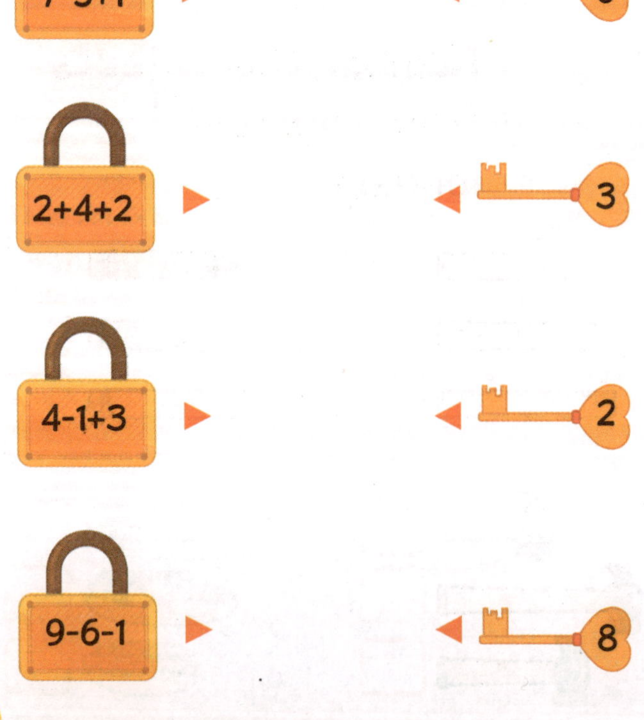

770 Help Miss Bunny get the carrots before Mr Fox reaches.

771 Count and circle the correct number.

772 Colour the cute dinosaur using the colour code.

1 2

3 4

5

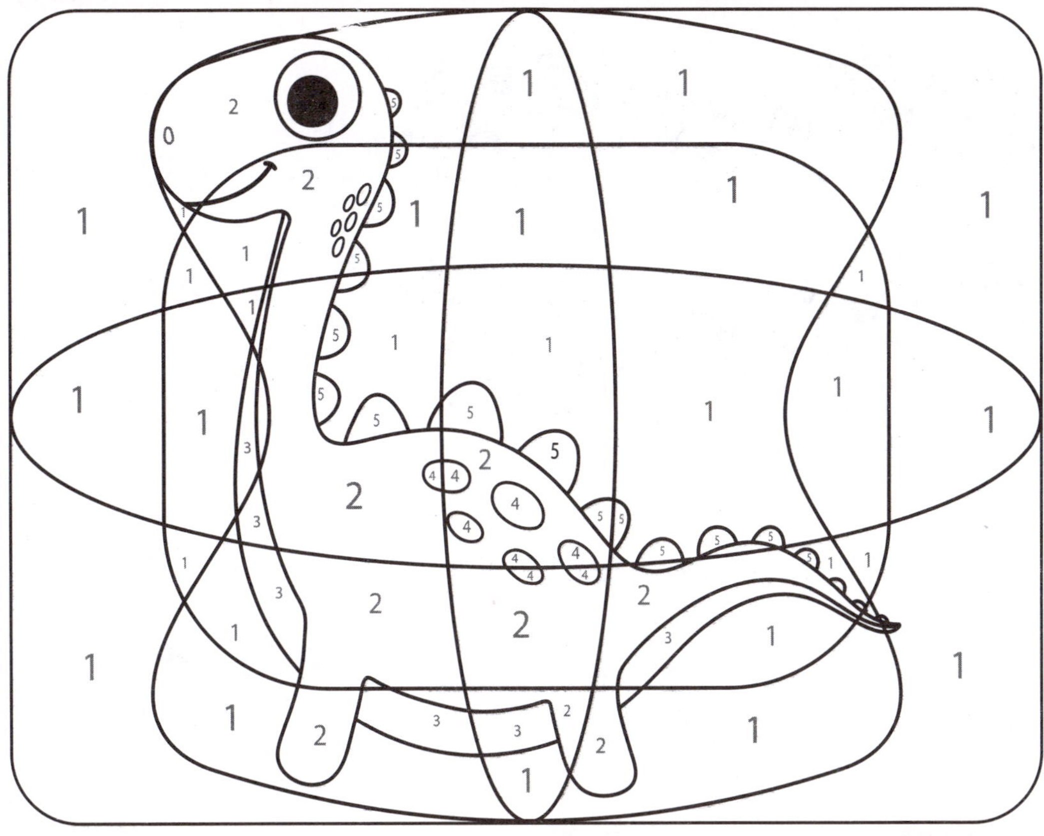

773 Solve the puzzle and match the answer.

+ + = 12

+ + = 13

+ + = 16

=

5 6 7 8

774 Place the trees in order from the tallest to the shortest.

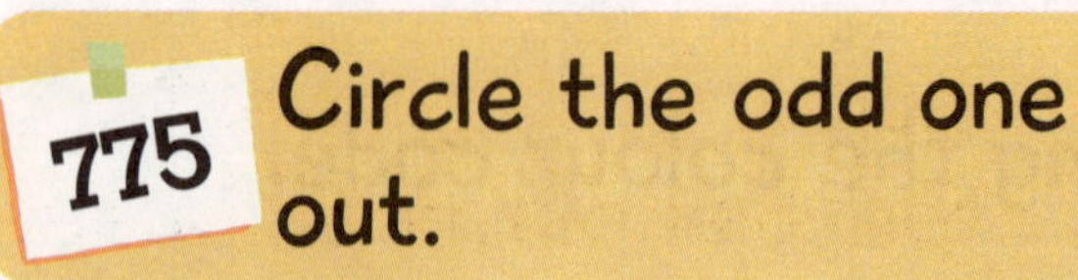

775 Circle the odd one out.

776 Count and add.

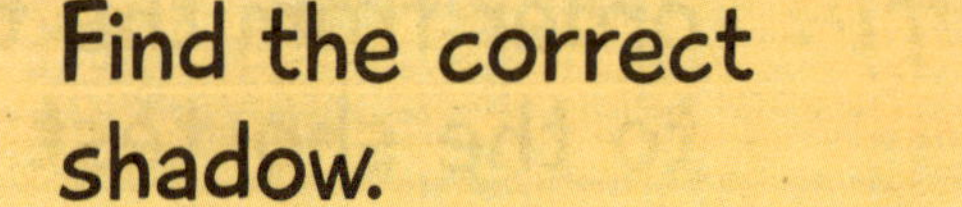

777 Find the correct shadow.

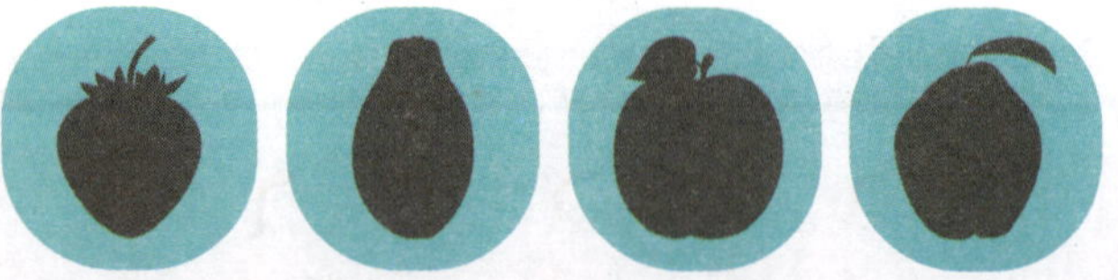

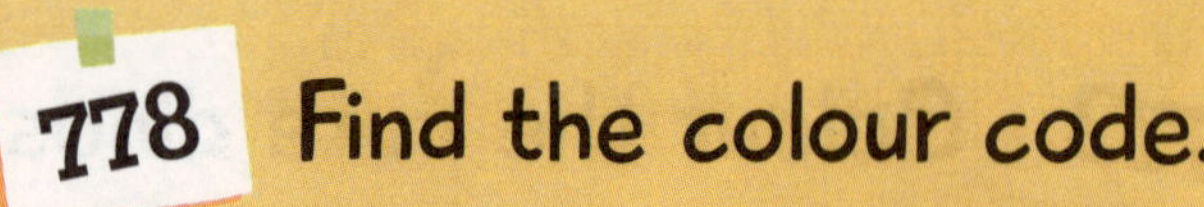

778 Find the colour code.

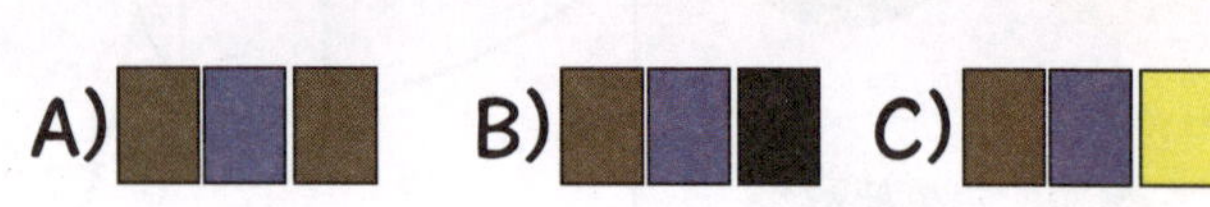

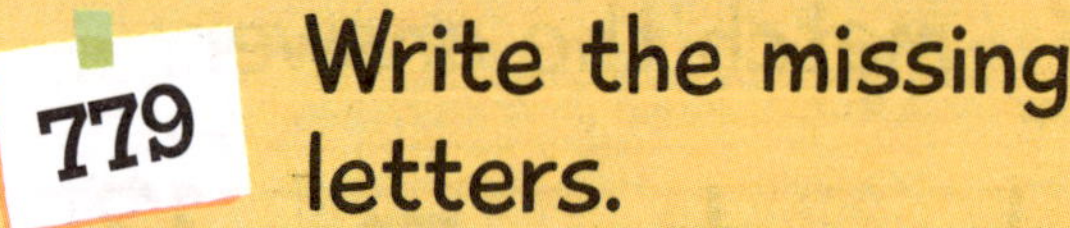

779 Write the missing letters.

780 Colour the picture.

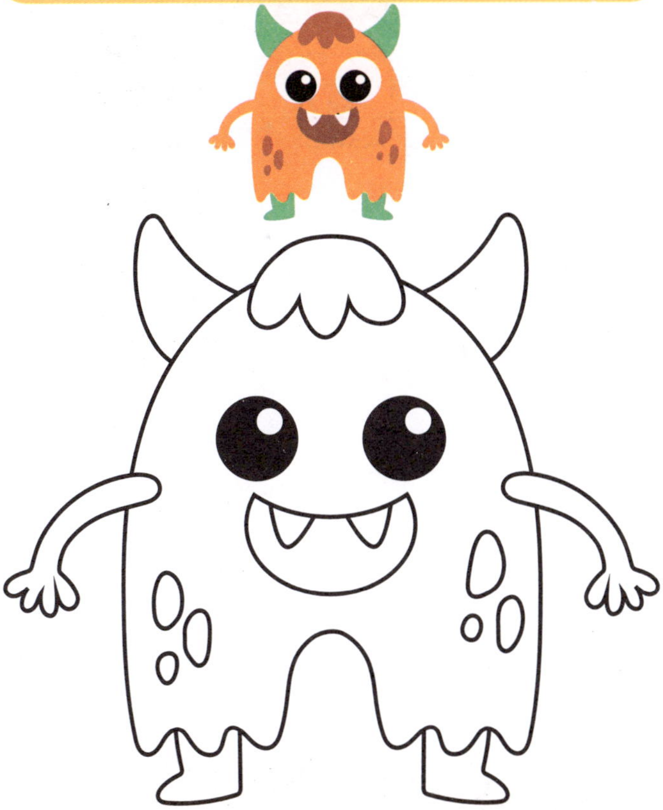

781 Match by count.

2 •

3 •

1 •

5 •

4 •

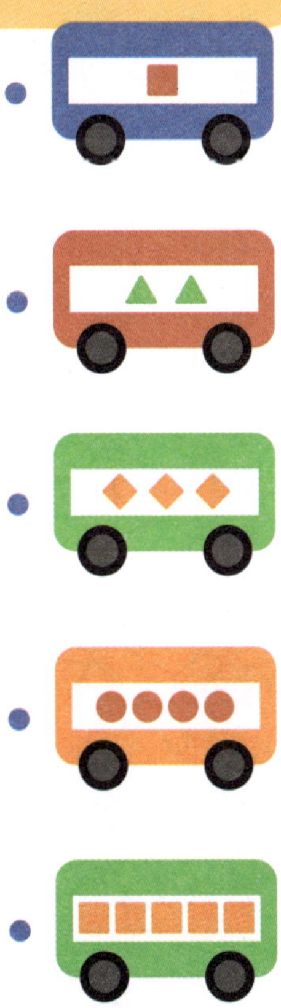

782 Tick the things that a football player will use.

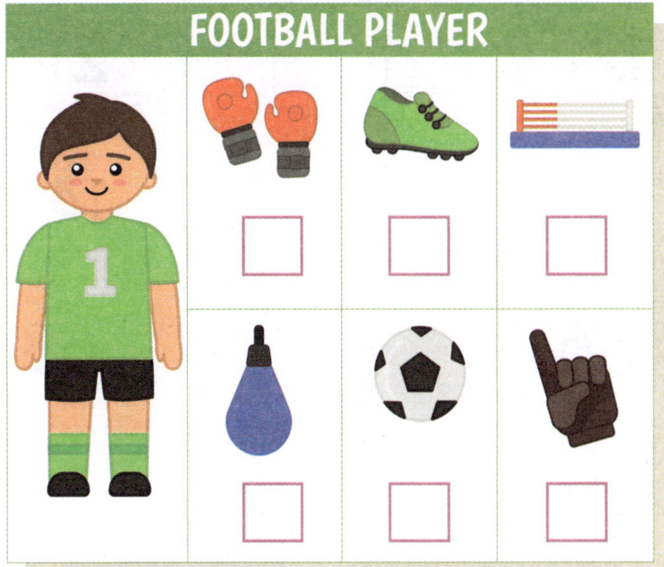

783 Fill in the missing numbers.

	11	12	13		15
23		25	26		28
	33	34		36	37

784 Count the astronauts and circle the answer.

2

3

5

4

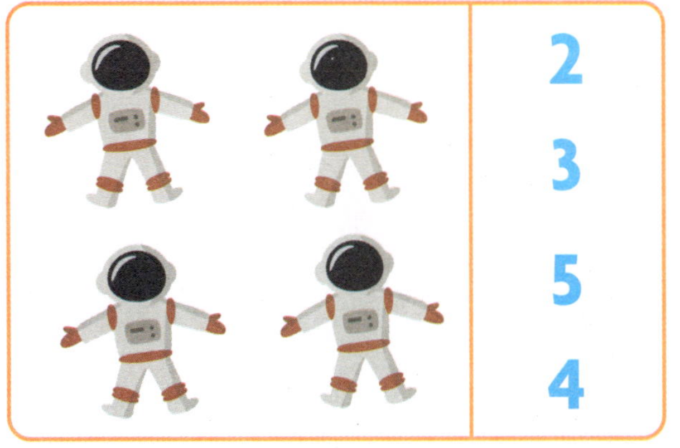

785 <, > or = ?

12	☐	21
14	☐	14
86	☐	68
39	☐	36
76	☐	69

786 Solve and match.

8+2-5	3+4
2+4+1	6-4
7-1-3	9-4
5+4-7	8-5

787 Trace the shapes.

788 Colour the strange alien!

789 Match the time on the clocks.

790 Unscramble to find the shape. Then, colour it.

791 Solve the maze.

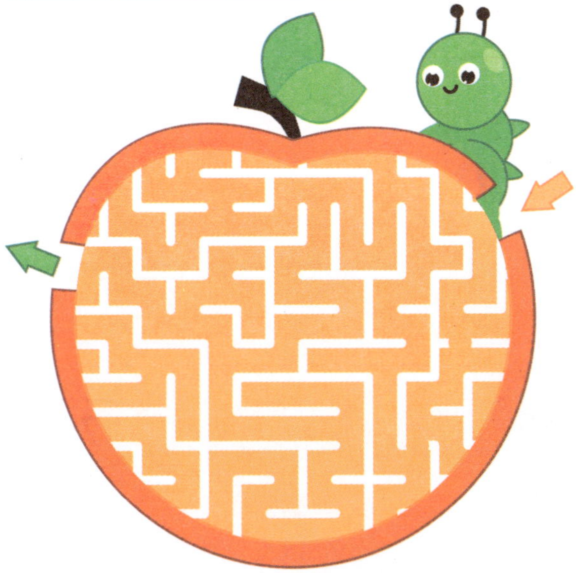

792 Which letter shows the exact shadow?

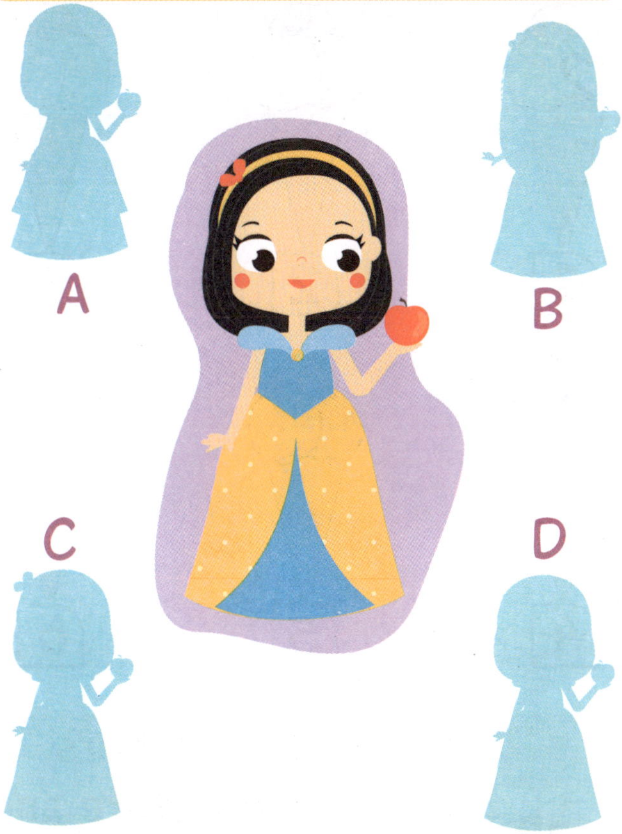

A

B

C

D

793 Finish the other half.

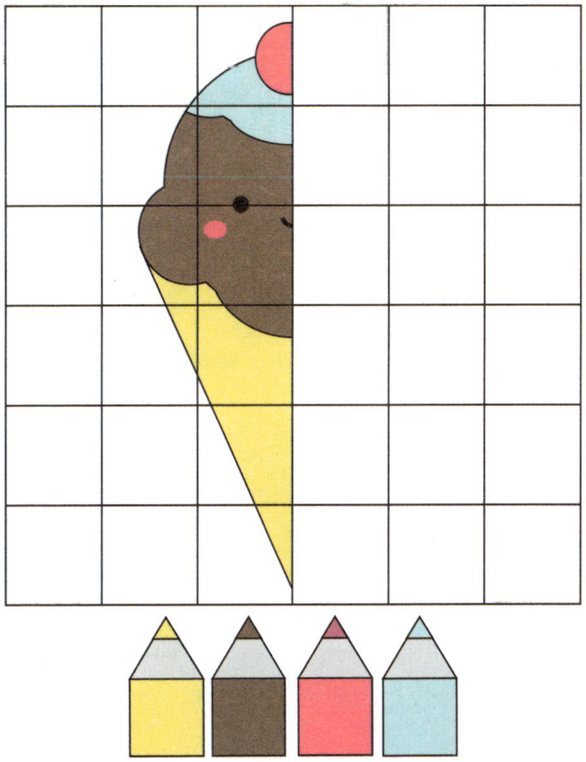

794 Which two are the same?

1 2 3

4 5 6

795 Write the numbers that come before and after. One has been done for you.

0 5 10

20

80

65

40

15

796 How many monsters are left?

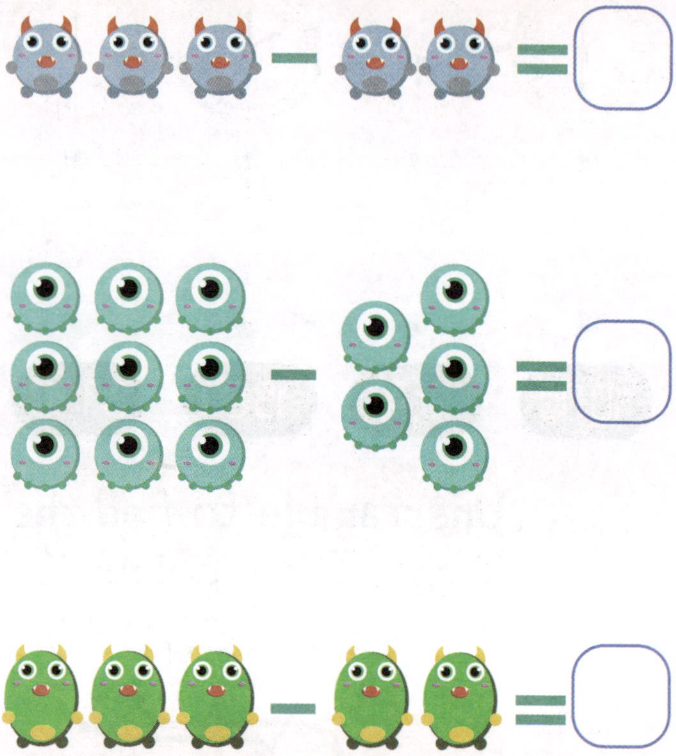

797 Match by the time shown.

3:00

2:00

7:00

798 Solve and find the colour code.

257 

591 

289 

281  

A) 

B) 

C) 

799 Find the mirrored copy for every picture.

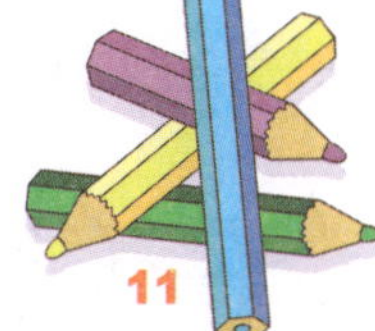

800 Which piece cannot be found in the given picture?

801 Circle what is not needed by a postman.

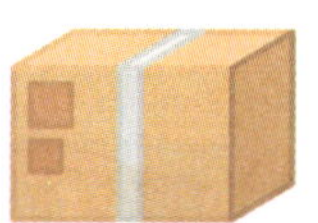

802 Colour by numbers.

1	1	1	1	1	1	1	1	1	1	1	1	1	1	1	1	1	1	1
1	1	1	1	1	1	1	1	4	3	1	1	1	1	1	1	1	1	1
1	1	1	1	1	3	1	1	4	3	1	1	1	1	1	1	1	1	1
1	1	1	1	1	4	3	2	4	3	2	2	2	3	3	1	1	1	1
1	1	1	1	2	2	3	3	4	3	2	2	3	4	2	1	1	1	1
1	1	1	2	2	2	2	3	4	4	3	4	3	2	2	2	1	1	1
1	1	1	2	2	2	2	4	3	3	3	3	4	2	2	2	1	1	1
1	1	2	2	2	2	4	3	4	2	2	4	3	3	2	2	2	1	1
1	1	2	2	2	2	3	2	2	2	2	2	2	4	3	2	2	1	1
1	1	2	2	2	2	2	2	2	2	2	2	2	2	2	2	2	1	1
1	1	2	2	2	2	2	2	2	2	2	2	2	2	2	2	2	1	1
1	1	2	2	2	2	2	2	2	2	2	2	2	2	2	2	2	1	1
1	1	2	2	2	2	2	2	2	2	2	2	2	2	2	2	2	1	1
1	1	1	2	2	2	2	2	2	2	2	2	2	2	2	2	1	1	1
1	1	1	2	2	2	2	2	2	2	2	2	2	2	2	2	1	1	1
1	1	1	1	2	2	2	2	2	2	2	2	2	2	2	1	1	1	1
1	1	1	1	1	2	2	2	2	2	2	2	2	2	1	1	1	1	1
1	1	1	1	1	1	1	2	2	2	2	2	1	1	1	1	1	1	1
1	1	1	1	1	1	1	1	1	1	1	1	1	1	1	1	1	1	1
1	1	1	1	1	1	1	1	1	1	1	1	1	1	1	1	1	1	1

1

2

3

4

803 Find the colour code.

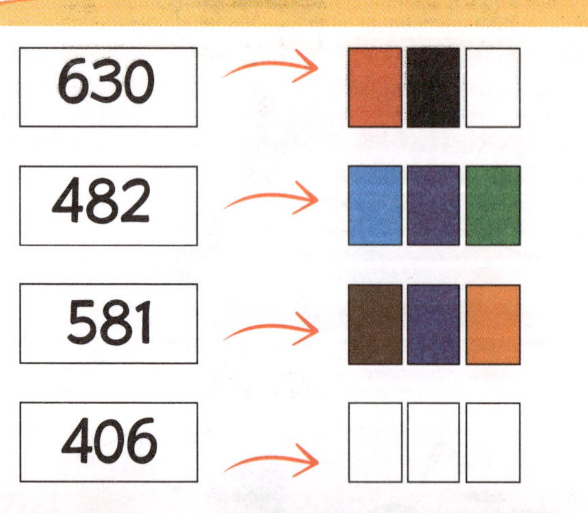

804 Paint by numbers.

805 Solve the puzzle to find my name.

G	S	H	P
M	U	R	D
T	O	O	L
C	M	B	N

806 Which house matches the one in the middle?

1 2 3 4 5 6

807 Write the missing letter.

_AINBOW

T

R

P

808 Find the right glasses for the straws.

809 Find the matching shadow.

810
Find the colour code.
715
603
594
304
A)
B)
C)
811
Colour the picture.
812
Find the exact front as House no. 1.
2
1
4
5
6
3
7
813
Match the opposites.
CLOSED
SLOW
LIGHT
OPEN
CLEAN
DARK
FAST
DIRTY
814
Which two pieces were used to make the picture in the centre?
1
2
3
4
5
6
7
8

815 Which piece cannot be found in the given picture?

817 From 1 to 9, which are not the fragments of the picture given below?

816 Solve the sports sudoku puzzle.

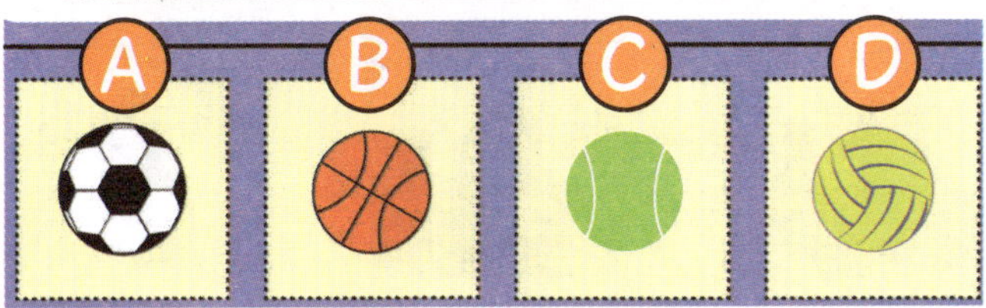

818 Find 10 differences.

819 How many figures can you see here? Count and write.

820 Solve the stationery sudoku.

821 Find the colour code.

A) B) C)

822 Colour the pair.

823 Find the matching shadow.

824 Match the pairs.

825 Turn right at green, drive straight at red and turn left at blue. Where will the red car and the taxi arrive?

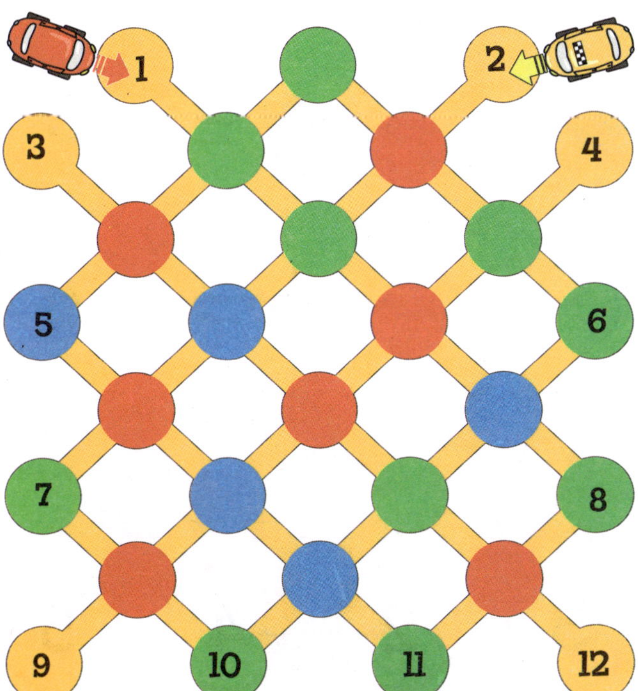

826 Take the colour pencils to the drawing at the centre.

827 Find the matching shape.

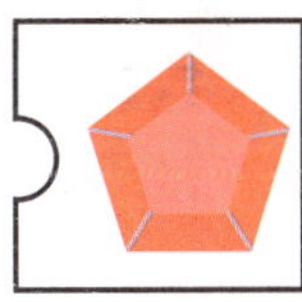
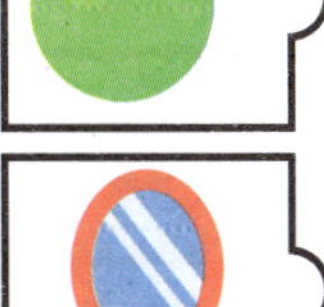

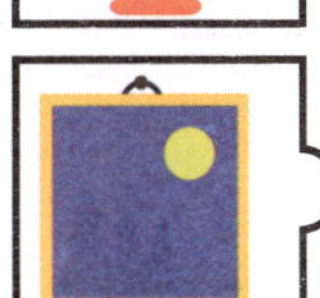

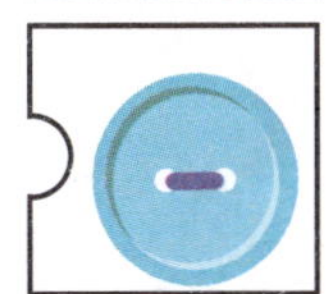

828 Match by their top views.

829 Complete the names.

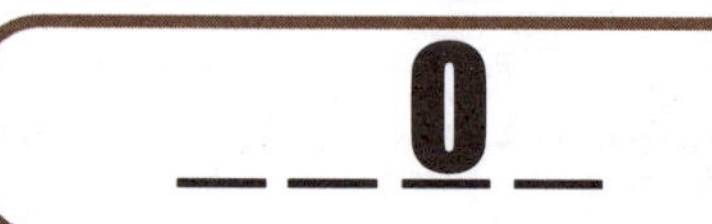

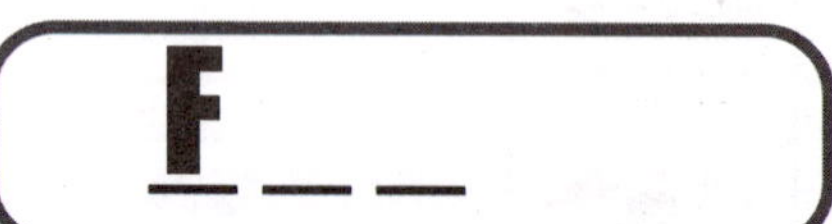

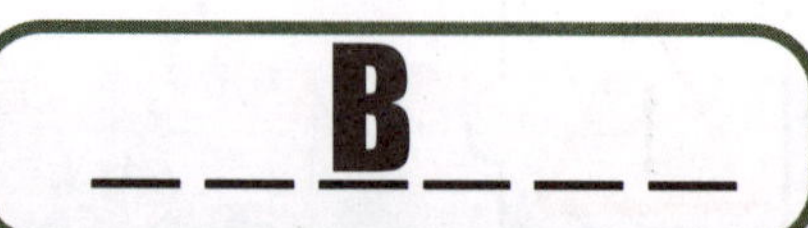

830 Find the mirrored copies.

831 Decode and solve.

☀ + ☀ + ☀ = 9

★ + ☀ + ★ = 5

☾ + ☀ + ★ = 6

☾ = ☐

832 Solve the number sudoku puzzle.

4		2	
1	2	4	3
3	4	1	2
	1	3	

833 Find the matching shadows.

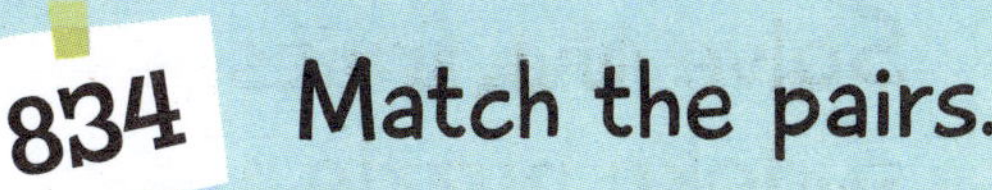

834 Match the pairs.

835 Solve the sudoku puzzle.

836 Solve the fruits sudoku puzzle.

A

B

C

D

837 Decode and complete the series.

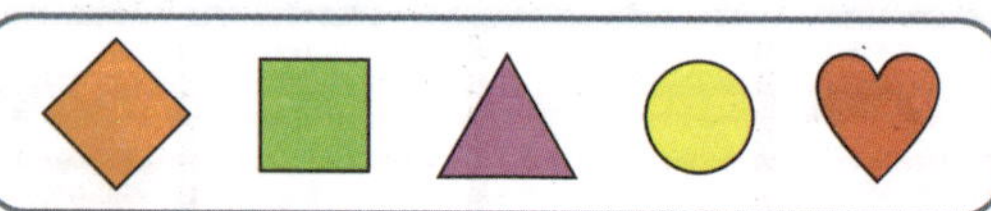

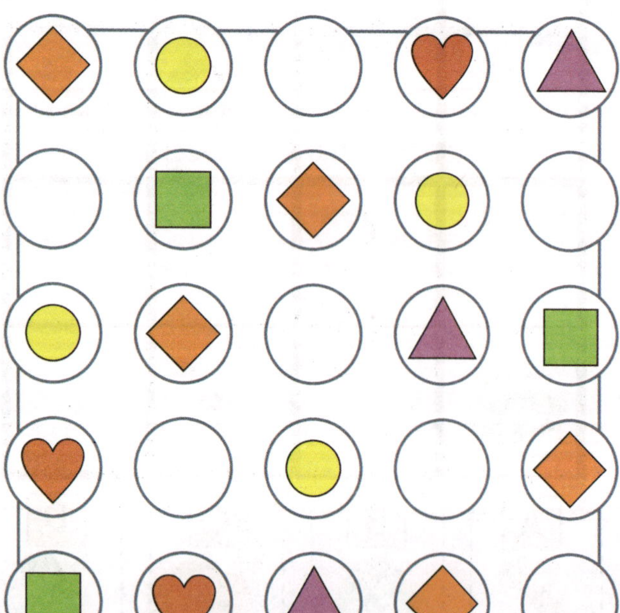

838 Decode and solve.

⚽ + ⚽ + ⚽ = 3

🏐 + 🏐 + ⚽ = 9

🏀 + 🏐 + ⚽ = 10

🏀 = ___

8 4 7 5

839 Find the mirrored copies.

840 Match by contents.

841 How many shapes of each colour?

842 Fill in the missing letter.

_RANUS

843 Write the letters from the biggest to the smallest in size to find the name of the fish. Then, colour the picture.

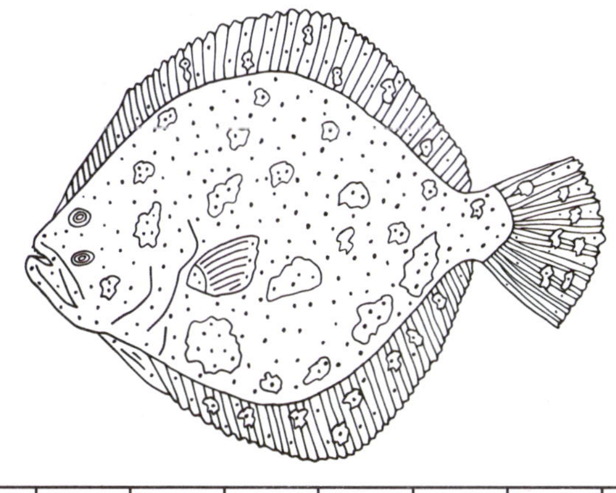

U N D E R O L F

844 Trace and colour the picture.

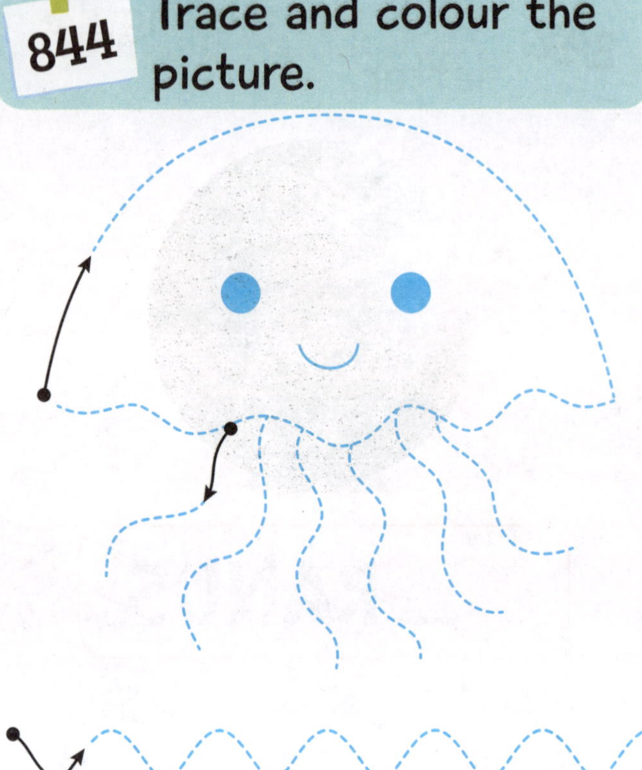

845 Colour the picture.

846 Circle the objects not needed by a doctor.

847 Find the matching shape.

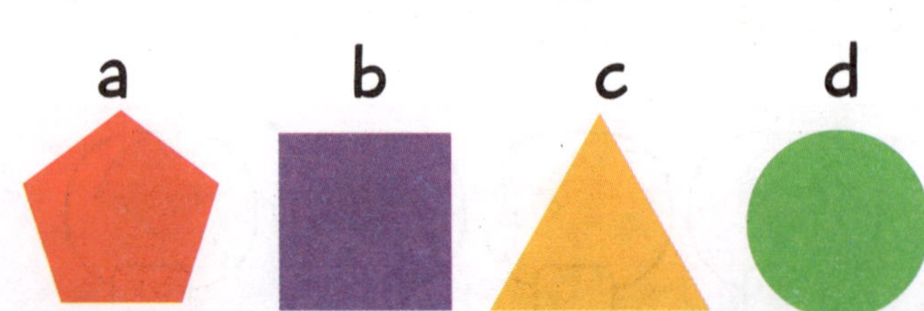

848 Decode and solve.

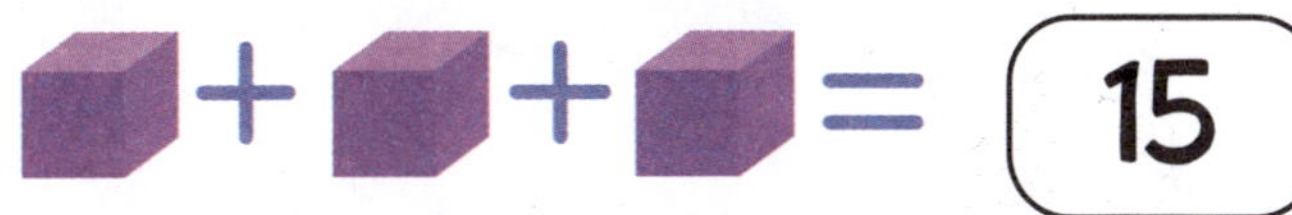

15

9

13

=

6 9 4 7

850 Colour the picture.

849 Count and write.

851 Match the ones that are of the same size.

852 Match the taste with the image.

I taste with my tongue.

Bitter

Sour

Sweet

Salty

853 Match by size.

854 Trace the shapes.

855 How many squares? Write in the box.

856 Colour the picture.

857 Decode and solve.

◇◇◇ + ◇◇◇ + ◇◇◇ = 6

品 + ◇◇◇ + 品 = 8

田 + 品 + ◇◇◇ = 6

田 = ☐

858 What are these pieces of? Match appropriately.

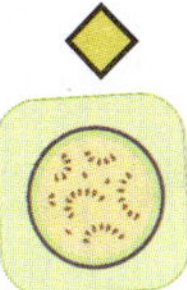

859 Count and write the sum.

860 Identify and count the number of shapes.

862 Colour the picture.

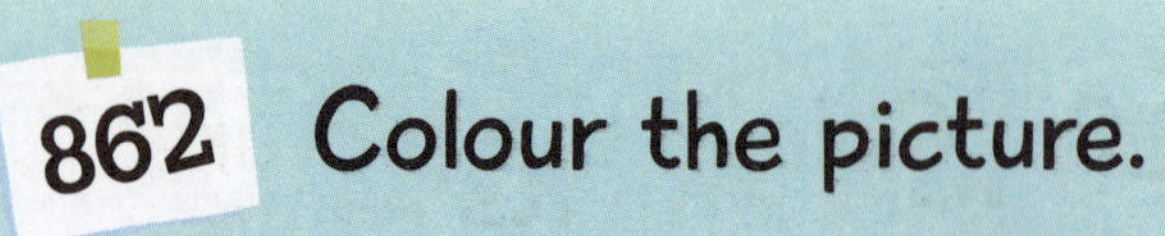

861 Place the chocolates into their moulds.

863 Sort the insects by type.

864 Match the body part with its name.

 • • nose

 • • head

 • • toes

 • • eyes

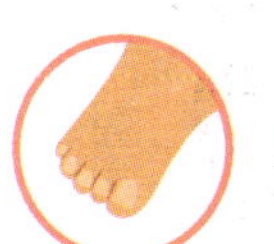 • • hand

865 Match the professionals with the equipment they use.

  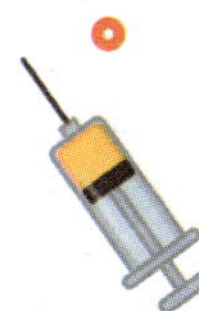 

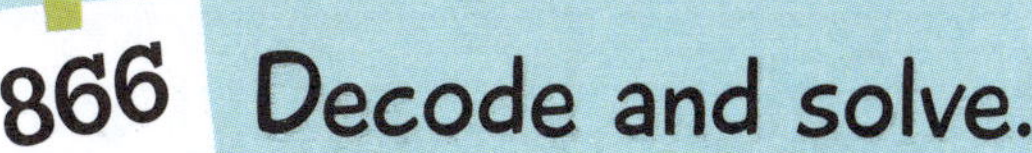

866 Decode and solve.

+ + = 9

+ + = 5

+ + = 8

=

867 Circle the objects not needed by a policeman.

868 Colour the picture.

869 Tick the things that a tennis player will use.

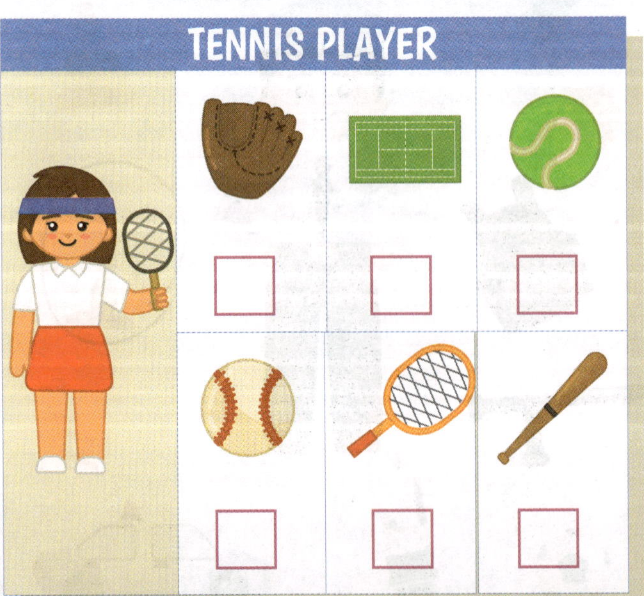

870 Solve the sudoku puzzle.

871 Count and circle the answer.

872 Sort the even and odd objects.

Even	Odd
 4	 9

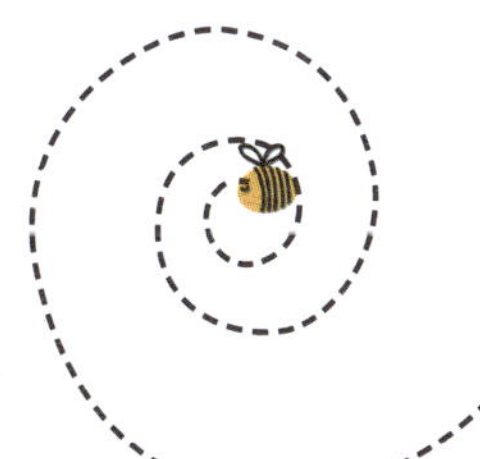

873 Trace the path.

874 Match the fronts to the backs.

875 Subtract and solve the sum.

876 Find the names of these sports in the grid.

X	I	X	Z	B	Z	M	H	G	V
R	F	A	V	S	V	K	M	N	O
J	E	A	R	I	G	Y	E	I	L
G	T	F	H	N	H	B	O	M	L
S	A	P	V	N	N	G	D	M	E
G	R	P	C	E	O	U	T	I	Y
S	A	X	O	T	Z	R	N	W	B
P	K	S	Z	X	E	L	V	S	A
S	O	C	C	E	R	B	F	T	L
V	P	K	F	L	O	G	N	W	L

877 Tick the things that a race car driver will use.

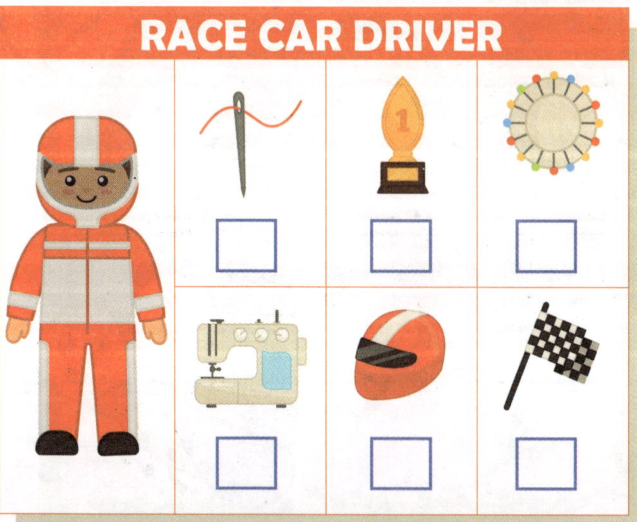

878 Circle the objects not needed by a basketball player.

879 Trace and colour.

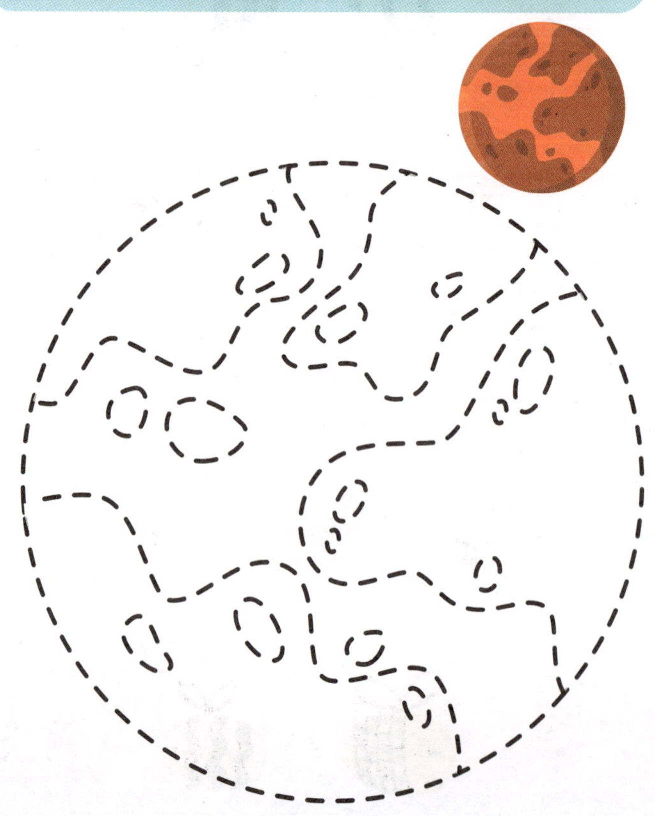

880 Match the pictures to their names.

 • • Eggs

 • • Eye

 • • Earth

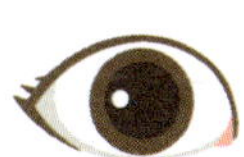 • • Eraser

881 <, > or = ?

882 Find the sum.

 +  = 

 +  =

 +  =

 +  =

=1 =2 =3 =4

883 Colour the picture.

884 Solve and write.

886 Help the ladybird reach the leaf.

885 Tick the things that an archaeologist will use.

887 How many circles?

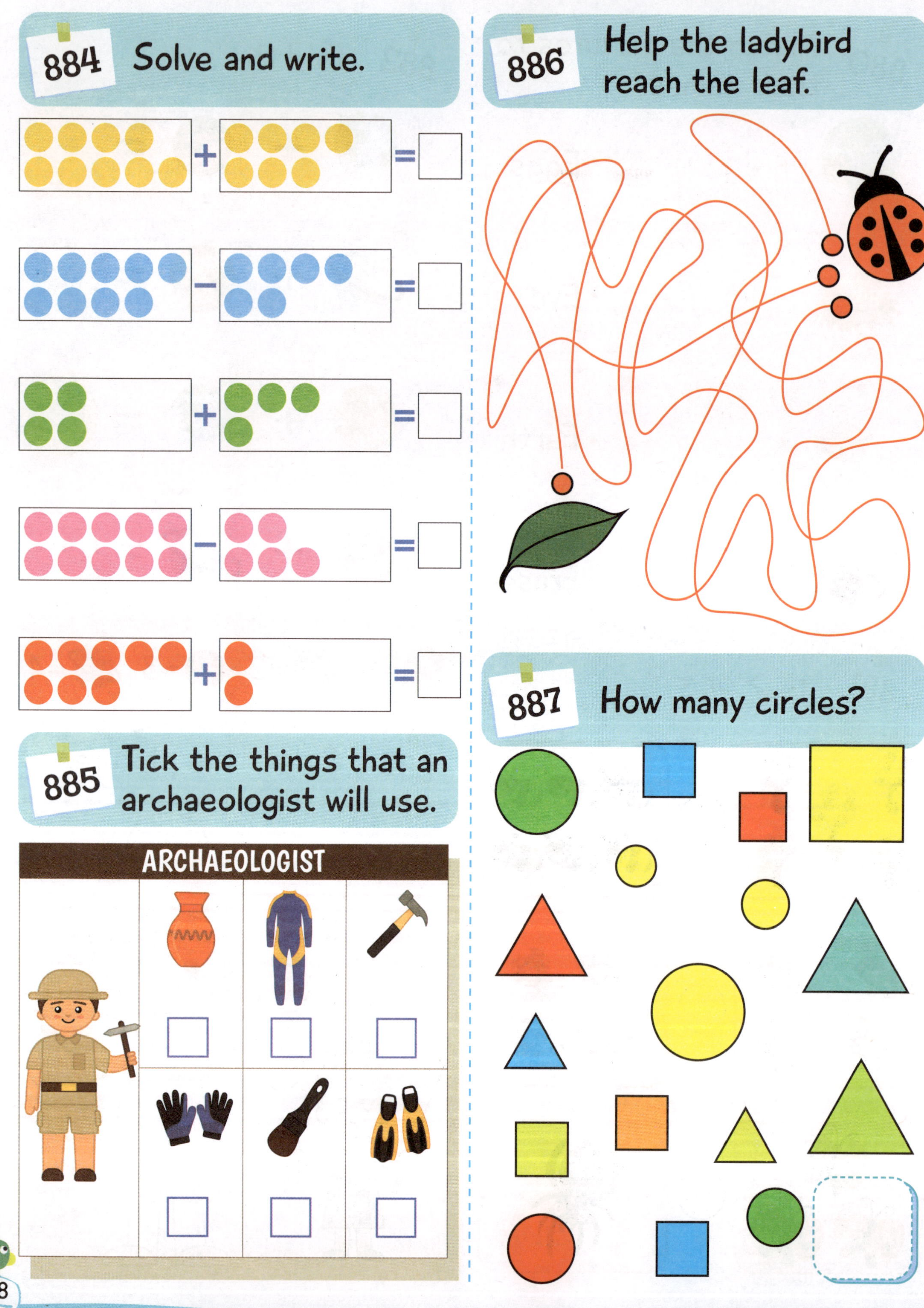

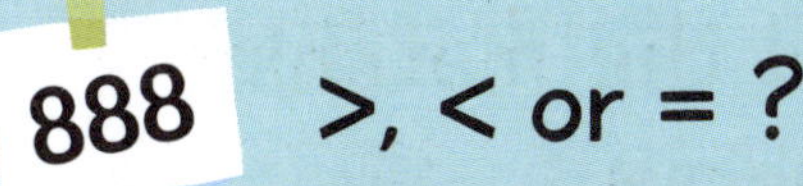

888 >, < or = ?

889 How many look to the left and how many look to the right?

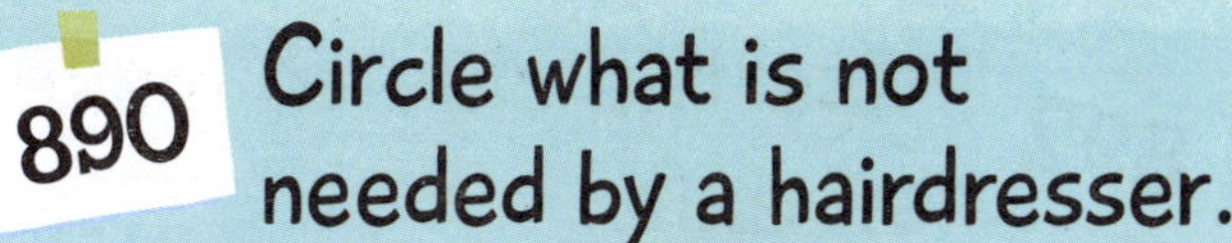

890 Circle what is not needed by a hairdresser.

891 Colour the picture.

892 Use the clue to make an exit.

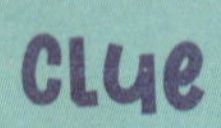

893 Colour the picture.

894 Find the matching shadow.

895 Solve the magic crossword.

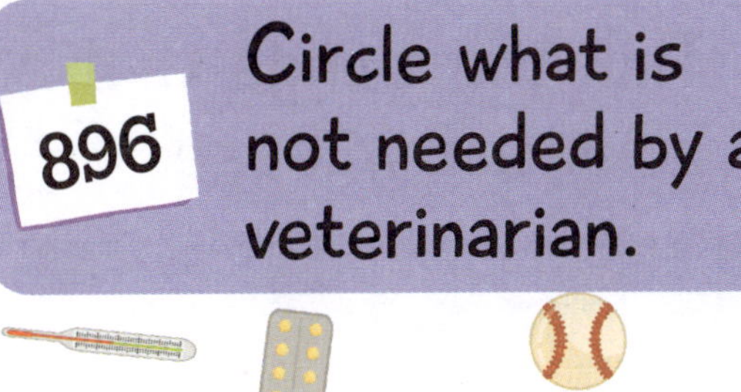

896 Circle what is not needed by a veterinarian.

897 Find the missing letter.

898 Colour by numbers.

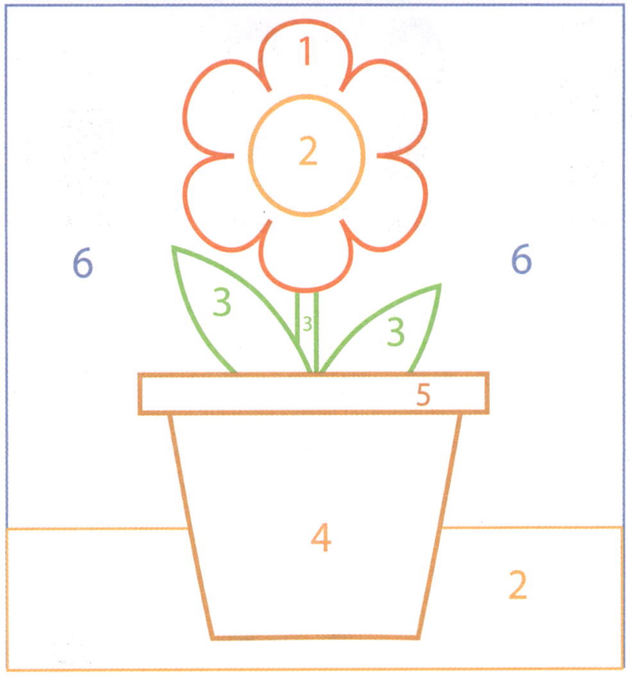

1 2 3 4 5 6

899 Which part cannot be found in the given picture?

Match them to the equipment they use.

How many each?

Tick the things that a scientist will use.

903

Colour by numbers.

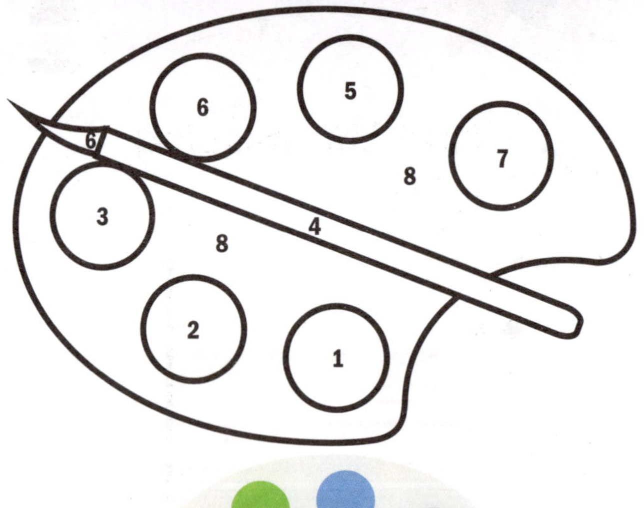

904 Help the astronaut get back to Earth.

905 Which planet is each rocket headed to?

906 Circle what is not needed by a fisherman.

907 Which one is his vehicle?

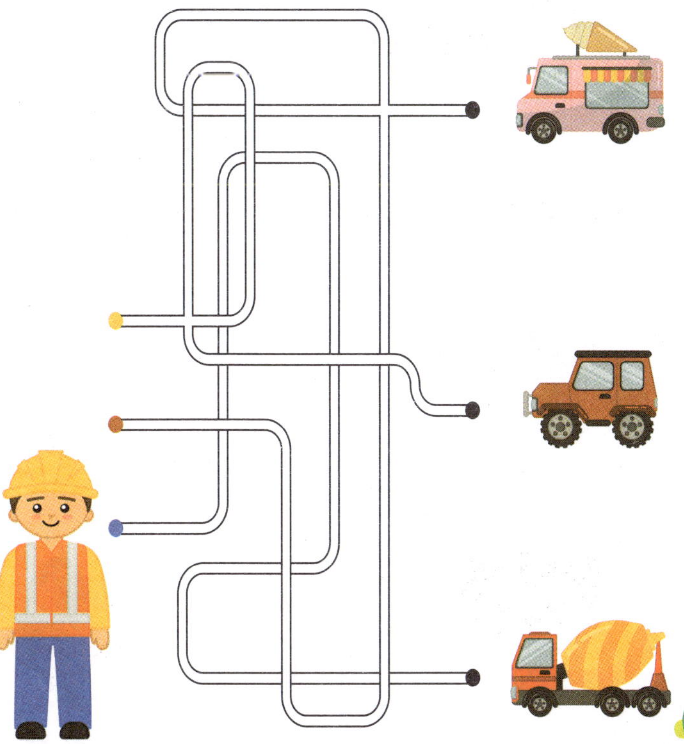

908 Identify the body parts and solve the crossword.

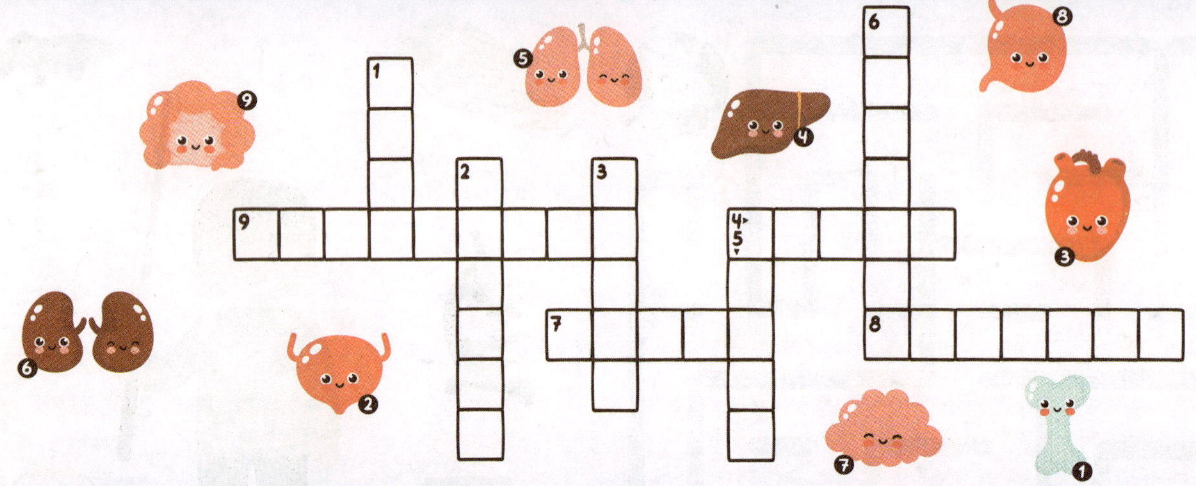

909 Count and write.

910 What sounds do they make?

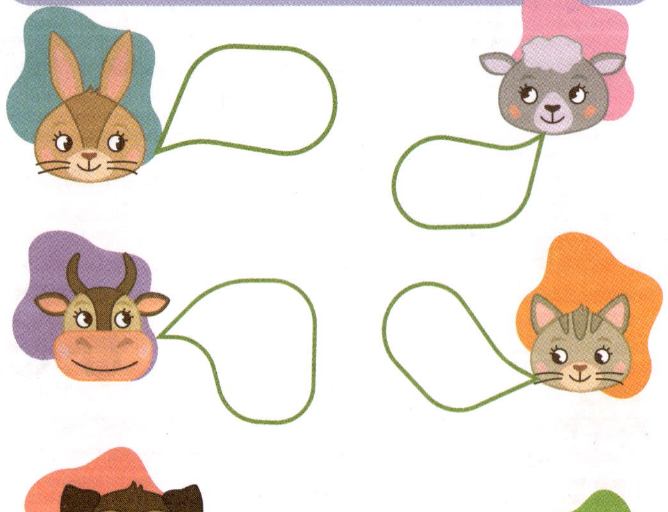

911 Circle what is not needed by a judge.

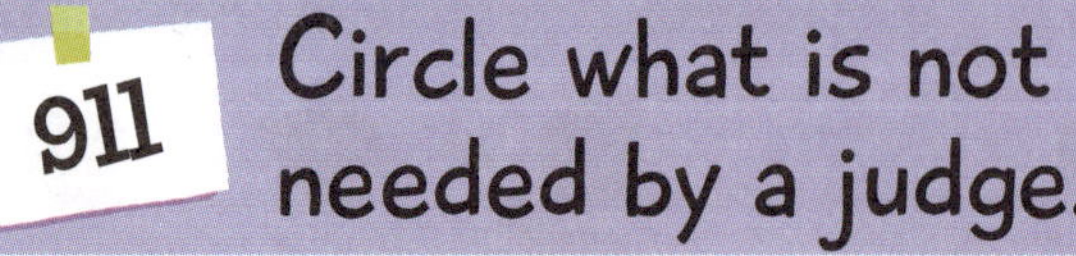

912 Find the correct shadow.

913 Match the objects to their users.

914 Colour the picture.

915 Write + or – to complete the equations.

4 ☐ 1 = 5

5 ☐ 4 = 1

6 ☐ 3 = 3

7 ☐ 2 = 9

10 ☐ 3 = 7

3 ☐ 6 = 9

916 Tick the things that a taxi driver will use.

918 Match the yarns with the patterns.

917 Match them to the things they use.

919 How many lions?

920 Help the kitten find its favorite food.

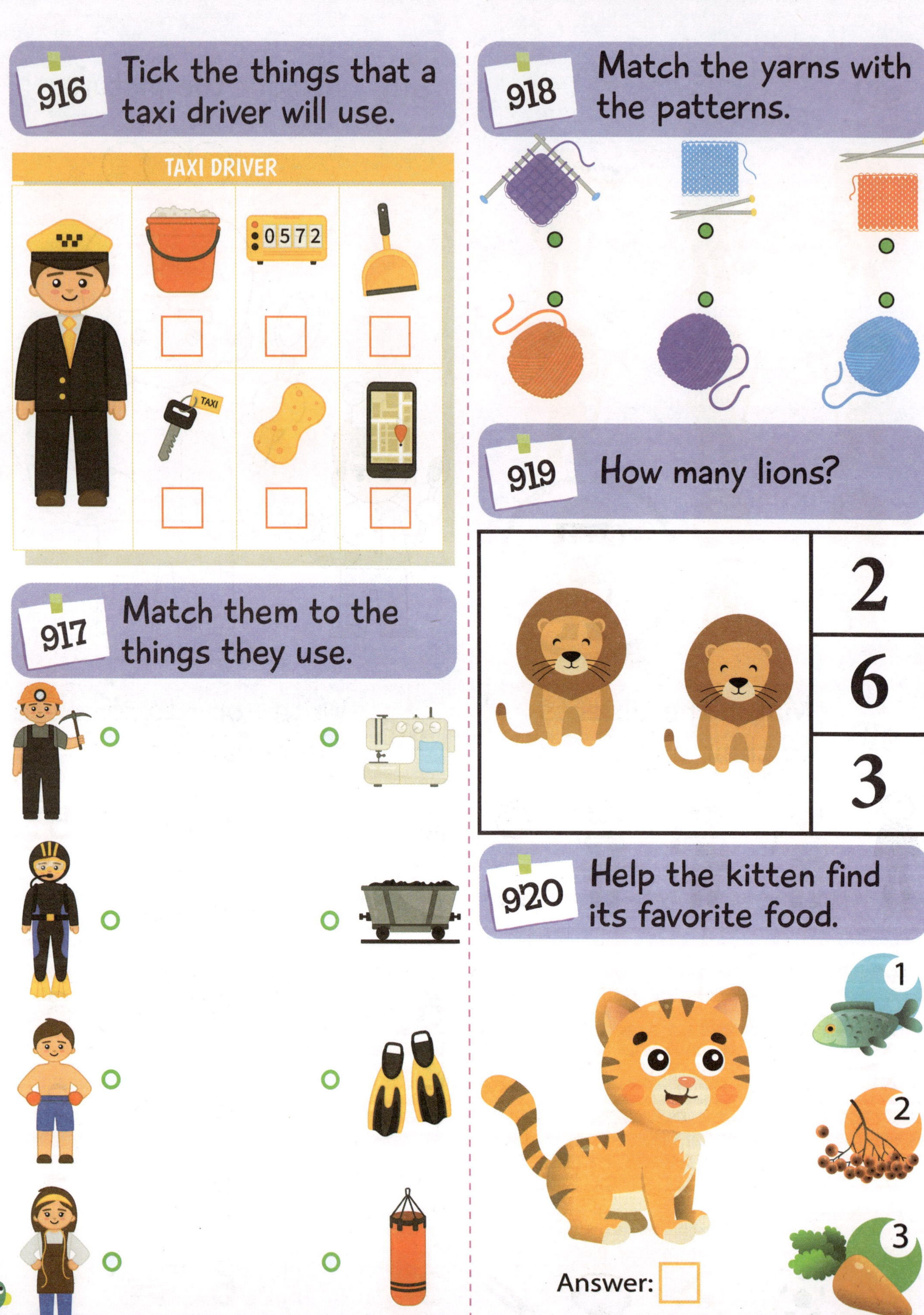

921 Find 10 differences.

922 Count and write.

923 Colour the picture.

924 Take the nurse to the patient.

925 Circle what is not needed by a ballerina.

927 Colour the creature.

926 Help the baker reach the cake.

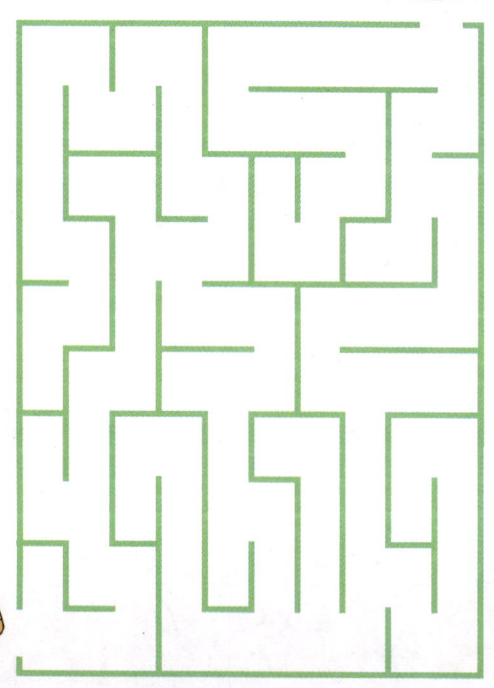

928 Match by their occupations.

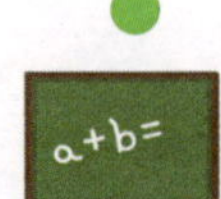

929 Help the driver get to his taxi.

930 Tick the things a pilot will use.

931 Count the different shapes.

932 Help the rocket return to Earth.

		2	3	4	5	9
		1	2	3	7	1
2	1	1	8	1	2	6
4	2	3	10	3	6	9
3	4	4	7	5	10	10
4	10	5	8	9		
10	4	6	7	10		

933 Circle the things not needed by the player.

934 Count and circle the answer.

935 Help the little goat to find his mum.

936 Solve the crossword puzzle.

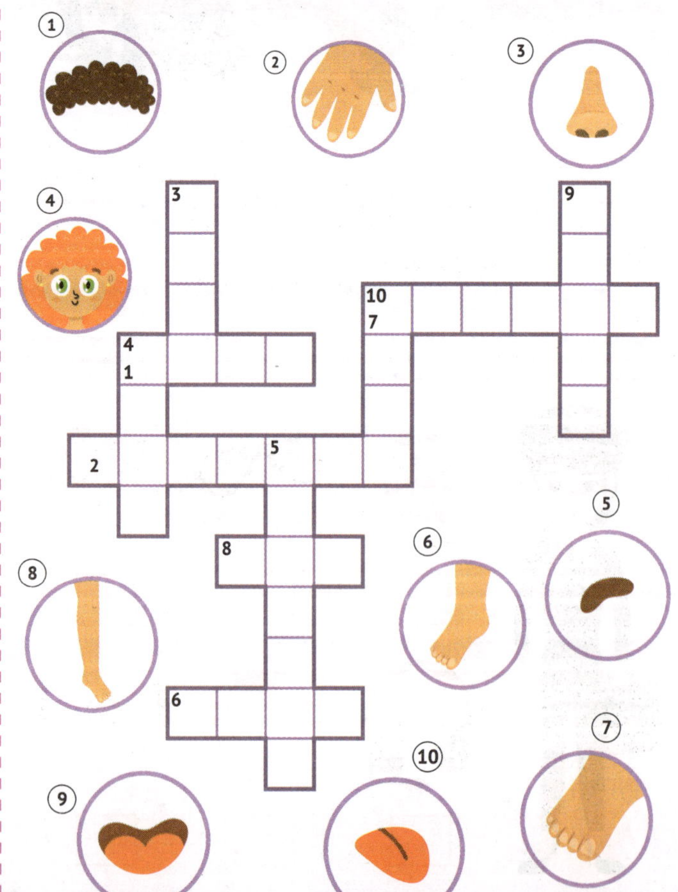

937 Trace and colour the picture.

939 Find the correct shadow.

938 Count and match.

940 How many each?

941 Can you find at least 10 professions in this maze?

Q F I R E M A N T U O A D U D
Y U H E O R A N G E L P L Y O
G F H P O S T M A N Z P E T C
A W P O I P S F R K Z A B M T
R O E R E Q R U C D H I C N O
D E N T I S T K H Z V N B X R
E A Q E Z V M P I L O T Y Z G
N A X R M K R C T M W E Y N P
E H L C F A R M E R U R W U I
R S Z A Q W S X C D E R F R B
Q W R S E C R E T A R Y L S P
A W Z C A V N P T O Q N S E D

942 Circle what is not needed by a mother.

943 Find the matching shadows.

944 Help the mason find his way to the top.

945 Find 5 differences.

946 Tick the things that a veterinarian will use.

947 Count and write.

948 Match the tools to their right shadows.

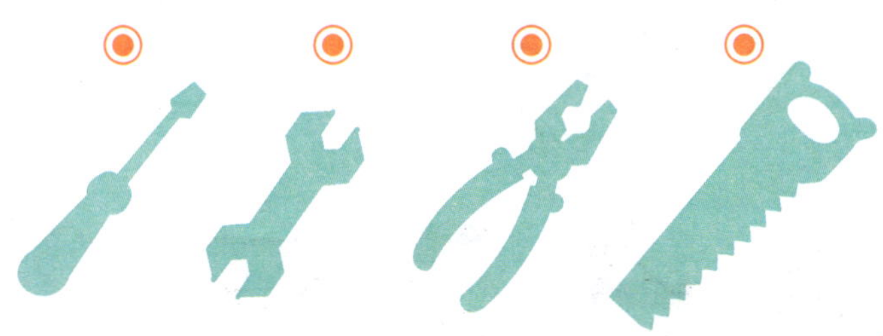

949 Find the matching shadow.

950 What is each professional looking for?

951 Trace and colour the picture.

952 Count and write.

953 How many triangles are there?

954 Match the image with its shadow.

955 Colour by numbers.

956 Count and write.

957 Find the matching shadows.

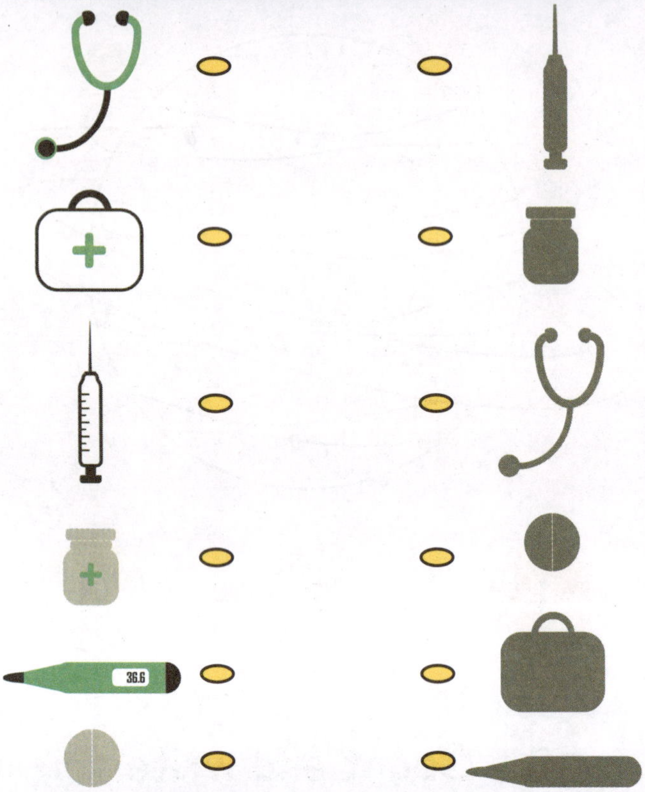

36.6

959 Colour the picture.

958 Trace the dashed lines.

960 Match the caps to the uniforms.

961 Help the loader to the truck.

962 Tick the things that a hairdresser will use.

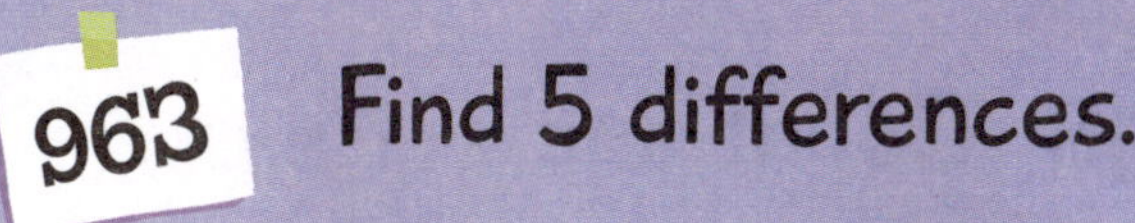

963 Find 5 differences.

964 Join the dots and colour the picture.

965 Complete the word.

966 Count and write.

967 By which way can the veterinarian reach the pet?

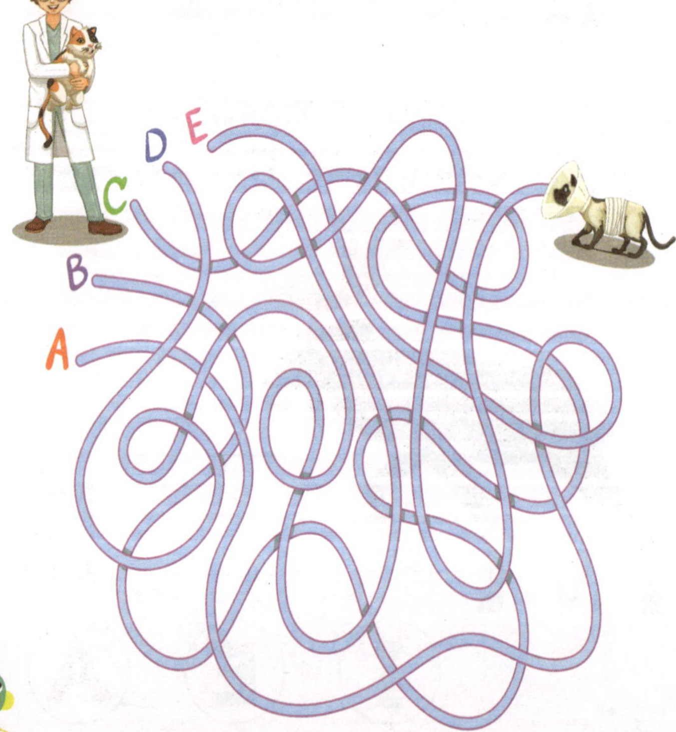

968 Find the colour code.

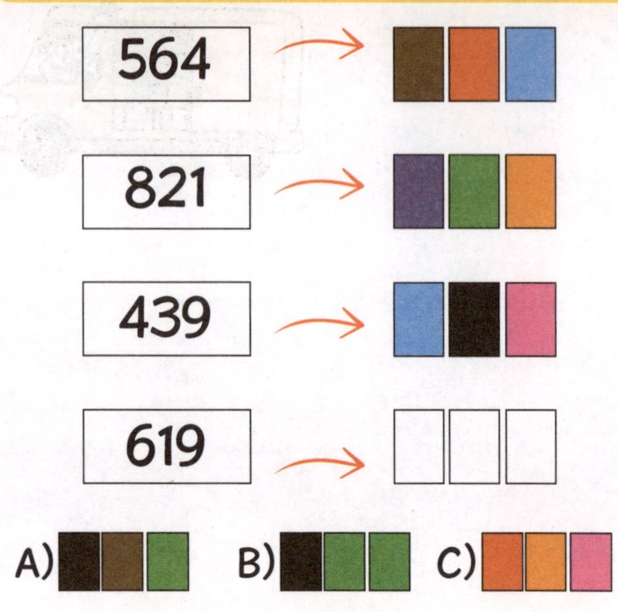

969 Colour the picture.

970 Identify the organ and write its name in the box.

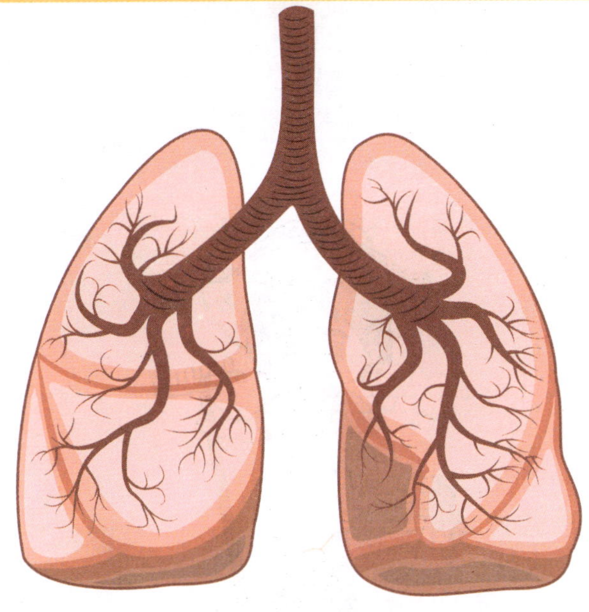

971 Find the correct shadow.

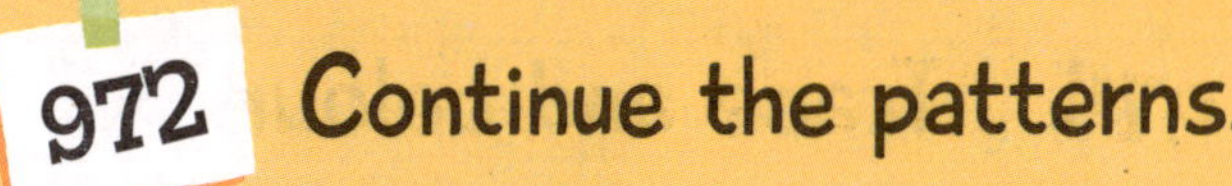

972 Continue the patterns.

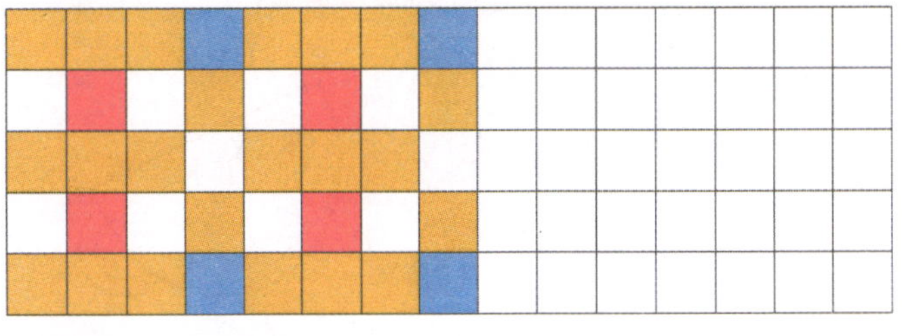

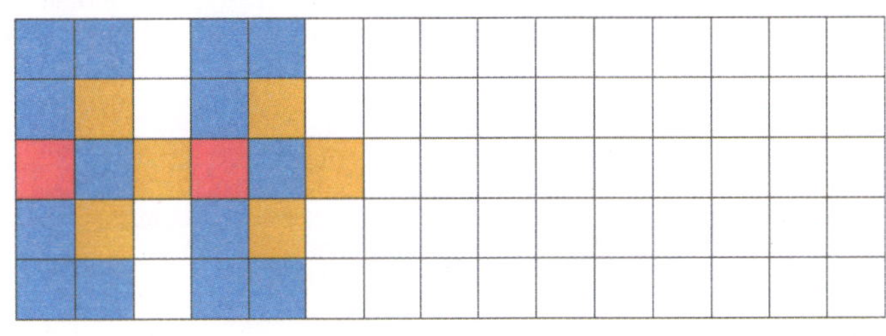

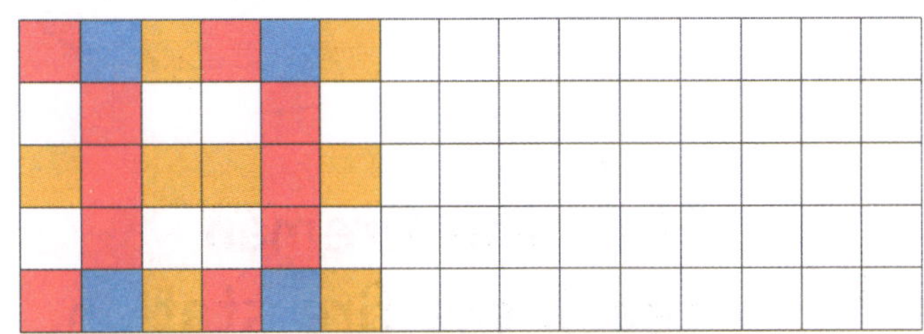

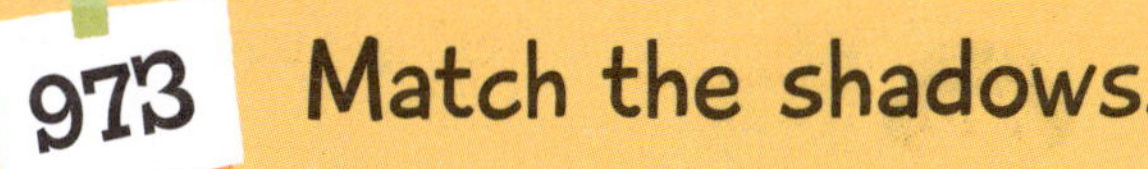

973 Match the shadows.

974 Trace and colour.

975 Help the fireman reach the fire station.

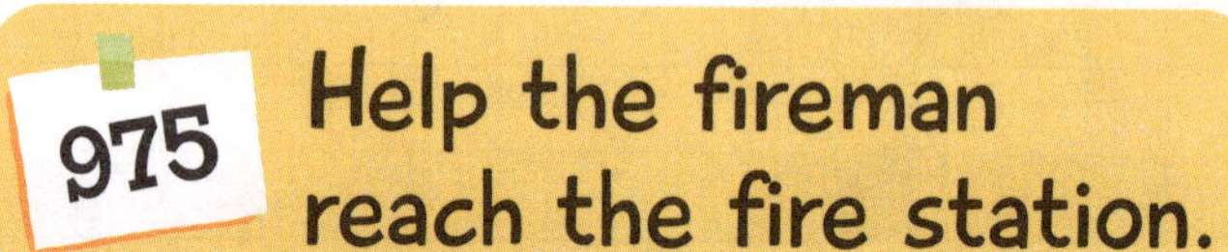

976 Which is the exact shadow?

977 Draw the other half and colour.

978 Circle what is not needed by a musician.

980 Outline the bricks and colour the picture.

979 Match by shape.

981 Copy the colour pattern.

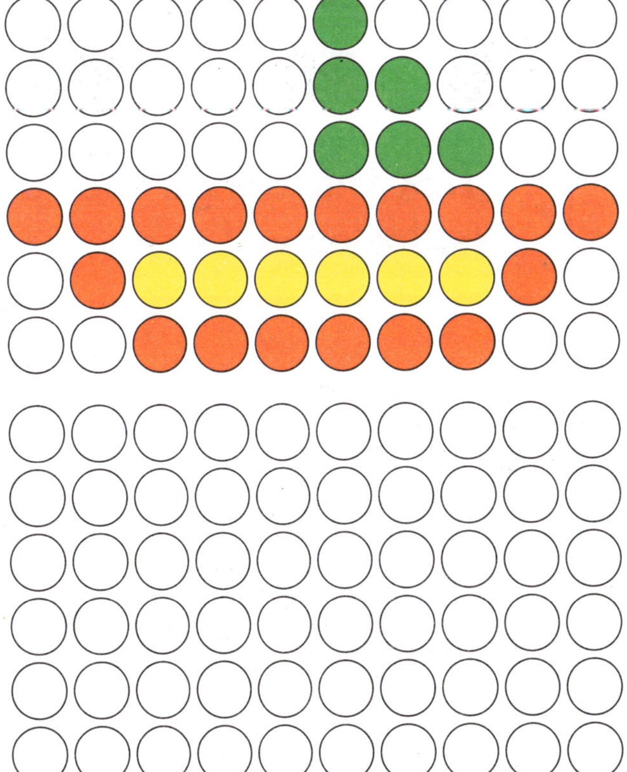

982 What is he called? Write in the box.

983 Find the colour code.

987	→
654	→
532	→
637	→

A) B) C)

984 Tick the things that a ballerina will use.

BALLERINA

985 How many look up and how many look down?

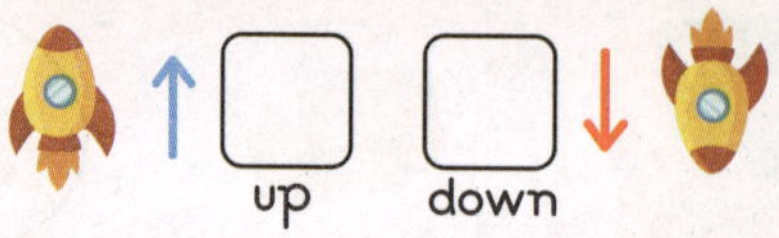

↑ up down ↓

986 Trace the 4 types of lines.

987 Colour the picture.

988 Find 7 differences.

989 Help the racer reach the trophy.

990 Match the fronts to the backs.

a b c d

a b c d

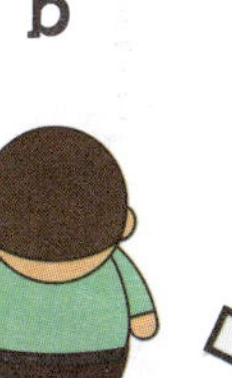  

991 Colour the fireman.

993 Match the musicians with their shadows.

992 Circle what is not needed by a race car driver.

994 Join the dots and colour.

995 Trace the rectangles and colour.

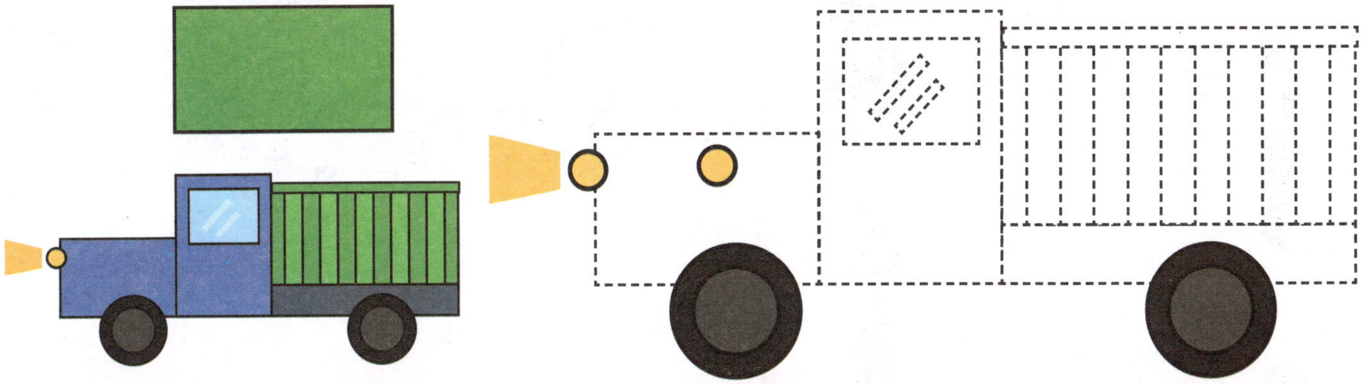

996 Fill in the missing letters.

DO_TOR

JANIT_R

SCI_NTIST

CH_F

997 Tick the things that a chef will use.

CHEF			
	☐	☐	☐
	☐	☐	☐

998 Circle the hammer among the tools.

999 Find these professionals in the grid.

H	C	E	K	H	J	S	T	N	K	D
F	R	N	B	E	O	W	A	H	H	E
I	E	J	R	H	I	M	H	F	A	N
R	T	C	T	O	E	Y	M	P	T	T
E	I	X	P	C	T	H	F	R	X	I
M	A	L	I	A	V	C	K	L	I	S
A	W	L	X	Y	P	H	O	Y	P	T
N	O	E	W	J	P	D	H	D	M	L
P	S	C	I	E	N	T	I	S	T	G
B	U	S	I	N	E	S	S	M	A	N
Y	H	H	S	H	U	E	X	T	Z	X

1000 Can you spot a captain's hat?

1001 Colour the picture.